Pledge of
Allegiance

Mark Lapin

Pledge of Allegiance

To Laurence Michael,
& to Rose & Dave,

in memory of the
day of the funeral.

Mark Lapin

A WILLIAM ABRAHAMS BOOK

DUTTON

DUTTON

Published by the Penguin Group
Penguin Books USA Inc., 375 Hudson Street,
New York, New York 10014, U.S.A.
Penguin Books Ltd, 27 Wrights Lane,
London W8 5TZ, England
Penguin Books Australia Ltd, Ringwood,
Victoria, Australia
Penguin Books Canada Ltd, 2801 John Street,
Markham, Ontario, Canada L3R 1B4
Penguin Books (N.Z.) Ltd, 182-190 Wairau Road,
Auckland 10, New Zealand

Penguin Books Ltd, Registered Offices:
Harmondsworth, Middlesex, England

First published by Dutton, an imprint of New American Library,
a division of Penguin Books USA Inc.

First Printing, April, 1991
10 9 8 7 6 5 4 3 2 1

 REGISTERED TRADEMARK—MARCA REGISTRADA

LIBRARY OF CONGRESS CATALOGING-IN-PUBLICATION DATA:

Lapin, Mark.
    Pledge of allegiance / Mark Lapin.
      p.   cm.
    "A William Abrahams book."
    ISBN 0-525-24979-6
    I. Title.
PS3562.A628P55   1991
813'.54—dc20

Printed in the United States of America
Set in Garamond No. 3

Designed by Steven N. Stathakis

PUBLISHER'S NOTE

To my son Daniel,
and my father Adam

Pledge of Allegiance

May Day, 1953

I could hardly wait to get back in from recess because Mrs. McMahon had promised to dismiss me just as soon as she finished calling the roll. I was going to a parade. I was the only kid in the whole third grade of P.S. 187, Washington Heights, New York, who got to go. But that was a secret.

My mother's note to the teacher said only:

Dear Mrs. McMahon,

Please excuse my son, Josh Rankin, from class at 10:30 this Friday morning.

Sincerely yours,
Elsa Rankin

If anyone asked where I was going, I was supposed to say: family business.

My mother had warned me not to tell about the parade. She had looked me straight in the eyes and warned me with her most serious voice, the one with a little quaver in it that she always tried to hide and that I tried not to hear because it gave me a weak, watery feeling way down in my stomach.

It was the voice she used to explain why we had moved all the way across the country from San Francisco to New York, and why my father couldn't live at home with us anymore, and why my sister and I were never supposed to talk about him to strangers, especially men with crewcuts and brown suits who might come up on the street and ask where he was staying.

That was such a big secret I didn't even know the answer. I just knew that my father was Underground. He was doing something important for the Party. My mother was in the Party too, and all her friends, and I guessed my sister and me and our best friends were in it, sort of, because of our parents.

All the good people were in the Party. But the bad ones wouldn't join even if you invited them, even if you explained everything in the clearest way in the world. They'd just get mad and call you "commie" and maybe beat you up or throw you in jail. They didn't even want to let us have a parade on May Day. They kept trying to take our permit away and we kept making them give it back and the story had been on the front page of the newspaper all week long, and on television too.

So I knew better than to tell Eddie Allen about the parade. But I couldn't help it. He made me mad during recess, and the secret just kind of popped out while we were flipping baseball cards in the little alley behind the school where the teachers couldn't see.

Eddie Allen was captain of the baseball team. He had blond hair and blue eyes, and he always wore fresh white polo shirts with red stripes around the collar, and he thought he was hot stuff because everybody liked him. I liked him, too, pretty much. He could be mean sometimes, but he was the one who first gave me a chance to play baseball.

That was a couple of months ago, just after we moved out of my grandma's house in the Bronx and over to our own apartment in Washington Heights. My first few weeks in the neighborhood, I brought my glove out to Fort Washington Park every day after school and moped around on the sidelines watching the kids play ball. They had a game every day. But no one would choose me because I was a short, shy, shrimpy kid with arms like toothpicks, and a stranger besides.

I had to wait till the guy playing right field got smacked on the ear by a line drive and ran home crying. Buddy Ryan said they didn't need him anyway. But Eddie Allen jerked his head over at me. "Okay, schnozzola," he shouted, "catch this and you're in." Then he hit the ball way up into the blue. Eddie could really mash it for a kid.

The ball went so high it turned into a little speck in the sky. Flies like that made me dizzy. They made me rush around in circles waving my glove in the air till I started to stumble and lose sight of everything and finally I'd just freeze and cover my head in panic while the ball plopped harmlessly at my feet.

But this time, maybe because I wanted to play so bad, or maybe 'cause I didn't like the way Eddie Allen called me "schnozzola," I planted my feet and let the ball come to me with a calm, almost sneaky feeling in my gut. First it was black; then it turned white; and when I saw the seams spinning, I pounced. The ball hit my glove with a sharp, clean smack that stung my palm and echoed across the playground and bounced back off the brick buildings as if people way up on the sixth floor were clapping for my catch.

So the kids let me play right field and bat last,

and it was funny, but after that I could catch. Not every time like Eddie Allen, but more often than before, and better than some of the other kids, better than Sidney Levin, for instance, who used to play right field. I thought he'd be mad at me for taking his place, but really he cared more about his dinosaur collection than baseball. Not me. Every afternoon I was the first one out at the park and the last one to leave.

Eddie still called me "schnozzola," and in school he usually ignored me, but when Buddy Ryan wasn't around, sometimes we'd flip baseball cards at recess. Mainly he won and mainly I didn't mind. A few cards were a small price to pay for my place on the team.

But this morning, May 1, the morning of the parade, Eddie got on a hot streak and cleaned me out, card after card, till I was all the way down to my last and favorite player—Pee Wee Reese, shortstop for the Brooklyn Dodgers. Pee Wee wasn't the biggest or the fastest or the toughest guy on the Dodgers, but he was the captain. He came through in the clutch. And he was fair. He was the one who welcomed Jackie Robinson when the other guys didn't want to let him play just because he was a Negro. And Pee Wee was a Southerner, from Tennessee, so that made it really special.

"Well," said Eddie, "what're you waitin' for? You still got one left."

I glanced down at Pee Wee. He stared back at me with soft brown eyes. I hated to risk him. But Eddie looked so stuck on himself, kneeling there on the blacktop pavement, with his hair all buttery in the sun and his white teeth sparkling above his white polo shirt and my cards making a big fat wad in his hand.

I took a deep breath and skimmed Pee Wee across the pavement. At the last second, just before hitting the wall, he caught a breeze, slowed, tilted, and came to rest leaning against the stones. I smiled at Eddie. He shrugged and flicked his card at mine like he didn't even care. It knocked Pee Wee over, slid in underneath, and stopped a quarter inch closer to the base of the wall.

Eddie picked Pee Wee up off the pavement, held him by one corner, and wrinkled his nose like the card was covered with dog shit.

"If you don't want him," I pleaded, "I'll trade you five guys to give him back."

"You don't got five guys," Eddie reminded me. "You're wiped out."

"I'll bring 'em tomorrow."

"Tough titty," said Eddie. "It's now or never. Whaddaya want a bum like Reese for anyway? Here's what they'd do to 'im on a good team like the Yankees." Then he tore Pee Wee in four little pieces and threw him in the trash can.

The card was kind of soft from all the time it'd spent riding in my back pocket, and it ripped with a sad, soggy sound that made me want to cry. But of course I couldn't cry in front of Eddie Allen, and I didn't dare hit him either.

So I pushed my chest up close to his and sneered in his face. "I don't care what *you* do, smart ass," I said, "because *I'm* getting out of school right after recess. And you know where I'm gonna be while you're sitting in class doing fractions? At a parade! I'm the only kid in the whole third grade who gets to go."

"Big deal," said Eddie, shoving me away. "Who cares? You're probably lying anyway."

"Oh, no I'm not. They're gonna have floats and a band and a big red merry-go-round. And I get to ride it."

Eddie stopped smiling. He stood on one foot and scratched his head and squinted at me kind of sideways, like he was trying to figure out if it was really possible that the great Eddie Allen could have any reason at all to envy a scrawny big-nosed shrimp like me.

I thought about the look I'd give him when Mrs. McMahon dismissed me for the day, and all of a sudden, losing Pee Wee didn't hurt half so bad.

I was the first one back in class after recess. The other kids were taking all day. Myra Simpson and a couple of her friends stopped right inside the door to compare the plastic barrettes in their hair, and everybody else had to squeeze past them one by one.

The minute hand of the clock above Mrs. McMahon's desk jumped to 10:33. I squirmed against the bottom of my chair. I looked out the window at the Good Humor truck parked by the lawn on the corner. It sparkled whiter than vanilla in the sunshine.

I slipped my hand in my pants pocket, grabbed the dime I had there and warmed it in my fist. I decided to buy an eskimo pie on my way home. I imagined the crisp chocolate crunching under my teeth and the cold lump of ice cream melting on my tongue as I skipped down the empty streets away from school. I glanced up at the clock again, just in time to see Eddie Allen's hand shoot into the air from the opposite side of the room.

"Just a moment, Edward," said Mrs. McMahon.

She rang her bell, calling the class to order. The three girls by the door dove for their seats. Mrs. McMahon was a stout, strict lady with iron gray hair that curled around her ears. She had a pale, puffy face and little black eyes that could drill right into your head when you were lying. I had never seen her wear anything but black high-necked dresses. It had to do with her son who wasn't coming home from the war in Korea. She had a picture of him in his Air Force captain's uniform. She kept it on her desk, right next to her silver bell and her metal-edged yardstick.

"All right, Edward," she said when the class had settled down. "what is it?"

"Mrs. McMahon," said Eddie, with a sideways smirk at me, "how come Josh gets to go to a parade today and no one else?"

My stomach dropped and my face got hot. I wanted to crawl under my desk. Or rush across the room and sock him one. But I couldn't do anything except watch Mrs. McMahon.

"What Joshua Rankin does outside of school is no concern of yours, young man," she said to Eddie. She frowned at him and shook her head.

I almost floated out of my chair.

But halfway through the shake, Mrs. McMahon caught sight of the calendar on the classroom door and her head stopped moving. The date monitor had circled May 1 in thick red crayon. I squeezed the dime in my pocket till my nails cut my palm and the cuts filled with burning sweat. Mrs. McMahon went right on staring at the date.

"Josh," she sighed finally, turning to face me, "did you tell Eddie you were going to a parade? *Today?*"

I gulped and nodded.

"Well, maybe you'd like to tell the rest of us about it too."

I shook my head no.

"Why ever not?" she asked, her voice still sounding friendly. "At least tell us what kind of parade it is."

"I dunno," I mumbled, careful not to meet her eyes.

"If it's important enough to miss school for, you must know what it's about," she insisted.

I couldn't answer. My ears flamed. The parade had to do with the Party, and everything about the Party was a secret. Especially from people like Mrs. McMahon.

"I'm waiting, Josh," she said. A thin smile stretched itself over her face, but I knew she was getting angry. Everyone knew by now. The whole class was listening.

I stared out the window at the Good Humor truck. It seemed miles away, but I could still see the little brass bells hanging on a wire above the cab. There was just enough breeze to make them shimmer in the sun. Maybe they were tinkling. I tried to hear.

Blamm! Mrs. McMahon's yardstick cracked down on her desk.

"I'm asking you a question, Joshua Rankin," she snapped. "And I expect an answer. What kind of parade is it?"

"For M-M-May Day," I mumbled. "They're gonna have a merry-go-round and everything."

"For M-M-May Day," echoed Mrs. McMahon. "Hhmmm. That's not one of the holidays we've studied, now is it? Maybe you'd be so good as to come up here in front of the room and tell us just what kind of people would want to march in a parade on May Day."

I slouched down till my eyes were about level with the chewing gum on the underside of my desk. "I have to go now," I pleaded. "My mother's waiting."

"You're not going anywhere till we get some answers," said Mrs. McMahon. "Come up here. In front of the room. This instant!"

I shuffled forward and stopped in front of the big glass aquarium next to Mrs. McMahon's desk. The aquarium was full of ants and sand. You could look in and see the tunnels they dug.

"Not there, Josh," Mrs. McMahon said. "By the flag. Under the picture of President Eisenhower."

I stood under the flag in a slant of sunlight from the window. The gold tassels brushed the top of my hair. My scalp crawled. I could feel my curls flying out in all directions, and my outsized ears flaring red and a thick wet lump starting to form in my throat and a gob of snot working its way down to hang from the tip of my long Jewish nose. My shirttail draped sloppily over the seat of my pants, which were not quite long enough to cover my socks, which sagged down over my unlaced sneakers.

I tried to face the class with a just-us-kids-against-the-adults smirk. But thirty pairs of vulture eyes stared back. Eddie and Billy and Buddy, the other kids on the baseball team, Myra Simpson and the girls with plastic clasps in their hair—they were all enemies, all eager to see me cry.

"We've been studying holidays ever since the term began," Mrs. McMahon said to the class. "We've studied Washington's birthday, Lincoln's birthday, Easter, Thanksgiving . . . But we've never studied May Day. Why not? Who knows what it's all about?"

Everybody sat on their hands.

"Then who wants Josh to tell us?"

Arms waved from every desk. Eddie Allen flapped both of his like he was trying to fly.

"You see that, Josh," said Mrs. McMahon. "We're all ears."

I swallowed and shuffled. I wasn't going to talk, and I wasn't going to cry.

"Well," she prompted, "are you going to the kind of parade we have on Columbus Day to celebrate the discovery of our country? Or Veteran's Day to honor our boys who died fighting for freedom?" Her voice wavered when she talked about the veterans.

I shot a glance at her face. It seemed to soften for a second. Maybe if I just said something, anything. "It . . . it's for labor," I told her. "You know . . for the unions . . . the workers. And for strikes."

"Oh, no it's not!" her voice whipped back. She was standing up now, towering over me, the big black bulge of her titties jabbing at my face. "Don't you dare get up in my classroom and tell me it's for the unions. That parade is for countries like Russia and Red China and East Germany where they don't have any unions at all. Do you know who's behind that march?"

Now it was coming. I could feel it. The word that was worse than "pussy" or "asshole" or "fuck" or "shit." The word that she was going to smear all over my face so that even if I stayed in her classroom a thousand years I'd still stink from it.

"No wonder you're ashamed," shrilled Mrs. McMahon. "May Day's not an American holiday. You're going to a parade for *Communists!*"

The kids gasped and snickered, elbowed each other and pointed at me.

"And the great thing about our country," Mrs. McMahon went on, turning to the class and holding up her hands for silence, "the great thing is that we let them celebrate it. We have plenty of parades for good citizens. But if Josh wants to march in one for our enemies, we can't stop him. It's his free choice. Do you really want to march with those people?" she asked me. "Do you? Well . . . DO YOU?"

I couldn't hold back any longer. The tears came hot and wet and shameful like pee in the middle of the night. "No," I sobbed. "No, honest, no. I don't want to go anymore."

"Well, you just tell that to your mother," said Mrs. McMahon, waving me out of the classroom with a big sweep of her arm. "Go ahead. You're dismissed."

2

Wiping my nose on the cuff of my shirt, I plodded down the block away from school. Halfway to the corner, I crossed the street to avoid the Good Humor man. He had a white uniform and white hair and a walrus mustache that curled when he smiled. On the door of his freezer was a picture of a polar bear reaching into an igloo to pull out an eskimo pie. I didn't want one anymore. I knew it wouldn't taste good.

A few blocks from school, I came to the park where we played baseball. It was tucked in between rows of brick apartment buildings, mostly six stories high with trees in front and courtyards. The park was surrounded by a black metal fence with spears on top.

I pushed through the gate, scuffed across the gravel, and climbed up on a step to reach the drinking fountain. I squirted the jet in my eyes and swallowed big gulps of water to rinse the salt from my throat.

Near the fountain were some swings. They dangled

over a sandbox and looked out on the diamond. It wasn't grass like the Dodgers had. The baselines were marked in fading yellow paint on a tar surface. The chain-link backstop was all pushed out of shape from where the big kids had tried to kick their feet through it.

I sat in a swing and started rocking. I didn't ever want to go back to school. I didn't want to go to the parade either. And I didn't want to go down to the subway where my mother and sister were waiting. I just wanted to sit in the swing and rock.

I closed my eyes. I kicked my feet softly against the sand, just enough to keep me moving. I could feel the sun and wind drying my face. The motion was making me drowsy. I let my head flop. Every swing carried me farther away from the classroom.

Already the scene under the flag was turning into something I remembered, not something that was happening to me right now. In a little while it would be just another picture in my head. Then I could forget it. I could push it way far down in the back of my mind and bury it under all sorts of other pictures and never let it come back up to the surface. I was good at that. I did it lots of times.

At least I didn't have to go to school again till Monday. Maybe by then nobody would remember how I cried. And if I didn't tell my mother, and went to the parade, and rode on the merry-go-round, and tried real hard not to think about it myself, then it'd be almost like nothing had happened at all.

"You're late," said my sister. She was standing with my mother on the subway platform wearing a dress with a lacy collar and a wide white skirt that she kept pressing down with her hands so it wouldn't get dirty touching the pillars. "You made us miss two trains, didn't he, Elsa?"

My sister was two years older than me. She called my mother Elsa and my father Ben because it sounded more grown-up. Her name was Vera. She went to a school for geniuses in Greenwich Village and had skipped a whole year. But when she got mad or scared she'd stamp her feet and pull her hair and cry worse than a baby. I didn't like her. She wore braces on her teeth and bit me when we fought.

"It's all right, Vera," my mother said, looking at her watch. "We'll be there before it starts."

"But I had to ride the train all the way up from the Village, and I got here on time." Vera stamped her foot. "He only had to walk a few blocks and he's late."

My mother put her arm around me and pulled me against her side. When I leaned into her, I felt the tears come up again just a little. She reached around and tucked my shirt into my pants. She patted a few of my curls into place.

"Where were you?" she asked.

I couldn't tell her about Mrs. McMahon. Not with the tear taste still in my throat and Vera standing there listening. "I stopped to swing in the park," I muttered.

"You what?" My mother pushed me away, giving an impatient slap of her heel on the platform. "Didn't you know we were waiting?"

"I knew," I said. "But . . ."

"But you thought the whole world could wait because it was warm and sunny and what's the point of getting out of school on May Day if you can't even take a swing in the park? Is that right?"

"Yeah, kind of . . ." I shrugged.

"Well, then what're you looking so glum about?" She held me at arm's length, scowling into my face. She had on a straight black dress with a turquoise scarf pinned over the shoulder by a silver clasp. She always dressed that way—dark with a few bright spots of color. Her face was shaped like a heart, with glossy black bangs and big brown eyes. They didn't bore into you like Mrs. McMahon's. They made you melt instead.

I looked away. I was glad for the dark of the platform.

During the ride downtown, Vera chattered with my mother while I stood up and looked out the little window in the door. We were in the last car, next to the brakeman's compartment. It was my favorite car to ride.

I held on to the silvery rail across the door and swayed with the train and stared out at the lights disappearing behind us. There were red lights and green lights and purple and gold. They all meant something different. I watched them curve away in the darkness. They made me think how big the subway was, how the rails branched and twisted as they streaked through the tunnels, running under the streets, under the rivers, running to places I'd never seen like White Plains and Flushing. Maybe the rails linked up with subways in other cities like Boston or Chicago.

Maybe if I jumped out of the train and followed the lights through the tunnels for a long, long time, I'd come to where my father was living Underground. I imagined a high, narrow room, with thick walls and books up to the ceiling and maybe a skylight instead of windows and my father tapping with two fingers at his big black typewriter, sitting knee-deep in piles of crumpled paper like I used to see him back home in San Francisco.

Someday soon, I was going to run away and find him. Maybe even today. Maybe instead of going to the parade, I'd just jump down off the platform and disappear into the tunnels before my mother and Vera knew what was happening. But I'd have to watch out for the third rail. One step on that, and you'd get fried and sizzled till smoke came out your ears and you were all black and crisp like bread stuck in the back of the toaster. I didn't want that to happen to me. But it did happen to people sometimes. And not just to people who fell on the tracks. They did it to bad guys on purpose. They did it to people they stuck in the Chair.

"Up you go young fella," said the man with greasy hands who leaned over to lift me onto the merry-go-round. It was one of the dinky, portable kind that they mounted on the back of a flatbed truck and drove around to carnivals in small towns.

My mother and Vera were standing on the sidewalk below. We were downtown in Manhattan. But it wasn't the fancy part where the Easter parade went. I saw crumpled-up newspapers and men with bottles sitting on the sidewalk and on one corner a big hole where they'd torn down an old building and hadn't put up anything yet but a fence.

Vera wouldn't ride the merry-go-round because it was for kids. She was going to march with my mother. She was holding my mother's hand and trying to pull her away to where a bunch of adults were forming up for the parade. Jody's dad Leo was over there. I saw his reddish hair flashing up and down as he knelt to hammer a big banner to a pair of poles.

The banner had a painting of longshoremen with big muscles and white caps. They were opening a drawbridge to a stream of ships with flags from all over the world, including Russia. The writing said TRADE AND JOBS. NOT WAR AND DEATH.

My mother didn't want to leave. She was staring at me, worried because I hadn't said a word ever since we got on the subway. The sun made her eyes gold.

"Don't you dare get off till we meet you at the end," she said. "Leo's driving us up to a picnic after the parade."

I smiled and waved. She blew me a kiss, then let Vera drag her away.

The second they were gone, the grin slipped off my face. I was disgusted with the merry-go-round. I'd imagined something like the one my father took me to just before we moved away from San Francisco, the one in Golden Gate Park that had gold and mirrors on the walls and horses with leather reins and unicorns with jewels in their eyes and pictures of fat ladies taking a bath on the ceiling.

This old thing wasn't even as good as the wreck on Macy's roof at Christmas. My mother had promised it would be red, but the only red part was the housing of the motor, and that was so covered with grease you could hardly tell what color it was to begin with. The motor sat in the middle of the truck bed with metal spokes sticking out from it like spider legs. The horses were attached to the spokes. They were made of plaster and barely big enough for a baby. Most of them had broken tails or taped-on legs or scratched-out eyes.

I swung onto a red stallion with one missing ear and looked around for Jody. He wasn't there. I'd seen some of the other kids at rallies and marches. A Negro girl with pigtails and a frilly pink party dress was riding the horse in front. Her name was Lonnie Mae. The ribbons on her braids flopped against her shoulders as she bounced in the saddle. She caught me looking, flashed a smile, and flicked her pigtails in my direction.

I heard a whistle blow. The banner at the head of the parade began to move. The truck jerked forward. The merry-go-round started spinning to a scratchy recording of carnival music. Our horses didn't bob up and down. They just turned in a circle and not even fast enough to make the buildings whirl. Even so, I let a cheer slip out my throat.

The adults chanted, "Fight the Fare Hike!" "Free the Rosenbergs!" "Bring the Boys Back Home!" They sang "Solidarity Forever." When they came to the chorus everybody shouted at the top of their lungs. I shouted too: "For the Union Makes Us Strong!"

Our voices bounced off the buildings. But somehow they didn't sound loud. No one came to look out the windows. The skyscrapers blocked the sun, and the street was so wide our march couldn't fill it. The kids on the merry-go-round called to people walking down the sidewalk, but they pretended not to hear us. It felt like we were parading through an empty city in a dream.

Finally I heard a crowd roaring up ahead. Everyone heard. The whole parade perked up. People linked arms and stepped all together and hollered their heads off. The men holding the poles made the banner dip and ripple. Picket signs waved in the air. I stood up in the stirrups of my horse to see the crowd. But it was out of sight, around the next corner.

When our banner turned the bend, the shouts rolled back like waves beating against the buildings. The truck sped up. The merry-go-round tilted as we followed the banner around the curve into the sunlight.

First it was almost too bright to see. I blinked at the crowd—a white mass, packed onto both sidewalks, pressing against wooden barricades, yelling and waving. Policemen on horseback lined the street, huge and shadowy in their long blue capes.

This was what I'd been waiting for. I sat very straight on my red stallion, soaking up the noise, the excitement, the whirling and calliope music, the faces and hands and flags blurring past in the sun. No matter what had happened, no matter what anyone had said, I was riding a merry-go-round in a parade and Eddie Allen was doing fractions back in class.

I waved to the crowd. I wanted to remember their faces. My horse swept past a man wearing a white shirt with rolled-up sleeves and four pens in the pocket. He was holding a shopping bag. He had horn-rimmed glasses and bristly gray hair that stuck straight up from his skull. He was shouting so hard that his forehead wrinkled and his eyes narrowed to slits and his throat turned red.

And suddenly, as if I'd just pulled my fingers out of my ears, I heard what the man was yelling.

"Commies!" he screamed. "Filthy, rotten commies!"

And he wasn't waving either. He was shaking his fist at us. They all were. All around, on both sides of the street. It was like the merry-go-round had whirled me around so fast that I landed in a different parade.

Up ahead where my mother was, I saw a bunch of men in purple soldier hats jump the barricade. They disappeared into the march swinging sticks. The banner at the head of the parade fell down. The truck stopped. The kids screamed. The police horses reared and kicked. The march broke down into knots of people spinning and shouting and shoving.

The man with the shopping bag was throwing tomatoes. He passed them out to the people around him. They aimed right at the merry-go-round. Right at us. We couldn't get away because the truck was blocked. Women were throwing too. Some of the kids ducked under their horses or covered their heads with their hands. I just sat there, too scared to move, my mouth wide open and no sound coming out.

The tomatoes made dark streaks across the sky. They smashed with a splatter of seeds and slop. One caught Lonnie Mae right in the chest. Her pink dress turned red. I got creamed on the side of the face. The tomato hit hard as a punch and stank like warm sewer water.

By the time I wiped the slime out of my eyes, our truck was moving again. The men had picked our banner up off the street. Lonnie Mae was staring at her dress and bawling. The crowd still roared, but we were turning a corner, leaving it behind. "Faster," I whispered, gripping my stallion's one good ear. "Faster. Faster. Faster."

3

Leo had a big blue Buick with soft seats and wood on the dashboard. It was jam-packed with people from the parade. They were all talking at once, telling where they were and who was next to them and what they did when the trouble started.

Vera sat up front, still whimpering even though nothing had happened to her except seeing a woman get socked in the stomach. I was in back, sitting on my mother's lap by the window. I didn't feel scared anymore, but I hated May Day worse than ever now and I was mad at my mother.

When we met at the end of the parade, she saw the red stuff all over me and practically fainted. Then she realized it was just tomato. She kneeled down and cleaned me off and hugged me and told me over and over that I was all right and she was sorry and we wouldn't do it again, ever. I just stuck my lower lip out at her and pouted. Even now, in the car, I tried to make myself all sharp and bony as I sat on her lap.

But once we started rolling down the Henry Hudson Parkway, I realized it was going to be a long trip. All the people made it warm in the car, and the windows had a shadowy blue tint, and even the voices died down after a while, except for Leo who kept talking on and on about a bail drive for the people who got arrested at the parade.

My mother's arms folded across my stomach and my hands crossed on top of hers. I felt the humming of the tires through her lap and the warmth of her breath blowing past my cheek. The window rattled against my forehead so I slumped back and let my head sink into her shoulder. There was a funny, tingly moment when I couldn't tell where my hands ended and her arms began, and I knew I was falling asleep.

The next thing I knew we were bouncing down a dirt road to a gate where some big fat union men with cigars and tattooed arms leaned into our car to collect money from Leo. Clouds of barbecue smoke drifted over the trees as we pulled into the dusty parking lot.

Leo jumped out and stretched. He was almost as tall as the guys with tattoos but thinner and harder than they were. He used to be on the wrestling team in college and a sailor in the war, but now he was a lawyer. He had curly reddish hair and a big Band-Aid with a splotch of blood over his right eye where he got conked on the head during the parade. He saw me staring at the bandage and winked.

"I saw him coming, Josh," he said. "But I wouldn't drop my side of the banner. So I just let him hit the hardest thing around. Broke his stick right in two. I guess you would've done better, huh Mighty Mouse?"

He always called me "Mighty Mouse" because I was small. Leo was like that. He found out what you hated to be teased about and kept reminding you of it. Sometimes he scared me too because I'd seen him get real mad at Jody and then his face turned purple-red and his hands looked like big heavy boards at the end of his arms. But when he came running up to the merry-go-round at the end of the parade, I was plenty glad to see him.

"End of the line, folks," he called out now, holding the door open for the others to climb out of his car. "Just close your eyes and follow your nose. And as for you, Lady Vera, control that wild appetite of yours and don't eat up all the food before I get back."

He always teased Vera about eating too much because she was so fussy she hardly ate anything at all. She gave him her turn-green-and-die look.

When we were all out, Leo jumped back in the Buick and my mother slid into the front seat next to him. They had to go back to the city to work on the bail drive. They were together all the time now since my father went Underground and we moved to New York.

My mother stuck her head out the window. "Here," she said, giving Vera and me a dollar each from her purse. "Buy anything you want to eat. Have a good time. I promise we'll be back before dark."

"Do you absolutely have to go?" asked Vera, brushing the dust off her skirt.

"You saw what happened at the parade," my mother said. "There are people in jail. Someone has to help them. Don't worry. You'll have hundreds of friends at the picnic."

The picnic was at a private campground down by the Hudson, and we had the whole place to ourselves. A green meadow sloped down to the river between thick rows of bushes. There were picnic tables on top of the slope and maybe a thousand people strolling around, or sitting on blankets, and kids darting across the grass, and even a few dogs, one with a yellow balloon tied to his collar. The barbecue smoke came from a row of booths with bright union banners and long lines of people in front.

I still hated May Day, but the smells were making me hungry. They were selling all kinds of strange food including stuff from the Philippines and chili with red beans and shish kebab and okra with corn bread and salad with something called Green Goddess dressing. The money went to families on strike so their kids could eat.

I started out with a cheeseburger and french fries. Then I went over to the United Electrical Workers booth for a root beer. I recognized the woman behind the counter. We called her "fat Peggy." She gave me a free soda and a big smile. Vera said Peggy was obese, and I knew my mother didn't like her much either, but I thought she was okay except for pinching me on the cheek sometimes and trying a little too hard to be friendly.

"Did you go to the parade?" she asked.

"Yeah."

"Was it scary?"

"No."

"Not even a little?"

"I got hit by a tomato."

"You did?" said Peggy. "You got hit by a tomato?" Her hands flew up to her wide red mouth. She had on a brown sweater that stretched way out over her boobs and blond hair and flabby arms and a little squeaky voice that didn't fit with her blimp-sized body. "Then you're a Wounded Veteran. A proud survivor of the parade," she said. "Come on. We can't hide a thing like that. We have to let people know."

She tore a strip of red crepe paper off the front of the booth and tied it around my head. The ends hung down in back like an Indian headdress. "That's your decoration," she said. "And if anyone asks what it's for, you look straight at 'em with those big green eyes of yours and tell 'em you're a Wounded Veteran of the May Day Parade."

I ate my hamburger standing by Peggy's booth. It came with a dill pickle that was so sour I blinked when I bit it. Every time people came to buy sodas, Peggy told them I was a Wounded Veteran of the May Day Parade and asked for an extra contribution. She said it so often, we shortened it to initials: WVMDP. She printed them with a black felt marker on my headdress.

Finally I got bored and went over to show Mary Lou my ribbon. She looked okay now. She had changed out of her party dress into red jeans and a T-shirt and was talking to four kids at once with her mouth half full of pecan pie.

"Hey, Lonnie Mae, we're Wounded Veterans," I said. "This's my decoration. It's for getting clobbered at the parade."

"Hhmmpph," said Lonnie Mae. "If you think you're something for gettin' hit by one measly tomato, Josh Rankin, then I'm something *else* cause I got beaned by two of the biggest ol' tomatoes anybody ever saw."

"Just like in the movies," I agreed. "They went *pow! pow!* And she got all red and fell off her horse. Like Cochise in *Broken Arrow*." I acted it out in slow motion for the kids. I was a pretty good actor for scenes like falling off a horse and dying.

"An' I didn't even cry," added Lonnie Mae, flashing me a wink. "Me an' Josh, we were right up there in the middle of everything with stuff flying every which way at our heads and we weren't even scared. Cause we're the Wounded Veterans and we're tough. Right, Joshie?"

She put her arm around my shoulder.

"Right!" I agreed.

"But I'm the toughest of all," said Lonnie Mae. "So I oughta be wearing that ribbon."

She snatched it off my head and jumped away, and then we were chasing her through the crowd, around picnic tables, in between family groups, over blankets and baskets. By the time we reached the open grass by the river, we must have had a dozen kids in the pack.

Lonnie Mae held the streamer so it whipped out behind her. She had long skinny legs and ran fast for a girl, but I would've been able to catch her, or at least keep up, if I really felt like playing. But the cheeseburger was still bouncing around in my stomach, and my legs felt like I was running in mud, so I lagged behind the other kids and was actually looking for a place to stop and mope around by myself, when Jody popped up out of nowhere and started trotting by my side.

I knew it was him even before he gave me a pat on the tush because Jody's the only kid I know who likes to run and sing at the same time. He had his shirt off and his pants rolled up to his knees, and his red brown hair flopped in his freckled face, which was giving me a big loony grin. He sang:

Glory, glory hallelujah,
Flush the teacher down the sewer
Bop her on the bean with a rotten tangerine
And the truth goes marching on.

When he finished the chorus, he passed me, caught Lonnie Mae in a couple of easy strides, and snatched the red ribbon out of her hand. Then we were all chasing him and I didn't feel like quitting anymore.

He'd let us come up almost close enough to touch and then pull away, and it was a funny feeling to be moving your arms and legs twice as hard as he was and yet see him smiling back over his shoulder as he danced out of reach.

He led us around the big log campfire they were setting up for folk songs and through the bushes along the side of the meadow and down a dirt path by the river and back onto the grass again. Nobody could come close to him, but somehow just chasing Jody was more fun than catching anybody else. The pack kept getting bigger and wilder, and even some adults and dogs joined the chase, and finally Jody doubled back and dodged through everyone till he swooped past me again.

His big gooney eyes locked on mine, and he gave me this look like "Hey, dummy, what're you waiting for?" and I kicked off my shoes and felt the grass squish between my toes and saw the sun bouncing along the cliffs on the other side of the river like a big orange balloon and I was just thinking that maybe May Day wasn't so bad after all when I noticed that all the other kids were dropping behind and without even trying I was floating, flying, going faster than I ever even dreamed about until it was just Jody and me skimming over the grass way out in front of everyone.

Later, when the sun went down, they had a campfire and folk songs. A tall skinny man named Pete stood up in front of a microphone and played the banjo. He knew lots of songs for kids and hopped around and clapped while he sang them.

My mother and Leo had come back, so our two families sat together like we always do. Vera sat with Jody's sister, Simone, and I sat with Jody, and Leo sat in between Elsa and his wife, Kaye. The night made my ears cold, but we were all bundled up in blankets, and on the sad, slow songs, we leaned against each other and rocked. Once I heard sirens wailing down the highway in the dark, and they made me think of the parade and school, but that all seemed far away and a long time ago.

We sang "Have you heard of the ship called the Go-od Reuben James?" and "Dark as a Dungeon Way Down in the Mine," and "Nobody Knows the Troubles I Seen" and "Follow the Drinking Gourd." Pete sang the words and we all did the chorus and sometimes we just listened to his banjo.

Finally we sang "Down by the Riverside." Everybody stood up and put their arms around their neighbors, and Pete told us to sing real soft so we could hear the Hudson flowing through the music, but I was too sleepy to stay on my feet and couldn't keep my eyes open even to watch the orange sparks flying out of the fire into the night.

I didn't think about school again till after "The Ed Sullivan Show" on Sunday night. The TV was in my mother's room, by the window looking down on the street. We lived on the sixth floor at 156 West 180th street.

I had turned off all the lamps in the room so I could play with my spacemen during the commercials on Ed Sullivan. My spacemen glowed in the dark. You held them up to a light bulb till they got warm, and when you turned off the lamp, they glowed purple-green. They didn't look as real as the picture in the comic book that got me to send in $1.25 for the set, but they were pretty spooky in the dark.

I had them stationed all over the room, some camped in moon craters that I punched in pillows, some walking in formation on the bookcase and windowsills, some guarding the antenna on top of the TV, some setting up an ambush under the mirror on my mother's nightstand. But the most important soldier of all was out of sight, controlling everybody from his hiding place under the sofa.

That was Captain Bob—the leader. I named him after Bob Thompson, who won a medal in the war and who came to our house for dinner one night and even shook my hand. Whenever someone told me communists weren't brave and patriotic, I remembered how Captain Bob wiped out a whole Japanese battalion with just his pistol and a couple of hand grenades before the government put him on trial and made him go Underground, like my father.

"Josh," my mother called from the kitchen, where she was sitting over the *New York Times*, helping Vera clip out articles for her current events report. "Josh, the program's over. It's bedtime."

"I'm not sleepy."

"Well you will be when it's time for school tomorrow morning."

"I'm not going," I said. The words just kind of popped out. My mind had made itself up over the weekend without even asking me.

"Jo-osh!"

"I want to go to Vera's school."

"Don't be stupid."

"Then I want to go to school with Jody."

My mother came into the room and turned off the TV and turned on the light. My spacemen stopped glowing.

"I thought you liked school," she said, leaning against the door with a cigarette in one hand and the other on the hip of her dark blue slacks.

"I hate Mrs. McMahon. She's just like the people at the parade. Like the man with the shopping bag who threw tomatoes."

She came over and sat down with me on the sofa and pulled me against her shoulder. She had been extra nice all weekend, but kind of far away too, like she was trying real hard to concentrate on us but had lots of other things on her mind. She put her cigarette out in an ashtray.

"Are you still thinking about that man?" she asked.

I wasn't but I could tell she'd feel sorry for me if I said so.

"I dreamed about him," I said. "I dreamed he was waiting for me on the way home from school."

"That can't possibly happen," she told me. "That man can't hurt you because he doesn't know your name or where you live or go to school or anything about you."

"But he was looking right at me. He saw my face."

"Now you listen to me, Josh," she said, putting her hands on my cheeks. She had long fingers, one of them with a ring that felt cool on my skin. The ring had a turquoise stone in a silver setting. It was made by the Navajo Indians. "Maybe you thought that man was looking at you, but he wasn't. He wasn't really looking and seeing. Because nobody could really look at you and see what kind of boy you are and then try to hurt you. Do you understand?"

"But he called me 'commie,' " I said.

"Well, is that so bad?" my mother asked. "Is that the very worst thing to be called in the whole wide world? No matter what you do, some people are going to call you names. You don't care what Vera calls you."

"But that's different."

"Even if it is different, tell me what you say to Vera."

"Sticks and stones," I mumbled.

"Is that all?" she smiled.

I said the whole thing. "Sticks and stones may cause some groans, but if you call me names I'll break your bones." I said it to her and then I said it to myself while I was picking up my spacemen and then I said it to Vera on my way through the kitchen. She just snorted at me without bothering to look up from her clippings.

4

Elsa

The hardest times are at night after the children go to bed. It is in the sudden quiet that I sense Ben's absence most. Our friends have been wonderful, of course, especially Leo. But what we thought was a temporary disruption has gone on for over a year and settled into a way of life. I look ahead and see no end to it, or else an end that I prefer not to contemplate. During the daytime, at least, I'm too busy to think.

In the mornings, there is the typical rush to pack the children off to school and myself to work. Josh is no problem. He demands the same bag lunch every day—peanut butter and jelly, a Hostess cupcake, potato chips, and a dill pickle. He complains bitterly if I try to change it. But Vera insists on variety. Yesterday's swiss cheese is no longer acceptable today. Sliced mortadella was edible last week, but now tops her list of indigestibles. She is really extremely nervous and high-strung and expresses it these days mainly through eating. Or rather through not eating. I suspect she throws away half of what I fix her.

Mornings, we walk to the IRT station together, Vera and I. That is a good time for her. Without Josh around, she blossoms. The quick lift and turn of her head, the words rushing off her tongue as if she does not have time to say them all, the soft shine of the sun on her young skin—all this gives me hope that somehow she will weather these times and emerge in a few years as a self-confident young woman.

At Fifty-ninth Street, we part company, I to the office and she on to her school in Greenwich Village. Her frightfully expensive school, I might add, which does her undeniable good, yet strains our finances beyond the breaking point. How so many left-wingers can afford to pay so much for their children's tuition is quite beyond me.

As for my job, what is there to say? Certainly, I am lucky to have it. What with the blacklist and the courteous attentions of the FBI, I am unable to find work outside our circle. My salary does not approach a living wage, but few movement jobs pay even as well as mine. The chief attraction has always been that Leo is more a friend and comrade than a boss. Yet that comfort has now become a fearful complication, particularly after the events of this weekend. Although so far as that goes, neither of us would allow our personal relations to compromise our work for the movement, and if such a situation should ever arise, we would certainly know where to draw the line.

The fact is that I do the work of three secretaries for the salary of one. I spend my lunch hour commuting to the courthouse on Foley Square. My afternoon coffee, I drink with one hand while taking dictation with the other. I put in an hour of unpaid overtime every day, and at the end of it all, the pile of memos, briefs, and affidavits on my desk is higher than before I began.

It is not, perhaps, the pace of the work that drains me so much as the sense of hopelessness that sometimes creeps in, especially in the late afternoons when the office is stifling and everyone's nerves are worn to the quick. Each week brings us new Smith Act indictments and fewer ways to defend ourselves against the absurd charge of "conspiring to advocate the violent and forcible overthrow of the federal government." Not actually doing anything violent, mind you. And not even advocating it. But conspiring to advocate—a vague and shadowy phrase that includes activities as innocuous as recommending Marxist literature. Any one of us could be indicted and convicted on that charge, which is precisely the point the government wishes to make.

It would be helpful if the children took on the chore of preparing dinner. But Vera needs her after-school piano lessons, and the mess Josh makes while trying to help hardly justifies his contribution.

I am content if he simply comes in to sit at the kitchen table and chat with me while I work. He will try to cheer me with nine-year-old humor when I am down, or listen seriously, his wide green eyes glowingly reminding me of Ben's, while I recount the latest maneuvers at the trial. His opinion is that the ten Smith Act defendants in New York should take advantage of their numbers, overwhelm Judge Dimock, and beat him into submission with his own gavel. I doubt that he will be a lawyer when he grows up. His ambition is to play shortstop for the Brooklyn Dodgers. I have promised to take him to a game at Ebbets Field before the season ends. Perhaps Chester McDowell, sportswriter for the *Worker*, will even use his connections to wangle Josh a meeting with one of his heroes.

I do not know why, but dinner is never simply a meal with us. It is either a delight or a disaster. On good nights, Vera and I succeed in discussing the latest news, or some new book or play, in a way that interests Josh as well. Ben's presence hovers over the table then for this is what we always did when he was with us. Refraining from direct mention of the Underground, I try to help them grapple with the complexities of our situation and accept whatever consequences may flow from it. Dinner over, the children are only too eager to jump up and do the dishes, working with each other in the most comradely fashion. Then I can rush off to my meeting secure in the knowledge that my family is united behind me.

But too often our attempts at reasonable discussion degenerate into childish bickering. Since our move to New York, the rivalry between Vera and Josh, present from their earliest days, has intensified into a bitter, unhealthy feud. For the most trivial comment, a child-ish joke or pun, an interruption, a dropped fork, she whirls on him in a teeth-gnashing frenzy, or tears into me for some imagined display of favoritism. Plates fly off the table, glasses smash to the floor. I struggle to keep my patience, to extend my endurance. But at the crucial moment, Josh finds some way to goad Vera to new displays of temper and my own nerves come unfrayed.

Hours later, while I sit at my club meeting dis-cussing quotas for the *Daily Worker* subscription drive or plans for the next Rosenberg demonstration, or our latest reading assignment, the scene still echoes through my mind. I hear my voice raging at Vera and wonder why she bears the brunt of my anger when truly both of them are at fault, or neither. Then I force my atten-tion back to the meeting.

Peggy Mendolsohn is praising the ace sub-getters of Brooklyn who have already met their quota, while we Washington Heights laggards have fallen 60 percent behind our goals. I look around at the worn faces of the men and women gathered on the threadbare sofas.

What am I doing here with them, I wonder, while my family is disintegrating at home? Yet some of these people have been my comrades for years. Some have husbands or wives already in jail, or on trial at this very moment. I recall picnics and outings that Ben and I have taken with these friends over the years, triumphant campaigns in happier times, shared family occasions. I remember how they found our apartment for us in Washington Heights. How they helped furnish it from their own homes with items that they carried up six flights of steps on their backs. How some of them pressed money into my hand while still panting from the climb. My eyes mist over.

"Elsa, Elsa," someone will say, "are you listening? What's wrong with you tonight?"

And I volunteer for new responsibilities, pledge to sell five more subs that weekend, commit myself to write the leaflet announcing the next demonstration, sign up to distribute it door to door.

But back home after midnight, I realize that the subscriptions I have volunteered to sell, the leaflets I must write, will disrupt my plans for the weekend. I will not be able to go to Vera's piano recital or take Josh to his precious baseball game. I will not even be able to spend a few hours catching up on the bills and balancing our checkbook. So I pull out the file of bills and sit down at my wobbly desk by the window to go over the hopeless additions and subtractions. With Ben's meager salary from the paper, mine from Leo, plus small sums from each of our parents (accompanied by disapproving advice) and occasional supplements from well-meaning friends, we are almost able to meet our daily expenses. But summer is coming. The children want to go to camp. Vera needs braces. There is no money for any of that. Not to mention a new summer dress for myself, a new scarf or hairdo, even a compact and lipstick.

*   *   *

I take two sleeping pills and go to bed. Each night, I hope the interval between lying down and falling asleep will be short. Yet each night, despite the sleeping pills, it seems to grow longer. I listen to the old apartment house groan and settle in the night. Sometimes, when I'm on the verge of sleep, a creak in the hall outside the door jolts my body with the force of an electric shock. I jerk upright in bed. My hand flies up to the scar on my forehead.

Sweating from a terror far deeper than my fear of the FBI, I remember a little Jewish village near the city of Minsk in Russia, a typical shtetl of hilly, muddy streets lined by poor houses. I see the lopsided shacks with their straw roofs ablaze in the night. I imagine the flames gleaming on the flanks of horses as the Cossacks gallop through the streets. I see them kicking down the door of our house with their boots, charging inside with sabers drawn. One stabs my mother in the side. Another rushes at my father. He stands before a curtained alcove. He will not step aside. The Cossack runs him through with such force that the blade pierces his body, comes out his back and cuts through the curtain behind him. The bright, bloody point slices into my forehead as I cower there in the alcove, a child of three, huddled with my sister, too terrified even to cry.

5

Monday morning wasn't half as bad as I expected. Nobody jumped me in the schoolyard. The kids didn't stand around in a circle calling me names or throwing tomatoes or anything like that. They just ignored me. Even the creeps I usually ignored walked away when they saw me coming—freaks like Herbie Griscomb, who had ringworm so bad they shaved off all his hair and made him wear a stocking cap to school, or fat Janet Frankel, who has one leg shorter than the other from polio. When the first bell rang and we lined up on our numbers facing the iron steps into the building, my partner moved about five feet away and held his nose like I stunk so bad he couldn't stand it.

Mr. Klein, the principal, watched us from the top of the steps. He stood in front of the doors to the school, holding a loudspeaker in one hand and rubbing his pot belly with the other. He was taller than all the teachers, but his stomach stuck so far out in front of his dark blue suit that he could rest his hand on top of it like a shelf.

He called us class by class, starting with 1–A. We were supposed to march past him real quiet, looking straight ahead and keeping in step with our neighbors. When my class walked by, he stared straight at me. Mrs. McMahon must have told him about May Day.

In class, I could hardly get my voice out to answer when she called my name during morning roll. I was scared she'd start in on me again, or make me go up in front of the room and give a current events report about the commie parade I went to. But roll call was the only time Mrs. McMahon said my name all day long.

I saw her looking at Myra in front of me and Sidney behind me and out the window over my head. But even when she asked us where was the capital of Iran and the whole class was stumped, she wouldn't look my way. I knew the answer. My parents talked about geography all the time. But I didn't raise my hand.

I sat there rolling pencils down the slope of my desk. I had a round black pencil and a yellow one with six sides. I made them race. I'd give the yellow one a head start and watch it roll about halfway down the slope before I let the black one go. The black pencil always came in first because it was Jackie Robinson on the Dodgers and the yellow one was all the white guys on the Yankees who didn't like him 'cause he was a Negro but he could beat them anyway. Sometimes I'd let Jackie's pencil roll right off the desk and into my lap. Once it dropped on the floor and rolled over to the radiator next to the window and I had to sneak over to get it. Even then, Mrs. McMahon didn't look at me.

I knew she was giving me the silent treatment, but I didn't mind. I just ignored her and the rest of them right back. Maybe I was a commie and a crybaby too, but at least I wasn't a dirty stoolpigeon snitch like Eddie Allen.

After school, instead of playing baseball in the park, I bought a model airplane from Sweeny's candy store. It was on the corner up the hill from my house. Mr. Sweeny reminded me of a big white mole. He had whiskers and a high, squeaky voice and a pink nose and fat cheeks that almost hid his eyes.

Inside his store was dark as Underground, but he could see everything you did and watched your hands real close to make sure you didn't steal. On one side was a counter where you could drink chocolate egg-cream sodas and refill bottles of seltzer water and sit on stools with tops that spun. Along the other wall were shelves loaded with plastic models and paints and brushes and comic books and pink Spaulding balls they used for stickball and all kinds of candy you could get for a penny, including sugar cones and licorice whips.

Sweeny had boxes full of baseball cards too, five for a nickle with a flat piece of bubble gum thrown in free. I grabbed a couple of packs and held them while I looked for a model. I picked out an F-86 Sabre jet like they flew in Korea. The box showed it swooping in low over snowy mountains to shoot down MiGs and blow Red Chinese out of tanks. It had a clear plastic cockpit that opened and closed and wing flaps that moved and bombs you could drop out of the bomb bay. On the way up to the cash register to buy the fighter, I slipped the baseball cards into my pocket. Sweeny never saw. If anyone had to pay for those cards, it oughta be Eddie Allen.

Back home, I spread newspapers on the kitchen floor so I wouldn't get the linoleum dirty and sat in the corner near the window where the light was best for working. I leaned against the legs of the kitchen table and began to build the jet. First I separated all the pieces and lined them up by the numbers. Then I began gluing them together, starting with the two halves of the fuselage. The glue had a smell like rotten bananas, and after I had been working with it for a while the kitchen got kind of fuzzy around the edges and I felt like I was building an actual Sabre jet in a huge aircraft hangar somewhere thousands of miles from Washington Heights.

Then Vera came home from school. She stood in the door to the kitchen, holding an armful of library books and looking down at me. "This place smells putrid," she said, wrinkling up her nose.

"It smelled all right till you got here," I told her.

Then she saw I had her *New York Times* spread out on the floor. She came into the kitchen to see which section I was using.

"That's disgusting," she said. "That's the cruelest, most insensitive thing I ever saw. I'm going to tell Elsa."

"Tell what?" I said, watching her legs invade my workshop. She was wearing brown loafers with pennies in the flaps and knee socks. The socks were very white and the loafers polished and the pennies shiny because Vera always kept her things neat. She kept her room clean too. But then she had the best room in the apartment with three big windows, not a dark little hole like mine.

"In the first place," said Vera, "you're making a vicious, awful toy. It's a warplane that drops napalm bombs on innocent people."

"Yawn," I said, flapping my hand against my open mouth to show how much I cared.

"And in the second place," Vera's voice went up like she was real scared and real pleased at the same time, "You're putting it together right on top of an article about the Rosenbergs. Can't you even read?"

I could read all right. I could read as good as anyone in my class. I could read *Pinocchio* to myself and

Mighty Mouse comic books and all the words in the instructions for my model, even the big ones like "fuselage." But I couldn't see anything in the paper about the Rosenbergs.

"Right there," said Vera, pointing to a glue-smeared headline at the top of the page. It had lots of big words. But Rosenbergs wasn't one of them.

"CHIEF EXECUTIVE DENIES CLEMENCY APPEAL," Vera said in a voice like a radio announcer. "JUNE EXECUTION DATE STANDS FOR ESPIONAGE AGENTS. You don't even know what that means, do you?"

"It means you better get outta here and leave me alone."

"Oh, no it doesn't," Vera said. "It means they're going to put the Rosenbergs in the electric chair at Sing Sing. Just a few weeks from now. They're going to shave their heads and strap them in and . . . and . . . electrocute them with one hundred thousand volts of electricity."

I couldn't help watching her face now. She had glasses with light blue frames shaped like butterfly wings, and her eyes were real bright behind them. Sunlight coming in through the window glinted on her braces. She was chewing her thumbnail. The tip was all bitten down to the red.

"It's a slow, hideous, excruciating way to die," she said. "And if they can do it to the Rosenbergs just for being communists and Jews, then they can do it to Ben or Elsa or even a little brat like you."

"They'd do it to you first," I said. "They'd do it to you first because you're older."

Then I started making a noise like a siren. I was pretty good at it. I scrunched up my throat and curled my tongue against the back of my teeth and kind of pumped my stomach to make the sound wail out high and thin just like Joe Friday's siren on *Dragnet*.

"EEEEE-eeee-EEEEE," I wailed.

Vera backed away. She put her fingers in her ears. Sirens scared her. If she heard them at night, she'd wake up screaming and couldn't go back to sleep for hours. Sometimes she'd cry just 'cause she saw a police car passing in the street.

"They're coming to get you-oo," I said in a real creepy voice between siren wails. "They're gonna get you and take you to Sing Sing and put you in the Chair."

Vera had backed all the way to the kitchen door now. She had one foot in the hall. Her face puckered up like she was just about to cry. I picked up the fuselage of my jet and dashed at her wailing as hard as I could. She ran down the hall and slammed the door to her room.

When my mother came home, Vera stamped into the kitchen and told on me. "He's playing with war toys again," she said. "Why don't you make him stop? It's indecent."

My mother was taking groceries out of a paper sack. She still had her hat on. "Not now, Vera," she said. "Please. Can't you see I'm tired."

"But he was putting it together right on top of a picture of the Rosenbergs," whined Vera. "If you're so busy organizing their defense with Leo, you could at least keep your son from desecrating their memory at home."

"Squealer!" I said.

"Liar!" Vera shouted.

My mother came over and looked at the paper I was using. I had smeared even more glue on the head-line, but she could still read it. "Put your toys away now, Josh," she told me. Her voice had that tremble in it that I didn't like to hear.

"But there's no picture," I wailed.

"I don't care if there's a picture or not." My mother stamped her foot and shook her head just like

Vera. "Put that thing away and get ready for dinner. I have a meeting tonight and no time for nonsense from either of you."

"See, smarty," said Vera from the doorway.

My mother whirled around. "Well at least he's doing something constructive. You might try it yourself sometime instead of carrying on the minute I get home. Can't you say anything nice about him for a change?"

"Oh, you think he's just your little angel," yelled Vera. "But he's not. He's a monster. A sneaky little monster and you're too blind to see it."

She stamped back to her room and closed the door. After I put my model away, I stood outside her door and made the siren sound. I had figured out a way to wail and say Sing Sing at the same time.

"Stop it!" Vera screamed through the door. "Just you stoppit, stoppit, stoppit!"

My mother couldn't hear 'cause she was running water in the sink for dinner.

The silent treatment didn't work like I expected. I thought if I just let the kids at school ignore me for a couple of days and didn't do anything to make them mad or show I cared, somebody would have to forget sometime and talk to me and I'd talk back and then it'd be over.

But actually it kept getting worse. If I just touched another kid by accident, they'd make a big show of brushing off the cooties while everybody giggled. Every day was like the first day in a new school except then you still had a chance to prove you were okay and now it was too late.

I guess I could've put up with it though if they hadn't started talking about the summer baseball league. Buddy Ryan had the sign-up sheet and he made sure I saw him passing it around. He asked just about every other boy in class to sign, and somehow he was always standing near me when he did it. All week long, I waited for him to ask me too.

Finally, at recess on Friday, when he was showing the list to Sidney, who used to play right field, I went straight up to him and said, "I wanna sign. It's not fair. I can play better than Sidney."

We were in the middle of the playground where they had the circle painted for dodgeball. Buddy wouldn't turn around. He just kept talking to Sidney. "There's gonna be umpires and everything," he said. "We're gonna go around and have games with other playgrounds on Saturdays. Even during summer."

"I got tap dancing lessons on Saturday," said Sidney. Ever since getting beaned on the ear, he hated baseball.

"Hey, lemme sign up, Buddy," I said to the freckles on the back of his neck. "Come on, please. If Sidney can't play, I'll take his place."

Buddy made like he didn't hear. "The winners're gonna get trophies," he told Sidney. "A big one for the whole team and small ones for every guy on it. And even if we lose, we get ribbons."

"Sorry," shrugged Sidney. "I got tap."

"Please, Buddy," I said.

He started walking off. The sign-up sheet waved in his hand. I grabbed for it. He yanked it away before I could get hold and laughed. He shouldn't have laughed. I shoved him hard as I could in the back. He fell face first on the pavement.

Buddy Ryan had red hair and got mad real easy, but he was about my size and didn't scare me nothing. He picked himself up off the ground and put his head down and ran at me waving his fists without even looking. When he knocked into me, I got him in a headlock. Headlocks were about all I could do in fighting, but they worked pretty good. We spun around in circles for a while, and then we fell down but I landed on top and got my headlock real tight so he couldn't breathe. He kicked and squirmed and even tried to bite, but I just crushed his face against my hip till he stopped fighting.

When I let him up, his face was all red and his shirt mussed up. His lip was bleeding. He touched his face, pulled back bloody fingers, and burst into tears. But he still had enough breath left to call me "Commie, commie, commie."

Lots of kids were watching us now, with more running up to join the circle every second.

"You better take that back!" I said.

He stepped away and I stepped after him, and just as I was about to jump him again, a real strong hand grabbed hold of my collar and jerked me up into the air. My stomach dropped through my shoes. It was Mrs. McMahon. She marched me across the schoolyard, up the stairs, and down the corridor to the principal's office.

I shivered and sweated on the bench in front of Mr. Klein's office till my shirt was wet under the arms. I had to go to the bathroom but didn't dare. I felt the hard wood of the bench through my pants and couldn't stop thinking about the paddle that Mr. Klein kept in a drawer of his desk. He called it "The Board of Education."

I watched Mrs. McMahon talking to him inside the office. The top part of the wall was glass so Mr. Klein could look out and spy on the kids in the hall. Mrs. McMahon was standing up. Every once in a while, she pointed at me. Mr. Klein sat in a leather armchair with his elbows on his desk and nodded and frowned. I couldn't hear what they were saying, but I knew she was telling him I started it. Buddy Ryan didn't have to go to the principal. She'd sent him to the nurse.

The hallway in front of the office was empty and

much too quiet with sunlight showing the scuff marks on the brown linoleum and dust drifting in the sunlight. All the kids were in class. Way far off at the end of the hall, I could see a bright gold crack outlining the door to the street.

Mrs. McMahon didn't say anything when she came out, just raised an eyebrow and gave me a disgusted look and walked back to class with her heels clicking loud and angry down the empty hall. Her fanny looked like a big black box when you saw it from behind. Mr. Klein still didn't call me in. He was on the telephone now. He talked and talked. Then he pulled a folder out of a filing cabinet and looked at it and talked some more.

Finally he hung up. He wagged his finger to tell me to come in. My hand slipped on the doorknob. I'd never been sent to the principal's office before. Never in all the schools I'd gone to. I was too scared to look around. I kept my eyes on the carpet. It was thick and gray with specks of black and worn-out patches where chairs used to be.

"Sit down, Josh," said Mr. Klein. He had a big, deep voice.

I sat in the chair in front of his desk. It felt even harder than the bench. My feet didn't reach the floor. I saw scratch marks on the wood of the desk and thought maybe they came from the fingernails of kids who held on to it while Mr. Klein paddled them. My parents never hit me. They didn't believe in hitting. Or fighting either.

"Did you start some trouble with Buddy Ryan?" Mr. Klein asked.

"I didn't mean to," I said.

"I'm not asking if you meant to or not," he shot back. "Who touched who first?"

"He wouldn't let me see the baseball sign-up sheet but everyone else could so I shoved him and he jumped me," I said, trying to get it all out in one breath so at least he'd hear my excuse.

"In other words," said Mr. Klein, "you started it, didn't you?"

"Yes."

"Yes, what?"

"Yessir."

"Well, when someone starts a fight in this school," said Mr. Klein, "I usually give them a choice." He paused and I held my breath. "They can get paddled right here by me or have their parents come in for a talk."

My stomach dropped so hard I felt like I was going to puke all over his desk. The paddle scared me more than anything. But I didn't want my mother coming to school, either. She hated fighting, and besides I'd never told her what happened before the parade and Mrs. McMahon was sure to let the secret out.

Mr. Klein watched me gulp. He stood up, blocking out the sun from the window.

"But your case is just a little bit different," he said, walking around to sit in front of me with one leg over a corner of his desk. "Mrs. McMahon tells me you've been having some trouble with the other boys in your class. Something about a parade, isn't it? A May Day parade?"

I looked up at him. His head seemed about a mile above me. The window was behind his back, and in his suit he looked something like a dark blue mountain with sunlight shining on the bald top of his head. His hands rested on his knees, so close I could see the hairs growing out of the brown spots on his pudgy fingers.

I couldn't talk anymore. I nodded real hard to show he was right about the parade.

"You know, Josh," said Mr. Klein, "I've been looking at your records. All the way back to kindergarten. You're no troublemaker. You're a bright boy. A good boy. So I'm going to give you a chance. I'm going to ask you a question. And I want you to think very hard before answering. Ready?"

I sat forward in my chair and folded my hands in my lap and pressed the palms together and looked at Mr. Klein with big teary eyes to show him how much I wanted to get the answer right.

"What do you think is the most important lesson we teach in this school?"

I knew from the way he asked it that he didn't want me to say spelling or fractions or geography or anything like that. I swallowed hard and said, "Not . . . not fighting?"

Mr. Klein smiled. He polished his glasses on his sleeve. "That's part of it. But there's an even larger lesson. I'll give you a hint," he said. "This lesson teaches us when it's right to fight and when it's not. When it's right to go to a parade and when you shouldn't. When you have to keep a secret and when you should tell on someone who's doing something bad, even if that person is closer to you than your very best friend. Still can't guess?"

I shook my head.

"All right. I'm talking about citizenship. How to be a good citizen of your school and your neighborhood and your country. America. Do you know what citizenship is?"

"Sort of," I said. He was talking to me in a real friendly, serious tone, and I knew I wasn't going to get the paddle now, but somehow I still felt scared, just as scared as before, only in a different way.

"Well, let me ask you one more question," said Mr. Klein. "This is an easy one. Which would you rather do? Draw a picture or write a story?"

"Write a story," I said.

"All right then, why don't you write me a story about citizenship and someone you know who's a good example of it? I want your idea. Not your mother's or your father's. Or even Mrs. McMahon's. *Your* idea. You can stay after school and bring it here before you leave. And if you do a good job, we'll forget all about this trouble. Okay?"

"Yessir!" I said, looking up at him. He was nodding at me, and when he nodded the pink, soft skin under his jaw bulged out and hid the knot of his tie. I glanced around his office. He had photos of graduating classes up behind his desk and green filing cabinets near the door. A showcase full of polished trophies and plaques covered one whole wall. The gold eagle on top of his flagpole gleamed in the sunlight by the window.

"Now run along back to class," he smiled. "And don't forget to tell Buddy Ryan you're sorry."

Citizenship
A good citizen knows our country's holidays. He goes to parades on patriotic ones. They are Abraham Lincol's and George Washington's

One of the most fameous men in our land was George Washington. He was as barve as a lion and truthful as he could be. He went to the Frenclu and Indian War. He knew when to fight and when to not

One time when my family was happy we went to the Statue of Liberty. We took a friend. When we got there mother wanted to know if he wanted to walk the stairs or go on the elevater. He said the stairs We went all the way to the top.

The policemen, firemen, street cleaners and postmen are the helpers in my neighborhood. The policemen helps me across the street. The firemen saves people from fire A street cleaner cleans streets. Postmen bring mail

A holiday to honor is Memorial Day. There was a gigantic parade to celebrate it. Many Soldies

Sailors and othe r good people marched in it They showed they would fitht for our country. They show they love our country

A good citizen who fouthg for our country is Captain Bob Thompson. He swam the river and pulled the men across on a rope. He beat the Javanese in the War.

Thanksgiving is a jolly time. We give thanks then. We have gay feasts on Nov. 22 that is Thanksgiving day.

Mr. Klein liked my essay. He made me wait in his office after school while he read it. He circled the misspelled words and made me write them ten times each, right there on his desk. Then he said I could go. I ran out of his office so fast that I bumped into someone coming in. It was a man in a brown suit. He had a thick neck and a crewcut that made his head look square as a building block. He gave me a friendly smile, but I was in too much of a hurry to smile back.

6

I wanted to apologize to Buddy Ryan. Not that I felt bad about the fight. Considering all the trouble he got me into, I wished I'd given him a bloody nose to go along with his fat lip. But making up with Buddy was the only way I had to get back on the team.

I thought about it a lot. I thought about apologizing at recess or on the way home from school or even in front of the class so he'd have to be a good sport and shake hands. But Buddy always tagged along after Eddie Allen. And no matter how bad I wanted to get back on the team and wear one of the pinstriped uniforms they were planning to order from Fishel's Athletic Goods, I just couldn't bring myself to apologize in front of Eddie.

I couldn't stand to see him smirk and curl up his lips and toss his blond hair out of his eyes and snort through his nose at me, especially after he had started the whole thing by telling on me about the parade. I never would've snitched on him that way.

So I kept putting it off day after day. But that didn't work either because suddenly it was the best baseball weather we'd had all year and each afternoon lasted about a month and I had nothing to do but sit on the edge of my bed in my dark musty room and slam my fist into the pocket of my mitt and think about how bad I wanted to run up to the park and play. When Vera came home, I'd find ways to make her cry and when my mom got back from work, I'd do things to make her angry too, like rolling my softball down the hall while she was trying to plan meetings on the phone, and that was about the only fun I had.

Then one afternoon the sun came shining down the alley outside my window and turned the brick wall across the way bright red and crept across my dusty floor till it fell on my sneakers, and before I knew it, I was lacing them up, grabbing my mitt, and racing out the door.

No matter what happened, I had to go up to the park. I had to get back on the team and tear around after fly balls and circle the bases shouting at the top of my lungs and waving my arms like a pinwheel. I ran up the hill to Sweeny's, and just as I was turning the corner, a man wearing a Dodger's cap came out of the store and flashed me a big, friendly smile and I figured that meant it was my lucky day for baseball.

I darted across 181st Street against the red light and took the ninety-seven steps to the park three at a time. The weather was warm enough for T-shirts but not sweaty like it got in the summer and the sky was so clear I could look across the Hudson and see every stick of the elaborate crisscross frame of the roller coaster at Palisades Park.

If I could just get to Buddy before they started a game, I figured everything would be all right. I'd apologize as nice as he wanted and we'd shake hands and say we were even and then I'd ask him to toss me the ball a couple of times to show there were no hard feelings. And once we started playing catch, there was a chance, just the tiniest little chance but the best one I had, that even Eddie Allen would say bygones are bygones and let me back on the team.

I went into the park through the gate near the stairs. Down at that end, they had stone tables and benches for old people to sit around and play chess or feed pigeons under the trees. I started walking slow now because I could see the kids on the baseball diamond through the branches.

Eddie was batting, as usual. The batting cage was way down at the far end of the field, and the farther away Eddie stayed, the better for me. The rest of the kids were scattered around the field, some of them not even paying attention, but peeling the wrappers off Milky Way bars, or tying their shoelaces, or calling each other names. Buddy Ryan was by himself for once, patting his glove on the yellow line back of third base. He was wearing jeans and black high-top sneakers like everybody else and a New York Yankees T-shirt because that's who Eddie rooted for.

I didn't want Buddy to see me till the right moment so I stayed under the trees at the edge of the outfield and walked all the way around to foul territory behind third base. Then I strolled up the line toward him but keeping close to the fence, running my fingers along the links and looking out at the cars passing on Fort Washington Avenue. Buddy was kicking the toe of his sneaker at a patch of gum on the tarmac and didn't see me till I came up.

"Hey, Buddy," I said. He swung around and looked at me. His eyes got round and he took a half-step back like he was surprised at the way I snuck up on him or even scared I wanted to fight again.

"Listen, I'm sorry I jumped you," I said, holding my hands out palm up. "It was my fault. I started it. Hey, come on. You can hit me back if you want to."

I hunched up my shoulder and offered it to him. He stuck out his jaw and balled up his fist like he was going to swing with all his might. But then he looked around and saw no one was watching and pulled at his red hair till it made a peak on top of his head and kicked at the gum again and finally said, "Aw, fergetit." But he still sounded mad.

So I rolled the sleeve of my T-shirt up over my shoulder and said, "Go ahead, Buddy. I owe ya. I never should've shoved you like that. I bet you woulda won if I didn't jump you from the back and knock you down and all."

Buddy looked like he was trying to hide the three teeth that hung over his lips when he smiled. In another couple of seconds we would've been friends again, but just then Eddie Allen had to butt in.

"Yeah, Buddy," he called, stepping out of the batter's cage and starting to walk toward us up the third base line, "go ahead and hit him." As soon as the kids saw where he was heading, they all drifted in from the field to circle around us.

Eddie had his Yankees cap on and a baseball jersey with number 7 in front. Seven was Mickey Mantle's number. Eddie had a square jaw like Mantle's, and he walked like he could pump 'em over the centerfield scoreboard too, and he even tried to imitate Mickey's smile, but on Eddie it just looked mean.

"Go on, Buddy," he said, coming up close. "Slug him one for me."

Buddy did. He sucked in his breath and scrunched up his freckled face and bopped me a lot harder than I thought he could. He shook his fingers out and blew on them afterward.

"Do it again," I said, rubbing my shoulder.

Buddy took another swing, and this time the sting went all the way down to my toes.

"Okay," I said. "Now we're even. Right?"

"Buddy turned to look at Eddie.

"Yeah, now you're even. Now get lost," Eddie told me.

I started to say it wasn't fair, then turned around and started to go. But the only place I could go was back to my dark, stuffy room and it seemed like my room was miles away and I felt too miserable to walk that far. So I turned back again and begged. "Come on, Eddie, please. I still wanna play. Lemme chase fouls or carry bats or anything. I don't care."

"Aww, he still wants to play," Eddie said to the kids standing in a circle around us. "The commie still wants to get back on the team. What'll we do?" He asked like he knew what the answer was going to be, like they'd talked it all over beforehand.

"Show 'im the list, Eddie. Yeah, the list. Make 'im sign the list," said the kids, elbowing each other and snickering.

"Oh, yeah, right. The list." Eddie snapped his fingers the way you do when you've almost forgotten something important. He pulled a piece of paper out of his back pocket. It was folded in four and looked like he'd been sitting on it for about a week.

"See this?" he asked me. "It's the new list we hadda make 'cause *you* tore the one Buddy had. No one plays on our team unless they sign it."

"Then lemme sign," I said.

"You wanna sign, huh?" asked Eddie, unfolding the paper crease by crease and holding it close to his chest so I couldn't see or grab it. "The commie still wants to sign our list. Whaddya think of that?" he asked the kids. They all thought it was a scream.

"Okay." Eddie presented the paper to me with a flourish. "Go ahead."

I took the sign-up sheet. SUMMER SOFTBALL LEAGUE was printed in dark pencil on the first line. Right under that in red crayon came "No commies or liers allowed." Eddie's name was first on the list, and everybody else had signed under him, one name to a line.

I didn't care what the list said. I was willing to sign anything. But I didn't have a pencil. I patted all my pockets, feeling stupid while I looked for one.

"What's the matter?" said Eddie.

"I don't gotta pencil."

For some reason the kids thought that was a howler, too.

"Shut up, you guys!" said Eddie. "Someone give 'im a pencil."

Fat Chico threw a stub at me. I didn't have the nerve to ask to write on his back, so I knelt down and put the paper on the tarmac and started to sign my name. But Eddie slapped the sole of his sneaker right down on the middle of the page and knocked the pencil out of my hand.

"Can't ya read?" he said. "It says no commies or liars. You gonna tell us you're not a commie?"

"Yeah," I said.

"Yeah what?"

"Yeah, I'm not."

"You swear it? You swear on your mother's grave?"

"Yeah. I swear."

"Then you're a liar," said Eddie, slapping his knee. "And you can't play anyway because you lied."

Everybody laughed like Eddie had just told the funniest joke all year. My face got red and hot. I stood up and looked at them. Fat Chico laughed with his mouth open so wide you could practically see his tonsils. Buddy was slapping Victor on the back. Tony giggled through his nose, making high little snorts like a horse.

I turned to Eddie Allen. Standing there with one hand hooked in his belt and his white blond hair peeking out from under the brim of his Yankees cap, he was the only one not laughing. He was giving me the Eddie Allen sneer with his mouth twisted up to one side and his eyes narrowed down and a hard cold light shining out of the slits.

I could tell he hated me. I could tell he was behind the list and the silent treatment and even the fight with Buddy.

"I never did nothing to you," I told him.

"Get outta here," he said, stepping up toe-to-toe with his chest pushing against mine. I could feel him all tensed up and hard and ready to hit. He was opening and closing his fists. He scared me. "No commies or liars allowed," he said.

I backed up. I wanted to run. I knew he'd keep me off the team and give me the silent treatment and make my life miserable as long as I went to P.S. 187, so I might as well run before he bashed my face in for good measure. But before running I just had to say the one thing that I'd been saving up ever since May Day.

"Well, at least I'm not a stoolie," I jeered at him. "At least I'm not a dirty rotten stoolie snitch like you."

His mouth dropped open and his ears got red and his head jerked around to see how the kids were taking it. No one ever called the great Eddie Allen a snitch. But he was and he knew it and he knew I had the right to call him one and all of a sudden I realized that was why he hated me so bad.

" 'Mrs. McMahon,' " I said, imitating his whine, " 'Mrs. McMaa-hon, how come Josh gets to go to a . . .' "

He hit me first on the side of my head right over the ear and I howled. Eddie didn't fight like Buddy with his eyes closed and his arms waving. He didn't charge blind hoping to bump into me and knock me down and roll around on the ground till someone pulled us apart. He fought squinting straight at me and swinging his balled-up fists with all his might and hurting me every time he swung.

Each one stung more than the last, and they came so fast I couldn't even put my hands up to block. I didn't have time to run. I couldn't reach him to use my headlock. I just stood there while he walloped me in the head about ten times and I saw black and red stars flashing behind my eyes and then I was swinging back, punching just like he did. I knocked the hat off his head and stood flat on my feet and threw my body into every punch, not even waiting for one fist to land before the other one looped down at his face.

And once I started swinging, I could hardly feel when he hit me. I could hear it more than feel it. I could hear his knuckles smacking me and mine smacking him and now we were right next to each other, slugging and hooking and grunting without either of us falling back, and I could tell he was surprised. I could tell he never expected me to stand up to him like that. And even though I was panting and bleeding and probably sobbing too, I felt glad, wild glad to be hitting back at him, and he didn't seem that much bigger than me now, and I didn't care anyway because everything was fading into a red misty hitting rage.

And then, I don't know if he got me one in the stomach or the nuts or what, but it was like that, all the air going out of me at once, and the red mist ripping apart, and right in the middle of it I saw my mother looking at me with soft brown eyes and shaking her head, and I saw my father, who never got mad no matter what we did, and I was still swinging but my arms felt weak now and Eddie Allen swelled up bigger and bigger till he towered over my head.

I could hear the kids cheering for him and sense them pressing tighter around us, and it seemed like the kids and the playground and the brick buildings on the street and the stones of the school and the whole neighborhood and the people at the parade and even Joe Friday on *Dragnet* and Superman—they were all lined up behind Eddie, all adding weight to his fists, all rooting for him to beat me down, and behind me there was no one, just no one and nothing but air.

And suddenly I was running, sobbing and running with Eddie on my heels and all the kids chasing me in a pack. I ran across the outfield and into the trees, and they were right behind, yelling and grabbing at me. I weaved through the tree trunks and broke away from hands and heard my T-shirt rip and made it to the benches by the entrance to the park. I dodged between the benches, but the pack split in two and came at me from both sides. I couldn't make it to the gate and I couldn't hop the fence because of the spears on top. I stopped, cringing and crying with my arms at my sides and my back to the bars of the fence. They closed in. Eddie came first, hands out to grab what was left of my shirt.

But just as he reached me, a man who'd been watching the whole thing from a bench under the trees stood up and dropped a warm solid arm around my shoulder.

"Hold it right there," he said to Eddie. "That's enough. Back off. All of you." He said it kind of soft. But he was a big guy and you could hear that his voice would be hard and scary if you ever made him mad. The kids looked around at each other and at the man and at me and then down at the ground.

"What d'you think you're doing?" the man asked Eddie.

Eddie stared at his toes. Then he looked up and said, "Don't trust 'im, mister. He's a commie."

"Oh yeah," said the man. "And what're you? A war hero like Audie Murphy 'cause you have the nerve to chase a kid half your size with a gang behind you? Go on. Get out of here. Go back to your game. And if any of you pick on my pal here again, you'll answer to me."

The man held me against his side while the kids followed Eddie back through the trees to the softball diamond. I was wheezing and panting, trying to catch my breath and stop my tears. His hand squeezed my shoulder. He gave me a handkerchief and told me to wipe my face. The handkerchief came away covered with snot from my nose and blood from my mouth. The man knelt down and wiped off what I missed. I recognized him now. He was the man with the Dodgers cap who smiled at me outside Sweeny's. Maybe I'd even seen him around somewhere before. He had bright eyes that kind of popped out of his face and a smile that showed lots of teeth and a thick neck that stuck up from the collar of his white shirt. His tie was loose.

"You okay now?" he asked me.

"Yeah."

"You want me to walk you home?"

I shook my head.

"Why not?"

"I left my glove over there," I said, nodding at the far side of the diamond. My mouth hurt. I could taste blood inside.

"Well, why don't you go over and get it?"

"I can't."

"Sure you can," said the man. "I'll watch from here. They won't lay a finger on you. Go on." He gave me a little shove.

It was a long walk over to the third baseline where I'd fought Eddie Allen. My knees wobbled and I kept my eyes on the ground the whole way, looking at the white splatters of pigeon plop on the tar. I hunched my shoulders up to my ears and wished I could pull my head down like a turtle. Any second, I expected the kids to start screaming and chasing me again.

But no one said a word. I didn't even hear the sound of the bat on the ball. I picked up the glove and slipped my fingers inside and felt the warm, soft leather. On the way back, I had the nerve to look up. Buddy Ryan was still playing third base. He gave me plenty of room to pass. Eddie was batting again, but no one seemed to be having much fun.

The man in the Dodgers cap was still waiting when I got back. "Come on," he said, "I'll walk you down the stairs."

He put his arm around my shoulder, and we walked out through the gate of the playground. My head came about up to his waist. His slacks were brown and he had a thin belt made out of brown snaky leather. He walked with a bounce in each stride.

"You did okay," he told me as we started down the steps to 181st Street. "You did okay with that kid. Maybe another couple of seconds and he wouldn've run instead of you."

I didn't say anything. I was busy feeling my face. I had lumps all over my head, especially a big tender one above my right eye.

"Well, you gonna tell me what it's all about?" he asked.

"Nothing."

"If it's nothing," he said, "how come they were calling you 'commie'?"

I blushed. I couldn't explain the whole thing, and even if I did, the man might get mad at me like they did.

" 'Cause they don't want to let me on the team," I told him.

"You like baseball, huh?" said the man. "You like it enough to get all tangled up with a big kid like that? Hey, who's your favorite team, anyway?"

"Brooklyn," I said.

He stopped on the landing halfway down the stairs, took off his baseball cap and ran his hand through his crewcut. The sandy blond bristles stuck straight up from his skull and popped back into place as soon as his hand passed. "What do you know?" he said. "The Bums're my team, too. Who do you like best? Duke Snider? Preacher Roe? Not one of those Nee-gro guys like Robinson?"

"Pee Wee Reese," I said. "He's gonna win the Golden Glove this year, for sure, and maybe hit .300 too."

"Reese, huh?" said the man. "Then I guess you wanna play shortstop like him?"

"Yeah, but I'm scared of grounders," I said.

We were at the bottom of the stairs now. Buses and cars rumbled up the hill. The sidewalks were crowding up with women shopping and men coming back from work.

"Don't sell yourself short, pal," said the man. "Maybe you just need practice. You think Reese got good without practice? All you gotta do is come out every day and . . ." Suddenly he stopped talking and hit himself on the forehead with the heel of his hand. "Now I get you," he said, bending down and putting both hands on my shoulders and looking at me with bright eyes that kind of bulged out of his face. "You can't practice 'cause they won't let you on the team. Is that it?"

I nodded.

"Well, I tell you what," said the man, brushing his thumb across his flat nose like a boxer. "I don't toss the ball around much myself nowadays. What do you say we practice together sometime? Just you and me?"

"You mean it?" I asked, pounding my glove.

"Sure," said the man. "Sure I mean it. Why don't

you bring your ball out to the park tomorrow? Is it a deal?"

"Yessir!"

"Okay, then guy, put 'er there."

He squeezed my knuckles hard enough to make them pop when we shook.

"Aren't you even gonna tell me your name?" he asked as I started walking down the block.

"Josh," I told him, looking back over my shoulder.

"Okay, Josh," he said. "I'm Dale. Now we're buddies."

7

I snuck into the house because I didn't want Vera to see I'd been fighting. But she heard me open the door and came out of her room and stood down at the end of the hall, watching me without saying a word. I held my glove up to my mouth and tried to push past her into the bathroom. She noticed my shirt first.

"Yuuuck," she said in her disgusted voice. "Aren't you embarrassed to run around like a street urchin when Elsa works so hard to . . ."

Then she saw my face. "What happened?" she asked. "You're injured."

"Leave me alone," I said, shoving into the bathroom.

But she followed and watched me splash water on my face at the sink. I wasn't tall enough to bend over the basin so most of the water splashed on the floor.

"Here," said Vera. "Come on. You can't do anything right." She turned on the light and took a washcloth and ran hot water on it and dabbed at my face. She pressed a little on the sore spots. It hurt, but I could feel the warm wetness drawing out the sting. Water dripped on her white blouse, but she didn't seem to mind.

"Sit down," she told me.

I sat on the floor, leaned against the tub, and tilted up my face to her. She got cotton out from under the sink and iodine.

"Close your eyes," she said. "This may result in temporary discomfort." She sounded kind of happy about it.

After, she made tea with honey in it and lemon. The drink burned a little on the raw spots inside my mouth. Vera asked if I wanted to lie down, but I said no so she brought out her jacks and we sat on the kitchen floor by the window bouncing a little rubber ball and scooping up handfuls of red, blue, and silver jacks. Vera's hands were white and very quick. She could scoop up ten jacks in one bounce. The best I could do was six, but then I was still shaking a little from the fight and thinking about Dale and wondering if he'd really show up to play with me.

The funny thing about Vera was that as soon as my mother came home she forgot all about playing jacks and jumped up to squeal on me.

"He's been fighting," she told Elsa. "He came in with his shirt ripped to shreds and blood virtually gushing from his face. He'd be in a coma by now if I hadn't administered first aid."

My mother dropped her grocery bags on the counter. She pulled me over by the window where the light was best and took my chin in her hand and turned my face from side to side. First she looked scared, but when she saw that Vera was just making a federal case out of a couple of cuts and bruises, her eyes turned soft.

She brushed her fingers very gently across the lump over my right eye. "Does it hurt?" she asked. "Do you want an ice pack?"

"No," I said.

"What was it about?"

"Baseball," I told her.

"Baseball?" she said, shaking her head with a sad little laugh. "How can you fight about a thing like that?"

Her laugh made me mad. If it wasn't for her and May Day and Underground and being a commie and all, I never would've had to fight in the first place. But that was too complicated to explain, especially with Vera listening in, and now there was the man named Dale mixed up in it too.

"They wouldn't let me on the team," I said. "I was just trying to make them."

Elsa hugged me against her, rumpling my hair and pushing my face against the soft cotton of her blouse, careful not to press on the bruises. "It's hard moving into a new neighborhood, isn't it?" she said. "Especially when Ben's not around and I'm too busy to play with you. But it'll get better. You'll see. And meanwhile, try to remember that there are better ways to fight than using your fists, and more important things to fight about than baseball."

That night I had bad dreams. They weren't dreams exactly. They were more like voices, voices calling me from Underground. They sounded nice to begin with so I let them lead me into this long, dark tunnel, but as soon as I got deep inside and heard the voices echoing down the damp, curving walls, I realized they weren't friendly at all. I jerked myself awake, but every time I closed my eyes the voices were waiting for me in the tunnel and each time it got a little harder to escape. Once I let them drag me way deep down into the darkness, and then when I tried to wake up, I couldn't move. I couldn't budge my eyelids or force a sound out of my mouth or even wiggle a toe, and it was just like being buried alive, and meanwhile the voices kept getting closer and louder and laughing and calling my name, calling "Joo-oosh, Joo-oosh, Joo-oosh," and they just didn't sound friendly at all.

After that, I gave up on sleeping and lay in bed, looking around my room. It was dark, but not black dark like in my dream. If I wanted to let it, the stain on the ceiling over my bed could look like the mouth of the tunnel in my dreams. But I knew the stain came from leaky water pipes. I knew that all I had to do was keep my eyes open and think good thoughts till the voices got tired of waiting in my dreams and then I could go back to sleep again.

I felt around at the bottom of the bed with my feet to find the lump under the mattress where I kept my mitt with a baseball snuggled in the pocket. I sat up and took the mitt out and rolled the ball around in the pocket and ran my fingers over the smooth oily leather and thought about the Dodgers. We were burning up the league this year. We had just swept three in a row and knocked the Giants out of first and Pee Wee was hitting .300 and if we won the pennant like everybody said, I just knew we were going to kill the Yankees in the series. We were going to cream 'em four straight, and I couldn't wait to see Eddie Allen's face when we did it. But right now, I didn't want to think much about Eddie Allen because it made the places where he hit me ache and I was trying to keep good thoughts in my head.

I looked at my model airplanes parked on the windowsill at the foot of my bed. The F-86 Sabre in the middle had its nose cone pointing out the window to protect against sneak attacks, and the jets on either side were lined up to intercept invaders who came through the door. My spacemen were standing guard over the fleet, but they weren't glowing because I hadn't warmed them up, and besides Captain Bob had disappeared somewhere in the house. I was afraid the enemy had him, but maybe he was just on a mission so secret he couldn't even tell me.

Out the window, I could see the top railing of the fire escape—a dark line against the black wall of the building across the way. The fire escape went down past all the apartments and ended in an alleyway where we kept the garbage cans. I'd never climbed down to the bottom, but it was late now and I could probably sneak past without waking anybody up, and if I *did* climb down, I'd go get Jody. He had a fire escape outside his window too. One night we were going to climb down our fire escapes and run away back to San Francisco together.

Jody used to live in San Francisco, too, in the same neighborhood I did. It was right under Twin Peaks. Jody was two and a half years older than I was and had lots of friends, but he still liked to play with me. When a bunch of other kids came around he'd get all excited and maybe start running or dancing so they'd all follow him and have a good time, but sometimes when we were alone he could be real quiet and that's what I liked best.

8

The next morning I woke up with a shiner. It was a black ring starting at my nose, circling under my right eye, and ending in a bruise on top of my cheek. It wasn't a gooey purple-yellow mess covering half my face like I got creamed by Rocky Marciano. But you couldn't help noticing it, and that was lucky for me because it made Eddie Allen happy.

Everyone at school knew he gave it to me. They could just look at my face and see how tough he was. It wasn't much fun being a walking advertisement for Eddie. But as long as he felt satisfied, I felt safe.

After school I ran home for my glove and went up to the park to meet the man named Dale. I slipped in through the lower gate, trying to keep out of sight of Eddie and the gang. Dale was waiting for me on one of the stone benches under the trees.

He still had his blue baseball cap on, but instead of his shirt and tie, he was wearing jeans and a gray sweatshirt and sneakers. He had a big black first-base-man's glove, all scuffed and oily and soft. He whistled when he saw my shiner.

"Well, I bet you gave him a few lumps, too," he said.

"I didn't see nothing," I answered, shaking my head.

"Aw, they were probably under his hair. You'd be surprised how much you can bang up a guy without showing a mark. Anyway, never mind. Take a look at this." Dale pointed at a fading signature with lots of loops in the pocket of his glove. I couldn't read it.

"Gil Hodges," said Dale. "Signed it for me himself out at Ebbets Field. Ever been there? No? Not yet? Well, you'll make it. Come on, let's toss the ball around."

I had my old softball, but it was mashed out of shape so we used Dale's—a brand-new hardball with red stitching and the official major league mark on its leather cover.

"Okay," he said. "First we stand close and throw soft. Then we move back till you can't reach me any-more. Then we come close again. Get it?"

I threw the first one over his head. It rolled under the benches and all the way to the fence. "You threw it, you chase it," said Dale. "That's the rules of this game."

I did a lot of chasing. But Dale was good. He scooped up balls off the gravel and jumped and stretched and twisted for them. He looked almost like a real ballplayer, leaning forward and waiting for my next wild throw with his feet spread and his hands on his knees and the sleeves of his sweatshirt pushed up to his elbows and his cap tilted back on his head. His face was kind of flat with nothing sticking out enough to get hurt even if a grounder bounced right up and hit him.

We played on the gravel around the benches at first, but then we needed more room so we moved through the trees into the sunshine on the baseball diamond. We stayed back in the deepest part of centerfield, near the fence where no one ever hit. But the kids could still see us playing and that made me nervous. I dropped easy ones and couldn't throw straight.

"Hey, I'm not a tree," Dale told me when I pegged the ball right at one. On the next throw he said, "Come on, guy, do I look like a lamppost to you?"

But he never got tired of playing. And once in a while I'd zing one right into his mitt.

"Hear that pop?" he'd say. "Pretty soon you're gonna be shooting 'em in that way every time. Just takes a little practice is all. Couple of three hundred throws a day and we'll put an arm like a bazooka on you. Right, guy?"

When he smiled, his pale blue eyes bulged out and gave him a funny, surprised expression, almost like a frog about to stick out his tongue and swallow a fly. I liked his eyes though. They were the only soft things on his hard, flat face.

The next day Dale brought a fungo bat. It had a long skinny handle like a drumstick with all the meat on top. He could hit anywhere he wanted with it. I practiced fielding. We started with grounders, and I couldn't do anything right. When I expected them to bounce, they rolled under my glove, and when they looked like rollers, they bounced up and hit me in the chest. I tried closing my eyes at the last instant, but then they rolled over my mitt, up my arm, and past my shoulder before I knew what was happening.

"Try another one," Dale kept saying. "You just have to hold your head down and watch it. Hang in there. You won't get hurt if you're watching."

I was about ready to cry when we switched to fly balls. That was more fun. Dale could hit high ones or liners or loopers or bloopers or pop-ups that twisted like leaves in the air. And sometimes I could catch them. And when I caught them, sometimes I could throw straight back to where he was standing even though we were much farther apart than before.

"Okay, little buddy," he'd tell me, "to your left." Then he'd snap the bat and hit one just far enough for me to reach if I ran with all my might. When I caught one at the end of a gallop like that, he'd say, "Way to go, killer. Good way to go."

I don't know if it was because he warned me where to run, or because he always gave me another chance when I missed, but by the end of the afternoon I was running flat out and snagging some beauties. I never thought I could play like that. And a couple of times, I knew the kids on the team were watching. That made me laugh because I was getting ten times better practice than they were. In fact, it seemed like in all the times I played baseball, I never really practiced up till now, never tried to do one thing, like catching flies, over and over till I finally got the hang of it.

But Dale could only play till about five o'clock. On the way down the stairs from the park, he told me, "Let's face it, guy. Pee Wee Reese, you ain't. And unless I miss my guess, you're never gonna be. But in the outfield, well, maybe you've got a shot. You're a fast little squirt, anyway. You've just got to learn about a million and one things like not holding your glove the same for a pop-up and a liner on your shoestrings. For the liners, see, you come in backhand like this. Or give yourself an angle on the ball. You know what I don't get, though?" He stopped, and took off his cap and ran his hand through his bristly blond crewcut.

We were at the bottom of the steps, leaning

against the big green box where the delivery trucks dumped the morning newspaper. I could see the tower of the George Washington Bridge above the red brick buildings by the river. Way up on top of the tower under the revolving light there was a little room with windows where I used to think that someone sat all the time watching our whole neighborhood through binoculars.

"What I don't get," said Dale, "is how come a good kid like you who wants to play so bad doesn't have his old man come out and teach him this kind of stuff. Doesn't he like ball, your dad?"

"Not that much," I said, kicking at the sidewalk. "Besides, he's away right now."

"Oh yeah?" said Dale. We started walking again, down the sidewalk past the candy-striped pole outside the barber shop where they always cut my hair too short no matter what I told them. We stopped for the traffic light on the corner.

"Well, when's he coming back?" Dale asked.

"After a while, I guess."

"I bet you miss him. Does he write?"

"No."

"Talk to him on the phone then?"

"No."

"Sounds like a busy man. He must be doing something important, right?"

"Yeah."

We had crossed the avenue and started up a narrow block between red brick buildings. They were shabbier than the ones near the park. They seemed to lean in and hang over the street, and it was dark in their shadow. Sweeny's store was up on the corner, and our apartment was just down the hill from Sweeny's. Suddenly it didn't feel good to be that close to home and talking to Dale about my father. I'd played with him twice, and he was about the nicest person I'd met since we moved to New York. But he was still a stranger. I wondered what my mother would say about him. Or Vera if she saw us together.

I tried to see him through their eyes. He had a thick chest and a dark wet circle around the neck of his sweatshirt and a few drops of sweat on his boney forehead. He tapped on the sidewalk with the fungo bat and stared back at me, looking out of the bottom of his bug eyes like he was trying to guess my weight. If it hadn't been for his eyes and his face being a little too flat, he could've maybe played the good guy in cowboy movies like Alan Ladd in *Shane*. But Vera would probably say he looked like an imbecile. And I guessed my mother wouldn't like him much either. And the really strange thing was that even though I liked him a whole lot, there was something about him, maybe just how quick and light on his feet he was for being so strong, that scared me a little too.

"I gotta go," I said, backing away.

He watched me, nodding his head. "You know what I like about you, Josh?" he said.

I stopped to listen.

"Your attitude. Most kids, they get beat up by a bully the way you did and right away they start hating. They'd be after me to teach 'em jujitsu so they could go back and murder the guy. Or else they'd blame it all on baseball and never play again for the rest of their lives. Or maybe they'd stay in their rooms and be afraid to go out on the street for the next two years. But you"—he pointed at me with the fat part of the bat—"you still want to be on the team. You want to get on it now even worse than before. Am I right?"

"Yeah," I nodded, surprised and kind of pleased that he could guess or even cared enough to try and guess what I was feeling.

"Well, that's the right attitude," said Dale.

"That's the right way to go. Don't hate. And don't quit. Just do your darnedest to get back on the team."

"But they'll never let me back," I sighed, " 'cause they've got this list and . . ."

"Forget the list," said Dale, waving his arm like he was throwing the list away. "You know what we're gonna do? We're gonna teach you to beat 'em at their own game. That's the ticket, Josh. That's the secret of success. Beat 'em at their own game, and one day they'll beg you to play on their team. You get me?"

I smacked the pocket of my mitt. "Can we practice batting tomorrow?" I asked.

Dale smiled his bug-eyed smile. "We're gonna practice batting till you got blisters on your hands as big as this." He showed me the calluses on his palm. He had small, thick hands, not cracked and dirty like a worker's, but hard. The calluses were mainly around his index finger.

"The only thing is, little buddy," he sighed, "I can't come up here and practice with you every day like I've been doing. Hey, don't look at me like that. You think your dad's the only busy guy in the world? I've got a job too. But I tell you what. It's Wednesday, right? How's about we meet up at the park every Wednesday afternoon right after school. That good enough for you?"

It wasn't, but I knew it was the best I could get out of him, so I tried to look happy anyway. After we said good-bye, I turned the corner and walked down the hill toward our building. The apartments got dirtier and older as I went down the block. There were garbage cans on the sidewalk and fat men in undershirts sitting on the stoops. I climbed the front stairs to our building, took the key that hung on a chain around my neck, and unlocked the door. Just before I let myself into the dark lobby, I turned and looked back. Dale was watching from outside of Sweeny's. I waved to him and he swung the hat around with his wrist as if it weighed about as much as a popsicle stick.

9

We were getting ready for a Party party at our house. That's what I called it when everyone who came belonged to the Party. We used to have them all the time at our apartment in San Francisco, but this was the first one my mother had given since we moved to New York.

I had cleaned up my room, and now I was helping out in the kitchen. My mother was baking piroshkis and frying Vienna sausages and slicing up carrots and celery and radishes for dips. She moved around the kitchen very fast, from the sink to the stove to the table to the refrigerator, holding a knife in one hand and a frying pan in the other, and talking to me while she chopped and stirred and fried and set out food on plates. I liked the way she could do everything at once and still look calm and pretty.

I sat near the oven waiting for the piroshkis to bake. I opened the door every couple of minutes to make sure they didn't burn. When I opened the door, baking smells and a faint whiff of gas curled around my face and the heat sent a breeze through my hair. The piroshkis were lined up in neat rows on a cookie sheet, little triangular pies full of meat and onions with white flour sprinkled on top. I liked them best when the dough browned just enough to make the edges crisp. I sampled one every time I opened the oven.

"Leave some for the party, Josh," my mother said. "If they're ready, take them out."

I huffed and puffed on my piroshki, trying to keep it from burning my mouth while I chewed. The crust still tasted doughy. "Not yet," I mumbled around a mouthful. After the last swallow, I looked at her kind of sideways and said, "I met a nice man at the park this week."

She was cutting the heads of radishes to make them look like red flowers with white petals on top. She stopped, brushed her bangs out of her eyes with the back of her hand, and said, "A man? What kind of man? What did you do together?"

"Practiced baseball. He's teaching me to catch."

"You have to be careful of strangers, Josh," she said.

"He's not a stranger. He's my friend."

"Why does he have time to play with little boys in the middle of the day?"

"How come you're always so suspicious?" I said, starting to feel sorry I'd mentioned Dale in the first place. "And besides, I wouldn't have to play with him if Ben was around."

My mother took a short, sharp breath. I knew she didn't like me to talk too much about Ben. She stopped slicing and came over to put her hand on my head. Her fingers felt wet through my hair.

"Do you miss your father a whole lot?" she asked, kneeling down so we were face to face.

I thought about it. I missed the times when we were all living together in San Francisco. But I didn't know if I missed *him* all that much. Sometimes it was nice just being with my mother. And even in San Francisco, Ben never had time to play catch with me like Dale. If he was just away somewhere, traveling or working or something, it might've been okay. But he was Underground, and that made everything different.

"Where's Underground?" I asked.

My mother sighed. She stood me up and hugged me and said, "I don't know, Josh. I can get letters to him if I have to, but it's better that we don't know where he is because then we can't tell anybody, even by mistake. But your father's fine. He's healthy and writing for the paper and he misses you very much. And he won't be Underground forever. One day he'll come back. We just have to wait and be strong. And while we're waiting, it's better not to think about him too much. Just try to put him out of your mind for a while, and before you know it, we'll all be together again."

She squeezed me against her, and we stood in the kitchen with the warmth of the oven on our backs, and I smelled her perfume all mixed up with the odors of piroshkis and radishes and Vienna sausages, and I could've stayed there a long time but the doorbell started ringing.

My mother jumped. "I told them not to ring," she said with an impatient stamp of her heel. "Be a good boy and run downstairs to let people in. The whole building doesn't need to know we're having a party."

I liked meeting people at the door. They all knew me and said something friendly about how fast I was growing or how much like my father I looked, and almost everyone brought something to eat on a big plate or in a paper sack or wrapped up in tinfoil. By the time I finished doorman duty, our kitchen table was covered with salads and sliced meats and platters of light and dark rye bread and bowls of rice and stuffing and potatoes and gravy. The desserts were on the counter by the sink. Someone brought angelfood cake with chocolate icing.

People put their coats in my room. That's why I had to clean it up. My bed disappeared under a heap of jackets and hats and purses. If I got tired during the party, I knew I could go in my room and lie on top of the pile or burrow into it and cover myself up with coats. It would be soft and dark, and I could rub the ones that felt like fur against my face and catch odors of ladies' perfume clinging to the linings.

Our hall was full of people now and the kitchen and my mother's room too. They didn't play music or dance or even laugh a lot. They just stood around smoking and drinking out of paper cups and talking. Everyone talked at once so their voices kept getting louder and louder as the party went on.

I took the platter of piroshkis and carried it through a forest of legs. Wally Jacks called me over with his big booming voice and scooped four piroshkis off my plate at once. Vera said Wally was coarse, but my mother told her all sailors talked that way and Wally had been a machine-gunner in Spain and shot down German airplanes so we shouldn't listen when he swore. I liked him because once he showed me how to make a noose using the draw cord of our Venetian blinds. It was a real noose with thirteen loops, and you could make it looser or tighter by pulling the end of the cord.

Wally was standing in the hall arguing with Chester McDowell. Chester was the sportswriter for the paper. He had gray hair and a beard, and he wore a green corduroy jacket with leather patches on the elbows. When Wally talked, Chester listened, puffing clouds of smoke from his pipe. They were arguing about the Rosenbergs.

"The fascists are going to fry those poor bastards, and you know it as well as I do," said Wally. "All our pleas and briefs and legal bullshit just make the lynching bee look more legitimate."

"Nonsense," said Chester. He took the pipe out of his mouth and shook it at Wally's chest, making sharp little check marks in the air with the stem. "People's lives are at stake. We'd be criminals ourselves if we didn't exploit every possible argument the system allows."

"I'll tell you the argument those bastards understand," said Wally. He popped the last two piroshkis in his mouth, stuck out his index fingers, cocked his thumbs, and made a spraying, sputtering sound like machine gun fire. Crumbs flew out from the corners of his lips.

"For chrissake, Wally," said Chester, snorting smoke through his nose. "This is nineteen fifty-three in New York, not nineteen thirty-six in Madrid. That kind of talk is totally out of line." He looked around to see who else was listening and spotted me holding the tray.

"Oh, *there* you are, Josh," he said. "Listen, your mother talked to me about taking you out to Ebbets Field one of these days to meet the players. Would you like that?"

"Wow, yeah, you bet!" I said, hopping up and down and getting so excited I almost dropped the tray.

"Okay, we'll work on it then. And in the meantime, be a good kid and get this wild man a drink to cool him off, will you?" He jerked his head at Wally. "A gin and tonic with plenty of ice. Get me one too, while you're at it." He gave me a couple of dollars for the drinks.

The bar was in my mother's room by the window. Fat Peggy Mendolsohn was bartender. She stood behind a card table covered with bottles and bowls of ice cubes and stacks of paper cups and a white coffee can for people to put their donations in. The coffee can had a label around it that said SMITH ACT DEFENSE FUND.

Before I reached the table, Joe Lester put his hand on my arm. He was the tallest man there. He bumped his head going through doors and kept his shoulders slouched over like he was trying to bring his face down to the level of other people's. He had a hook nose and a vein that stood out on his forehead when he got excited. The vein was pulsing now. He was arguing with a dozen people who stood in a circle around him.

"Let's ask this young man," he said, drawing me into the circle. "Now what do *you* think, young Josh?" He pointed a long finger at my face and looked at me seriously. "Is it really five minutes to midnight?"

I couldn't see why they needed to ask me the time when they all had watches and I didn't. But Joe Lester was always asking tricky questions like that.

"It's nowhere near midnight," I told him.

"How do you know?" he asked.

"Because the party just started," I said. "And by midnight it'll be all over."

"Out of the mouths of babes," said Joe in a loud satisfied voice, turning back to the group and pointing a finger at Leo. "Out of the mouths of babes. It's nowhere near midnight and the party's just started. I tell you, we have to . . ."

They started arguing again. My mother's room was hot and smokey, and I didn't feel like talking to grown-ups anymore. I put my platter down on top of the bookcase and squeezed through the crowd to Vera's room.

Her door was closed, so I knocked.

The door opened a crack and Simone's head peeked

out. Simone was Jody's sister and Vera's best friend. She was sleeping over tonight. She wore glasses and braces like my sister, but instead of reading all the time like Vera did, she carried a white slide rule everywhere she went.

"It's your brother," Simone said to Vera.

"You can't come in," Vera called, "unless you want to play Party Meetings."

"Groan," I said. But I went in anyway. I knew all about Party Meetings because the only time Vera and Simone let me play with them was when they needed somebody else for the game. Vera was crazy about meetings. We weren't supposed to listen when my mother had one at our house, but Vera would crouch on the kitchen floor with her ear pressed against one of the painted-over panels on the door to my mother's room and listen for hours without getting bored.

She was sitting on her piano bench with her legs crossed and a notebook on her knees when I came into her room. She had on red knee socks and a plaid skirt. They were all set up for the meeting with Monopoly money to pay dues and coffee cups from Vera's dollhouse and even ashtrays from the kitchen with rolled-up pieces of paper for cigarettes.

"I'm Org. Sec.," Vera told me. That meant Organization Secretary.

"And I'm Sec. Org.," said Simone. Sec. Org. meant section organizer. It was like chairman, so Simone sat at Vera's desk by the window with her slide rule in her hand to call the meeting to order.

"You're the rank and file," Vera said to me. "You sit with them." I sat down on the gray rug between the desk and the piano bench with four or five of Vera's dolls. They were the rank and file until I came along.

Vera started the meeting by taking role and collecting dues. I had to pay for myself and all the dolls.

Then Vera sold literature because she was lit. org., too. The literature was lined up on Vera's orange bed-spread. There were green-and-white pamphlets called *Monthly Review* and heavy sets of books with leather covers and gold print from our bookcase. Vera made me buy the thickest book of all.

"I'm sure you'll find it enlightening," she told me. "It'll correct your left deviationist tendencies," she added. "If anything can."

When Simone took over, she made us report on our activities. We had to tell about our work with Mass Orgs. and how many leaflets we passed out and how many "subs" we sold that month. The last time we played I said I sold a thousand "subs" to the navy, but they expelled me for that because "subs" weren't submarines like I thought. They were subscriptions to the Party newspaper and Vera said I ought to know about the paper because my own father edited it.

When you got expelled, first they brought you up on charges before the review committee. And if you couldn't explain what you did, they took a vote and threw you out. Then you had to leave the room and no one would talk to you and you couldn't go to meetings or Party parties anymore. Usually they found some way to expel me before the meeting was over, but I didn't mind because, after using Monopoly money to pay dues and buy books, all they did was talk.

They talked about Problems and Questions. There were lots of Questions. Like the Negro Question and the Woman Question and the Peace Question.

"Tonight," said Simone, "we will hear a report on the Negro Question from our junior member, who"—she scowled at me—"needs considerable education on the subject." She tapped her slide rule on Vera's desk and nodded at me to begin.

"The Negro Question's getting a lot better," I said. "Because before they wouldn't even let Jackie Robinson play in the majors. But now we've got five Negroes just on the Dodgers alone." I counted them off on my fingers. "There's Jackie, and Campanella behind the plate, and Newcombe and Black on the mound, and this season Junior Gilliam at second base. And he might even win Rookie of the Year."

Vera and Simone looked at each other, shaking their heads and making *tsk tsk* sounds through their closed lips.

"I think we have to bring him up on charges," Vera said.

"White Chauvinism if I ever heard it," nodded Simone.

"Don't you know that even if they let Negroes play a stupid game and get traded for money like slaves, they're still lynching them in the south?" Vera asked me. "Haven't you read your own father's articles on the Emmet Till case?"

"And what about Male Chauvinism?" said Simone, waving her ruler at me. "Did you ever stop to think that all your precious ballplayers are men? What about the plight of the colored woman?"

"He's left deviationist and right opportunist both at the same time," said Vera.

"Clear cause for expulsion," said Simone.

"Out," shouted Vera, pointing to the door. "Most definitely and incontrovertibly and irrevocably out!"

I was feeling a little tired after they expelled me from the Party, and our whole apartment was full of noise and cigarette smoke, so I decided to go lie down in my room. People would have to come in and get their coats off my bed before leaving, but they were still yelling like they could argue for a couple of hours yet and I wanted to nap in the meantime.

The door to my room was closed, so I pushed right in and hit the switch without thinking. My mother and

Leo spun away from the window and whirled around to face me. It happened so fast that I couldn't tell if they were talking or hugging or kissing or what. But I felt that awful awkward blush you get from barging into the bathroom while your sister or someone is using it.

"Hey, there, Mighty Mouse," said Leo, straightening his tie and giving me a lopsided smile, "don't you ever knock?"

"Knock? Whaddya mean, knock? It's my room! Can't I even go into my own room without . . ."

"Shhh, honey, don't yell," said Elsa. Her voice sounded calm and solid, but something watery was sloshing around underneath it, and her eyes looked extra bright like maybe she had been crying. "Of course, you can come in your room without knocking. We were just . . ."—she shot a quick look at Leo—"just looking for Leo's jacket."

"Then why didn't you turn on the lights?" I asked.

"Don't be smart, Sherlock," snorted Leo. He turned to the bed and began tossing coats and hats around till he found his jacket. He grabbed it and slung it over his shoulder so hard that something small and black flew out of its pocket. Neither of them noticed.

"I'll see you on Monday," Leo said to Elsa, squeezing her shoulder and giving me a clumsy pat on the head as he went through the door.

Elsa came over and rumpled my hair. "Are you getting sleepy?" she asked, not meeting my eyes or looking at my face. "They'll all be leaving soon. Why don't you lie down and doze for a while? I'll turn off the lights."

She went out in a hurry after Leo, darkening the room and closing the door behind her.

* * *

Much later that night, after the party was over and we were all asleep, the telephone rang in the hall. It rang for a long time before my mother woke up and hurried out of her room to answer it. "Who? What?" she asked. Her voice sounded sleepy and scared at first, but got more and more annoyed as she woke up. "Can't it wait till morning? No? But . . . Oh, all right. No, don't bother holding on. I'll call you back if we find anything." She hung up with a sharp click.

I heard her bare feet padding down the hall to my room. She pushed the door open a crack and stood there without coming in.

"Josh, Josh," she whispered. "Are you awake?"

"Maybe," I said. "What's wrong?"

She came into my room and sat down on the edge of my bed and smoothed the hair off my forehead. She hadn't turned on the light yet. Her face was a dim blur surrounded by the black of her hair and the white lace around the throat of her nightgown.

"That was Leo on the phone," she told me. "He thinks something fell out of his coat pocket in your room. He wants us to look for it."

"Now? In the middle of the night?"

"Shhh," she said. "Don't wake up Vera. I'm going to turn on the light."

The brightness hurt my eyes. Elsa got down on her knees and looked under my bed and felt around with her arm. She came up empty-handed. The sleeve of her turquoise nightgown was all covered with dust.

"You'll have to get up," she told me, brushing off the dirt.

"Why? What're we looking for anyway?"

"An address book," my mother said. "Leo thinks it fell out of his pocket during the party. He can't sleep from worrying."

"Well, does he have to wake *us* up just because *he*

can't sleep? What's the big deal about his stupid address book anyway?"

"There are a lot of names in that book," Elsa said in her serious voice. "If Leo didn't leave it here, he must've dropped it somewhere else. And if the wrong person finds it, there could be trouble. For all of us." She pinched her lips together and stared at me. Her hair was snarled from sleep. Her face looked sharp with dark shadows under her eyes.

I got up and helped her move the bed away from the wall. We didn't find anything except dustballs and a missing sock and a few spare parts from my airplane models and a used-up tube of glue. I felt cold standing around in my underpants. I hugged myself. Elsa reached out, rubbed the goosebumps on my arms, and frowned at the dust under my bed. She tapped her bare foot on the floor.

"Oh, all right," she sighed. "Get back in bed. We'll take another look in the morning."

After she left, I slipped back in bed, pulled my Indian blanket up over my head, and shivered comfortably in the dark. She could come back in and search all she wanted to tomorrow, but she still wouldn't find that little book with the gold lettering that said ADDRESSES on its black leather cover.

Because I'd already found it. I'd found it behind my radiator when I was still mad at Elsa for the way she walked out of my room without even telling me what she was doing with Leo. First I'd just slipped it under my pillow. But after, when the party had ended and everyone left and the house quieted down, I'd hidden it in my secret place in the cigar box under the loose floorboards in the darkest back corner of my closet beneath a pile of old skates and broken badminton rackets.

Of course, now that I knew how important it was,

I'd have to give the address book back. But why hurry? It served them right to worry for a couple of days. Or even a week or two. None of this would've happened in the first place if they hadn't been messing around in my room in the dark.

10

Elsa

I started working at night during my first year in high school. After graduation, I took a job as a secretary and attended evening courses at City College of New York. Soon I was going less for the lectures than for the political debates that boiled up in the cafeteria, swirled around the quad, echoed down the corridors.

There were hundreds of organizations. It was a threatening, ominous time, with Hitler rising in Europe and Depression here at home. Yet we had tremendous hope. We believed that the future could be fundamentally different, if only we had the courage to fight for our vision of it. The brightest, most active people on campus belonged to the National Student League. The NSL published its own newspaper nationwide. Ben was the editor, as well as the printer, distributor, advertising salesman, and staff photographer.

A thin, pale boy, with a headful of wavy black hair and glittering green eyes, he seemed to be everywhere at once. He was always up on the platform at demonstrations, rarely a speaker himself, but the adviser and brain-trust of the leaders. He was already famous for leading his first student strike at the age of twelve. By the time he reached college, he was a veteran agitator for the NSL.

We met when I bailed him out after a demonstration against Franco's fascists in Spain. He had a black eye and was quite proud of it. They'd hit him for signing his name on the police blotter as Citizen Tom Paine.

On our first date, he took me to the Cloisters in Fort Tryon Park. I gushed over the tapestries, the golden chasubles, the carved ivory altars. But Ben mocked me. "Of course they're beautiful," he said. "But beauty is beside the point. All this was owned by that old pirate John D. Rockefeller. He plundered the wealth of nations. And now he touts himself as a philanthropist for giving an infinitesimal fraction of it back."

Then Ben read me a poem he had written. It was about four poor Negro youths who had been snatched off a boxcar in Burleigh, North Carolina, and sentenced to death for the rape of a white woman whom they had never seen.

"That's where we have to find beauty now," he told me. "In the holes of a poor boy's shoes. In young eyes staring through prison bars at the hanging tree outside."

Ben's father was a poet, too, an important figure in the Jewish community. I felt very unsure of myself the first time I entered their home with its ceiling-high bookcases, its walls decorated with original paintings and etchings, its reputation as a center of Yiddish culture. Mama Rankin welcomed me with a hug. But Ben's father seemed a stern man, tall and aloof. Over dinner, however, I discovered his gentleness, his wonderful sense of whimsy. By the end of that first visit, he took a lock of my hair, held it up to the lamplight, and said to Ben in Yiddish, "Look at this shine. A raven's wing. If we didn't have Mama, I'd marry her myself."

There were other young women in the movement who were more articulate, better read, possessed of greater courage than I. Yet Ben believed in my potential. He was such an optimist. Around him, it was impossible not to feel the future as a great wave that would sweep us up, toss us around, and, after many a difficult trial, wash us ashore in some distant, shining land.

He finally proposed to me because of a steel strike in Pittsburgh. By that time, he had been expelled from college, recruited by the party, and hired as a reporter for the *Daily Worker*. They wanted him to cover the strikes sweeping through the steel industry, spreading from factory to factory across the heartland of America. But he refused to go to Pittsburgh unless I accompanied him. I was eighteen, a big revolutionary, but Ben was the first boy I ever kissed and he knew considerably less about it than I did.

Our wedding was a traditional Jewish affair, with both families in attendance. Ben and I stood up on a little wooden platform under a canopy. We sipped wine from the same glass. Ben was supposed to throw the glass down and crunch it underfoot. He stamped so hard that he broke not only the glass but the flimsy floorboards beneath it. The rabbi assured us this was an auspicious sign.

Our honeymoon we spent covering the steel strike. I could see the chimneys of the blast furnaces from our bed in a cheap rooming house in Pittsburgh. The whistle calling the scabs to work woke us at dawn. It rained constantly, and I was often alone while Ben roamed the grim factory towns along the banks of the Monongahela. In his columns, which ran on the front page day after day, he waxed poetic about the rows of factories brooding over the river like the fortifications of a doomed feudal monarchy, and the smokestacks pouring their plumes of red and orange flame into the starless night. But to my humble eye, Pittsburgh was a dirty, ugly city where poor people lived on narrow streets under a perpetual cloud of soot.

Yet for all that, I was happy. Within an hour of our arrival in the city, we had been welcomed into the inner circle of the Party. Ben's articles rapidly earned him a national readership. People sought him out—Party organizers, labor leaders, even congressional staffers on fact-finding missions from Washington. Our rooming house became a center of activity, and I, who had at first been overwhelmed by our articulate, impassioned guests, soon found my tongue and my place among them.

That was what the Party meant to me—the chance to meet, to work with, to spend my life among the brightest, most committed, most exciting people I knew. We didn't feel we were against America. On the contrary, we joined the movement to become part of America, to identify ourselves with all that was best and most progressive in the country.

From Pittsburgh, the paper sent us to Washington. Those were wonderful years, the highlight of our life in the movement. At twenty-six, Ben was a Washington insider and a correspondent for a paper with three hundred thousand readers. I remember him leaning over the railing of the Senate gallery, twirling that lock of hair on his forehead, scribbling feverishly on his notepad, and smiling to himself as he listened to a speech by some Dixiecrat senator whom he was planning to skewer in his column.

I, too, wrote for the paper occasionally, when I wasn't working as a secretary and trying to organize women workers inside the federal bureaucracy. Our apartment was hardly lavish, but it was a sunny place, better than many people had in those Depression years. I painted it with bright colors, decorated it with Navajo rugs and Amish bedspreads, with flowers and artwork from friends in the movement. I learned to cook, to throw parties, to make our apartment a gathering place for all the progressives in Washington. We lived at a tremendous pace, rushed everywhere, had hundreds of friends—writers, congressmen, lobbyists, professors, ambassadors. Some of them had to be careful about how publicly they associated with us. But the fact that we were communists in no way made us pariahs.

Sundays, we moved the dining table out onto our glassed-in porch and invited people for brunch. I remember the grapefruit halves with dabs of strawberry jam sparkling in the pale December sunshine the morning FDR came on the radio to announce the attack on Pearl Harbor. Everybody's spoon stopped in midair. Then there was a mad scramble away from the table as our journalist and political friends dashed off to their offices the moment he finished speaking.

Ever since Spain, the party had been agitating for Roosevelt to join the struggle against Hitler. Now, at last, we were in. Russia was our ally. Our policy was to suspend all strikes, to declare a moratorium on labor disputes, to work with any organization dedicated to winning the war.

Ben wanted to enlist along with the thousands of other party members who joined the service. I was already pregnant with Vera, but that would never have dissuaded him. The Party, however, insisted that he stay on the paper in Washington. They wanted him to expose those in the government, and there were many, who thought Stalin was the enemy, not Hitler.

The afternoon before Vera's birth, I wrote a pamphlet called "Parenthood and Political Activism. Can

They Co-Exist?" Many of our movement friends had started families, and we held earnest discussions along those lines. Vera's arrival certainly revised my thinking. An active, bright-eyed baby, she gave a whole new meaning to the word precocious. She was crawling at five months, speaking her first words at less than a year.

But she had an insatiable need for attention. No sooner would I begin an important phone call than she would demand to be picked up. And woe unto us if we tried to hold a meeting at home. That would trigger a three-hour crying jag, as would my attempts to attend meetings outside.

Since I was confined to the home in any case, we decided to have another. Josh was an easier baby, or perhaps I was simply more resigned to surrendering large chunks of my life to the children. As for Ben, it was all the same to him whether we had one child or two. He was gentle, even-handed, and patient, more patient in fact than I could be with Vera, but his time was limited and his work unquestionably came first.

The outcome of the war was now clear. We looked forward to raising our family in a postwar world where fascism had been defeated. We believed that the alliance between the United States and the Soviet Union would continue, enabling us to work for socialism as part of a broad progressive coalition. We rejoiced with the rest of the country when Hitler was defeated. We wept with the rest of the nation on the day that FDR died. We felt that the best days of our movement were approaching.

11

When the next Wednesday finally rolled around, I ran home after school, grabbed my mitt, and raced out to the park. Dale was waiting for me on a bench under the trees just like he said he would be. I wanted to rush right up and jump him, but I made myself stroll over real casual like I just happened to be passing by.

"Oh, hiya, Dale," I said, stopping in front of the bench. I could see he was all set for practice. He had his glove and bat and his tennis shoes on and a blue sweatshirt with U.S. MARINES CORPS printed across the chest.

"Don't gimme that 'Oh, hiya, Dale' stuff." He smiled. "I know you've been waiting on me to come back. Hey, I brought you a souvenir."

It was a key chain from Washington, D.C.—a green plastic disc with a picture of the White House embossed on the front and OUR NATION'S CAPITAL written underneath. As a key chain, it wasn't much. But coming from Dale made it pretty special.

"Wow. Thanks a lot," I said, slipping the disk in my pocket. "I was afraid you'd forget to come."

"Forget? Heck, no," he said, standing up and squinting at me with that look like he was trying to guess my weight. "I been thinking about you all week. How're things going with the gang over there?" He jerked his head at the kids on the baseball diamond.

I dug the toe of my sneaker into the gravel.

" 'Bout the same, huh?" he said. "Well, how about your old man? Any news from him?"

"Naw. He's still away."

"No letters? Not even a phone call?"

I shook my head.

"Okay," said Dale, picking up the bat and holding it out to me handle first, "then, I guess it's all up to us. Come on, slugger, show me your grip."

I showed him.

"Now, take a couple of cuts."

He watched me swing half a dozen times. Then he took off his cap and scratched at his sandy blond crewcut. "Whew," he sighed. "Have we ever got a job of work to do."

By the end of our first hour of batting practice, I almost wished Dale had never come back. He was making me toss the ball up and hit it. "Okay," he'd say, "toss, step, swing, and hit. One, two, three, and snap. Nothing to it."

I tried a couple of thousand swings and missed every time. The ball seemed to dodge around my bat like one of those fluffy white dandelion puffs that drift in the air and float away when you try to grab them. Dale gave me advice after every strike, but none of it worked. I wanted to break the bat in pieces and roll around on the gravel, kicking my feet and crying. But

I was afraid Dale wouldn't practice with me anymore if I did.

I could tell he wasn't having a good time either, and that made everything worse. He kept looking at his watch and sighing and scratching the top of his head. If he was playing with me just for fun, I thought, he would've walked away a long time ago and never come back. But he stayed.

Finally, he said, "Hey, Josh, it's all about confidence. You just gotta believe you're gonna hit it. Look, you trust me, don't you?"

"Yeah," I said, looking at him standing there balanced on the balls of his feet with the muscles of his arms popping out from the pushed-up sleeves of his Marine Corps sweatshirt.

"Well, I've seen kids much worse than you who learned to hit real hard. You want me to give it to you straight?"

I nodded.

"Okay. It just don't come natural for you," he said. "You're not one of these kids, like your buddy Eddie Allen over there, who creams the ball nine times out of ten without anybody ever showing 'em a thing.

"But don't get me wrong. You can end up hitting better than Eddie. Because he's gonna stick with what he knows and never let anybody teach 'im. But you're gonna make hitting a science. We're gonna turn you into one of these mind-over-matter guys who bat .300 by slapping dinky little rollers through the holes in the infield.

"Tell you what," he said, bending down to look at me with his pale blue eyes, "since we're at a tricky stage here and you're trying so hard and all, I'm gonna forget our once-a-week rule and come up here again tomorrow, even if it means getting in Dutch with my boss. Now just go home and relax. Get a good night's sleep, cause we're really gonna work tomorrow. And remember . . . Confidence!"

The next day, Dale had a good idea. "What the heck," he said. "You're not gonna be a home run hitter any-way. Let's try bunting. Just stick the bat out in front of you."

I held it out level, and he stood close and pitched the ball right into the bat. I felt kind of stupid, but it was better than striking out.

"Now run when you hit it," he told me.

We used a tree for first base. Dale pitched and scooped up my bunts and tried to tag me before I reached the tree trunk. He caught me when I bunted straight back, so after a while I learned to push the ball away from him. When we were racing across the gravel to the tree, I'd try to fake him out or dodge under his glove. I was pretty good at dodging. When I made him miss, we both laughed.

It was a bright day at the start of June. I could smell that soggy summer heat in the air. We got sweaty and loose from running around so much, and pretty soon I started taking soft little pokes at his pitches, and finally I got the hang of laying the fat part of the bat on the ball. Then the bouncers turned into liners and even when Dale leaped as high as he could some of them shot over his head.

Finally he said, "Okay, now this's the last pitch of the day. The one we've been building up to all along." He spun his big arm around like a pinwheel. "Just imagine it's got your good buddy Eddie's mug plastered all over it. I wanna see you dig in your heels and give it that killer swing."

He lobbed the ball up to me, and I watched it coming all white and smooth and kind of full of itself the way Eddie looked when he won my baseball cards. My whole body whipped around and a stinging shock ran through my hands and Dale ducked like someone shot a gun at his head and I saw the ball streaking on a line for the other side of the playground. It cleared the fence on one bounce and rolled out into the street.

I started to run after it. But Dale held me back.

"Forget it," he said. "Let some other kid keep it as a souvenir."

He dropped his arm over my shoulder and led me to the bench. "So? Now you trust me?" he asked, wiping the sweat off his face. "I said you'd get it and you got it. I bet your old man's gonna be proud when he comes back and sees you play. Heard from him lately?"

"It's like I told you before," I said. "He never writes."

"Yeah, but why don't *you* write him?"

" 'Cause I don't know his address."

"Well, why not ask your mom?"

"She doesn't know either."

"But you've gotta know what city he's in. Or what state, right? At least you know if he's in the country or not. I mean, he's not living in Mexico or someplace is he?"

"It's gettin' late now," I sighed, shaking my head. Happy as I was about knocking the ball out of the playground, it made me just a little nervous the way Dale kept asking about my father. "I gotta go home."

"Relax. I'll give you a lift," he offered. "Come on. There's something I've been meaning to show you."

Instead of going straight down the stairs like we usually did, Dale steered me down a short block at the end of the park, his hand on my back. Up at the corner, we crossed Fort Washington Avenue, and he led me to a shiny gray Ford parked outside one of the tan brick apartments facing the park. His car was a '52 Fairlane. I could tell by the taillights.

"Hop in," said Dale, unlocking the door. "I'll drive you home."

We tossed our gloves and stuff in back. Then Dale put the keys in the ignition. He had about a hundred keys on his ring. But instead of starting the motor, he just sat in the driver's seat and watched me out of the corner of his eyes. I'd spent a lot of time with him by now, but we'd always been in the park or out on the sidewalk around other people. Somehow he seemed different now that it was just the two of us, sealed off from everyone behind the tinted glass windows of his car. He seemed bigger, harder, more like a stranger. And it seemed like something was building up inside of him, some kind of pressure that made his eyes bulge out of his face even more than usual.

He wiped the sweat off his forehead with the sleeve of his shirt. Then he took a deep breath, opened his mouth to talk, shook his head, and let the air sigh out through his nose instead. I shifted around on the soft gray cushions. I pressed the button on the glove compartment, but it was locked. I guessed he was building up to tell me something I wouldn't like. Probably that we couldn't practice anymore.

"Josh," he said, finally, "you're an all right kid, you know that? How old are you anyway?"

"Nine."

"Nine, huh?" He pushed air out through his nose again and chewed a little on his lip. "Well, sometimes you act older and sometimes you act younger. I guess it has to do with your dad being away and all. Why don't you level with me? Tell me what it's really all about. Tell me where he is. Maybe I can help you all get back together."

I started fiddling with the chrome button on the glove compartment again. I pushed it in and let it snap out. The snaps were the loudest noise in the car.

"I'm not supposed to talk about him," I said.

Dale looked straight ahead like he was driving. "Why not?" he asked. "Who says you shouldn't talk about your own dad?"

"My mother."

"Oh, yeah," Dale nodded. "Your mom. You told her about me yet, about how we're practicing together?"

"Yeah."

"What's she say?"

"She says why do you have time to play with me. She says I should ask where you work."

"She's a smart lady, your mom," said Dale. "You oughtta ask. You *never* oughtta get in a stranger's car without finding out about him first. If you were my kid and pulled a stunt like this, I'd whale the living daylights out of you."

I looked at his small hard hands gripping the wheel and started getting scared. I thought about making a run for it. My eyes shifted over to the door. All of a sudden, I noticed there was no handle, no way to open it from my side. And just at that second, Dale turned the key in the ignition, stamped on the gas pedal, and jerked out into the traffic so fast my head snapped into the cushions of the seat behind me. The tires screeched as he made a U-turn in the middle of the block. He swung left against the light onto 181st Street and wheeled down the hill, driving so crazy I couldn't find my voice to scream. Before I really knew what was happening, we were on the approach to the Henry Hudson Parkway, going too fast to jump even if I'd had a way to open the door.

"You see what I mean?" He smiled over at me, letting the air hiss out of his flat nose. "A guy could do anything once he's got you in a place like this."

"Yeah," I gulped. My voice cracked. I was surprised I could get it out at all. "But with you it's different, right?"

"What makes you so sure of that, little buddy?" Dale asked. "You don't know the first thing about me."

He opened his eyes up wide and round and shot a look at me. It only lasted for a second or two before he turned back to the road. But his eyes were so pale and bright and cold that it hurt to look in them. And meanwhile, I knew he was searching way down inside of me, all the way down to the weak, watery got-to-go-to-the-bathroom-real-bad feeling sloshing around in my gut.

"You want me to tell you a secret, Josh?" he smiled. "Something I really shouldn't let you know?"

"No thanks," I said.

He laughed. "Don't you even want to ask what I do for a living? Like your mother says?"

"It's none of my business."

"That's where you're wrong, little buddy," he said. "That's just exactly where you're wrong. And I'm gonna show you why."

He jerked the steering wheel hard to the right. We cut across three lanes of honking traffic onto an exit ramp that curved around and up between trees, leading us to a parking area above the river. I let out a deep breath because there were a couple of other cars in the lot, and I figured now I could scream for help if I really needed to.

Dale took the keys out of the ignition, reached across the dashboard, and unlocked the glove compartment. He fished around under the maps and notebooks and a flashlight he kept in there and pulled out a little black wallet. He dropped it in my lap. The leather was grainy and worn around the edges.

"Open it up," he ordered.

I stared at the wallet, not wanting to look. I already knew that Dale hadn't been playing baseball with me just for fun. Maybe I'd known that right from the start. I didn't want to find out any more.

"Go on," he said. "Give yourself an eyeful." There was a low, hard rumble in his voice, like little steel balls knocking together.

I opened the wallet. Inside I saw a shiny badge with an eagle on top and a blindfolded lady holding scales and a sword in her hands. Between the eagle and the blind lady, the words FEDERAL BUREAU OF INVESTIGATION were printed in capital letters.

I stared till my eyes got watery. My breath kept catching in my throat. I had to try three or four times to gulp a lungful of air. In a way, I was almost glad he was FBI because at least that meant he wasn't some kind of crazy kidnapper nut. Mainly I just wanted to close the wallet so I wouldn't have his badge staring me in the face. But my hands wouldn't move. They just sat there holding the wallet in my lap.

"I know how you feel," said Dale. "Believe me, I know just how you feel." All of a sudden his voice was friendly again. And the second I heard that buddy-buddy tone he used on the playground, I went from being scared enough to pee in my pants to feeling like I wanted to kill him.

"No, you don't!" I shouted. "You don't know nothing. Let me out!" I threw his wallet on the floor of the car and grabbed at the door.

"Get a hold of yourself, Josh," he said calmly, watching me claw at the window. "I'll let you out in a minute. No one's gonna hurt you, I promise. It's just me, Dale, remember? The guy who's helping you get back on the team? And I still wanna help you. I wanna give you a chance to get on the right side for once in your life. You hear me?"

"It's a trick," I shouted at him. "A lie. You pretended to be my friend, and all along it was nothing but a rotten sneaky trick."

"Josh, for crying out loud, if I was trying to trick you, would I show you my badge?" He shifted around and put one arm over the back of the seat and faced me, keeping his voice soft and reasonable. "Would I tell you flat out I'm with the Bureau? I'm playing this straight. You didn't even want me to show you, remember?"

"You shoulda told me the first day. The very first time we met."

"Okay. Supposing I had. Then you would've run away and never talked to me again. We never would've got to know each other. Never would've had a chance to play ball. Are you sorry about all that?"

"Yes!"

"Why? You didn't tell me a thing. I could've got more talking to a lamppost than I did from you. You're a pretty tight-lipped little squirt. Hey, I bet you had me figured out right from the start, didn't you? Come on, admit it."

He smiled at me, but I wouldn't smile back. I sat on the seat with my lower lip pouting out as far as I could push it.

"Look," he said, holding up his hands, "so far, the way it stands, you got half a dozen free baseball lessons and I didn't get a thing. Maybe you won't believe me, but that's why I'm telling you now. While you're still free and clear. Call it quits today, and you're way ahead of the game. You can run home and tell your mom how you outsmarted the FBI.

"But once you tell her about me, Josh, it's over. We're never going to be able to see each other anymore. Is that what you want?"

"Yes."

"Okay. You've got it."

Dale clicked a lever under the steering wheel, and my door swung open a crack. I braced myself to jump out onto the parking lot. My feet pushed hard against the floorboards. My backbone dug all the way down to the springs in the seat. But somehow I didn't move.

"What're you waiting for?" asked Dale.

I didn't know. My mind kept telling me to get out of the car, but my arms and legs wouldn't budge. It was one of those dream feelings where a witch is coming at you with a hatchet and you can't move an inch to save your life. If Dale had talked or tried to touch me or coughed or anything, I think I would've jumped out of the car. But he just sat there, breathing as soft as he could, smiling and watching me with one arm over the seat. Finally, I couldn't stand it anymore.

"You're after my father, aren't you?" I asked.

"Yes and no," he said. "Are you ready to listen? Or you still think I'm a liar?"

"I'll listen," I said, folding my arms over my chest, and looking out the window at the river gleaming like hot metal in the late afternoon. "But I'm not gonna tell you *nothing*. Not now and not ever."

"Okay, tough guy," he laughed. "It's like this. No thanks to you, we know a lot about your dad. We know he's a nice peaceful guy who never owned a gun or got in serious trouble with the law or did anything except get himself kicked out of college and then go write for the Party newspaper. We don't much like what he writes, but in this country he can say anything he wants without breaking the law. So far, so good. You with me?"

I nodded and settled back in the seat a little.

"But here's the problem," said Dale. "Not everyone in the Party is as nice as your mom and dad." He sounded relaxed now. His voice flowed on nice and easy, almost like he was telling me a story. "The guys on top, the big guys, they're hard cases," Dale said. "They've been in the war. They know about guns and bombs, and they're planning to use them right here in this country. Okay, maybe you don't believe me. But we've got stacks of evidence this high." He stretched his arms out as far as they'd go. "Tapes and photos and everything. We put eleven of these people on trial right here in New York and got them convicted. And then some of them ran away. They went underground. Well, we can't let them do that. They broke the law and got convicted, and they have to pay the price.

"Now your dad, Josh . . ." He stopped and pointed a finger in my face, and I looked at the blunt nail on the end of it so hard I thought I'd go cross-eyed, "We think your dad's in touch with these big guys on our Most Wanted list. We think he's meeting with them, bringing them news, helping them run the show. And the way it works in our country, if you meet or help somebody who's breaking the law, then you're breaking it too.

"Your dad's getting in pretty deep, Josh," said Dale, shaking his head and pressing his lips together till they flattened out into tight white lines above his square, solid jaw. "But maybe there's still time to pull him out. If he helps us find the guys we're after, we'll let him come home and live with you, no problems, and no questions asked. But if he keeps on going like he's going, we're gonna have to put him away. I mean it, Josh." His hand clenched itself into a fist and pressed hard against the seat back. "He's working himself right into a ten-year term at Leavenworth."

"But what'm I supposed to do about it?" I wailed. "I don't know where he is. No one tells me things like that. Besides, he's my *dad*."

"I know that," said Dale, nodding his head and pursing his lips. "I know you'd never tell on your dad. And I'd never ask you to, believe me."

He ran his thumb along his cheek, and I could hear the sound of the bristles scraping against his finger. "I just thought that if you really wanted to help him, you could ask a couple questions for me. Just little things. You know. You'd be surprised what we can figure out from a little thing."

I shivered but didn't answer.

"Well, think it over, Josh. Don't answer right away. And whatever you decide, at least we had fun playing ball together, right?" He gave me a little poke in the shoulder.

I stared at the rubber-ribbed floorboards of the car. They were clean. Everything in Dale's car was clean, even the ashtrays.

"Can I go now?" I asked.

"Go?" said Dale. "Yeah, sure you can go. I'm sorry about locking you in before, but I just didn't want you to run away before you heard what I had to say."

I opened the door and stepped out onto the gravel of the parking lot. I looked around. The green hills of Fort Tryon Park rose up behind me. Below, I could see cars streaming out of the city on the parkway. Across the river, the sun was shining through the big roller coaster at Palisades Park. The frame looked like the skeleton of a burning building, all black and charred in the reddish light.

"You know where you are?" asked Dale, leaning across the seat. "You know how to get home?"

I nodded. I just had to follow the pathways along the river for a dozen blocks till I got back downtown to 181st Street.

"You sure you don't want a lift?"

I walked away without answering.

"Well, think about what I told you, little buddy," he called after me. "And in case you still wanna practice, I'll be waiting for you next Wednesday. Every Wednesday up at the park, just like before."

I studied the weeds growing out of the gravel to keep from looking back.

12

As soon as Dale was out of sight, I started running. First it was just a shuffle, then a trot; then my feet took over from my mind and I galloped as fast as I could go. I kept glancing over my shoulder to see if Dale was following. It was too late to get away from him now no matter where I ran, but my legs kept pumping anyway.

They carried me along a twisting path between trees and across a fenced-in overpass above the highway, then down a curlicue ramp and out onto a dirt trail on the bank of the Hudson. I ran along the trail till my side throbbed and my breath burned. Then I scrambled over a fence and plowed through thick weeds and thorns till a sheer stone wall blocked my path.

The wall held up one end of the George Washington Bridge. The stones rose high enough to hide the sun. They cut across the bank and sank down into the scuzzy, gray waters of the Hudson. The river reeked of rotten eggs. Traffic up on the bridge made a rumbling groaning roar. Little specks of black soot drifted down from above.

I found a beer bottle in the weeds. I picked it up and threw it against the stone wall. The glass shattered and sparkled and sprayed back at my face. I threw all the bottles I could find. When I couldn't find any more bottles, I picked up a rock and smashed the pieces of bottles I'd already thrown. When I couldn't find any pieces big enough to break, I cleared off a spot in the weeds and sat down with my back against the wall and settled in to think.

I thought about a lot of things all at once. I thought about Dale's badge and my father and Underground and the TV programs I wanted to watch that night and the chimneys of the tugboats steaming up the river and specks of black soot on the orange flowers growing in the crisscross shadows of the bridge. I thought that if Dale really was an FBI man then he must've had a gun and maybe I should've made him show it to me in the car but it was too late now because I wasn't ever going to see him again and I should've felt glad about that but I didn't.

I thought that I had to run right home and tell Elsa everything he said in the car. I had to tell her so she could warn Ben the FBI was after him. But Ben already knew. That's why he went Underground. And if I told my mother about Dale, she'd want to know how I managed to get myself into his car in the first place. She never let you tell just the thing you wanted.

So I'd have to explain all about baseball practice and how I trusted Dale because he saved me during the fight with Eddie Allen, and that would lead to why the kids were chasing me, and finally we'd get all the way back to Mrs. McMahon bawling me out because I bragged about the May Day parade at school. Whatever happened, I didn't want to tell about May Day because

I was ashamed of letting the secret out and crying in front of the class, and besides my mother would want to know why I waited more than a month before explaining something that involved the whole family and the Party and even the FBI.

She'd get that trembly sound in her voice. She'd think I'd given all sorts of other secrets away just because I'd blabbed about May Day and sat in an FBI man's car. But even Dale had called me "a pretty tight-lipped little squirt," and then I'd said, "I'm not gonna tell you *nothing*," and he had laughed and called me "tough guy."

That was the hardest part about telling. Dale was the FBI and looking for my father, and that meant he was bad and he scared me and I hated him for tricking me, but at the same time I liked him, and now that I knew he was the FBI, in an awful sneaky way, I liked him even more.

If the kids at school knew I had an FBI agent for a friend, they'd let me back on the team for sure. Or if he was down here under the bridge with me right now, we could maybe collect some more bottles and line them up and shoot at them with his gun. It would be scary to shoot a gun, and I probably wouldn't be able to hit anything at first, but Dale would teach me how to stand and hold my arms and squint my eyes and take a deep breath while I pulled the trigger. He'd be real patient, and finally I'd get the hang of it just like batting.

I wondered how it would feel to have a gun and badge and know that all the other guys with guns and badges and uniforms and walkie-talkies were on your side and you never had to worry about prisons and courts and handcuffs and gas chambers and electric chairs except to put the bad guys in them.

Dale thought the communists were bad guys, but my father said the guys with the guns and uniforms and badges were bad and the worst bad guy in the world was Hitler because he liked to kill people and the more people he killed and the worse he hurt them the better he liked it.

Sometimes, just to imagine what Hitler was like, I'd throw a milk carton into a fire and watch the wax on the walls begin to melt and hiss and bubble. I'd tell myself the carton was a house with people trapped inside and the people were Jews and Hitler had soldiers guarding the doors and nailing up the windows so they couldn't get out. I'd imagine the people running and screaming inside as the first flames licked through the brown spots on the walls of the carton, and I'd see the soldiers standing outside, laughing and joking, or maybe blowing on their hands because it was winter outside with snow falling all around. I'd watch till the walls finally collapsed in a sudden orange fireball. Then I'd suck in my breath, shiver in horror, and throw another carton on the flames.

I never wanted to get caught in a house like that. But if you were against all the guys with guns and uniforms and badges, some night they might pull you out of bed and throw you in one. And what if the only way you could get out was to tell them secrets, tell them where people were hiding, tell them where your own father was hiding? I was pretty sure I'd tell. And that pretty much meant I was bad.

But it didn't mean I had to tell Dale. He couldn't throw me in the flames or do anything at all even if I never talked to him again. Because we were in America and we didn't have Hitler for president, we had Eisenhower. Eisenhower had beaten Hitler in the war and killed him so America was free. But Vera said they were going to put the Rosenbergs in the electric chair on the last day of school and fry them till their eyes bubbled and smoke came out their ears. The Rosenbergs were innocent, and the only reason they were getting the chair was because a squealer turned them into the FBI. His name was David Greenglass. He squealed on his sister Ethel to save his own skin, and that was the lowest thing anybody could ever do even though if I had to squeal on somebody, I thought my sister Vera would be a pretty good choice.

But my father would never squeal on anyone. Ben wasn't tough. He wasn't all solid and musclebound and fast on his feet like Dale. He had a soft, round face and black curly hair thinning out on top because he was always twisting and twirling it around his finger and pulling on it while he listened to you talk. I'd never seen him get in a fight or hit anyone or even raise his hand in an angry way. When my mother or Vera screamed at him like they did sometimes, he just kind of shrugged his shoulders and walked away and came back when they felt better.

But no matter how Dale asked him about the Party, even if they put him in a room and handcuffed him to a chair and shined lights in his eyes and worked on him for days without coffee or cigarettes or anything, even if they gave him the Third Degree and hit him with rubber hoses and all, I just didn't think he'd talk. He wouldn't because he believed in acting good. He tried really hard. He tried harder than anybody.

He never sat me down and explained it all, but just from living with him and watching him, I guessed that the whole point about the Party and the paper and all was convincing everybody that they had to try and act nice and fair to everybody else all the time like he did. Then there wouldn't be any fights and everyone would share what they had and we wouldn't need jails or guns or armies or electric chairs and atom bombs anymore.

I knew it might be a little more complicated than that because my dad was always reading thick books and using words I couldn't understand and having arguments that lasted all night long about Russia and Stalin and China and the war in Korea. But basically, when you came right down to it, I figured my dad wanted everybody to act good like he did and the problem was they didn't want to. They liked being bad because it was more fun and the worse they acted, the more they hated my father for telling them to stop.

And even I could tell his way wouldn't work because here I was, his own son and all, and deep down inside, I felt sneaky scared and rotten. And maybe Ben knew. Maybe he disappeared without sitting me down to explain where he was going or why he had to leave because he knew he couldn't trust me.

And maybe Dale knew too. Maybe the FBI had a way of spotting people like that. Maybe Dale had picked me out from all the other kids with commie parents because he saw something in me, something bad and dark and twisted, something he could use to make me tell.

I stood up and shivered. I had goosebumps on my arms. The sun had gone down behind the amusement park on the other side of the Hudson. The water had turned battleship gray. It was gloomy in the shadow of the wall. Up on top of the bank, a scummy-looking man was wandering into the bushes. I didn't know the time exactly, but I had to be late for dinner.

I started walking back along the path toward home. I walked fast. I wished Ben was with me. I tried to think of something really fun we did together, but all I could remember was the morning in San Francisco when he took me down to see the paper where he worked.

First we rode the trolley all the way to the East Bay Terminal on Mission Street. Then we walked past shabby alleys where bums sat begging for quarters on the sidewalk in front of old brick warehouses.

The paper was at the end of an alley in a dark two-story building that smelled of ink. Ben showed me the printing press. I could tell he felt proud of it. The press was big and black and gleaming with grease. It had rollers and metal arms that clanked and clashed and looked like they might reach out to grab my shirt and pull me in if I wasn't careful. They kept it in a special room with a high ceiling and a man in a blue apron to feed it ink and paper.

Ben's office was up on the second floor. It wasn't a real office with a door. Just a little space between two frosted-glass partitions, both of them covered with taped-up notes. Some of the notes were turning yellow. My father had a folding chair and a scratched-up desk just about hidden under piles of paper. His big black typewriter sat in a corner, surrounded by coffee cups with cigarettes floating in them.

Offices like his ran around all four walls of a big room with rough wood floors. Sunlight came down through a dusty skylight, but it was kind of dim everywhere except right underneath where they had a bunch of filing cabinets in rows. I had to wait a long time while Ben worked on an article. Only a couple of people were working because it was Sunday.

Ben wore a green wool shirt that smelled of tobacco and had holes in the elbows. It was his favorite, and he wouldn't take it off even to wear the new one Elsa bought him for Christmas. He rolled up his sleeves and started typing. He typed with two fingers and made the spidery black keys of his typewriter move so fast they bumped into each other. Every minute or two, he'd jump up and walk out of his office and pace all around the room. He'd go in and out through the rows of filing cabinets, up and down in front of his office, pulling at the curls on top of his head, stepping over me as if I wasn't there, until suddenly he'd get a new idea and charge back to the typewriter and rattle off a few more words.

I played around, wheeling a toy truck through the canyons between the filing cabinets. I found some paper clips and rubber bands on the floorboards and shot them at my truck. I did everything I could think of and still got bored enough to cry by the time he finished writing.

On the way home, we went to a park near the bus stop. It was just a little park, but way up on a hill where you could see the city and the bay and the white buildings downtown. It had swings and a slide and a sandbox with parallel bars over the sand. I got hold of the bar and then swung my legs up to show my dad how I could hang upside down by my knees. It was a new trick I'd been working on for weeks.

Ben was standing right at the edge of the sandbox. From my upside-down position, I could see the tips of his brown canvas loafers digging into the sand. One of the shoes had a rip in the toe. I thought he was watching me swing. But when I craned my neck to look up at his face, I saw that his green eyes had gone cloudy and his finger was twisting around in his curls, and I knew he was thinking about his article again. And suddenly I felt so stupid and disappointed hanging there upside down that I just lost interest in the whole thing. My knees unlocked all by themselves and the sand rushed up and I fell face first into an explosion of orange stars. The fall took my breath away, and when I tried to get it back, I sucked up a mouthful of sand.

Ben picked me up. I was wailing and spluttering. He wiped the sand out of my eyes and nose and mouth and ears. He patted my shoulder in a clumsy way till I calmed down. Then he took my hand and led me out of the playground. But before we got half a block from the park, his hand went limp, and I knew his mind had circled back to his article and the Party and the

paper again. Dark was coming down, and his slack
fingers made me feel lonely and hopeless and sulky mad
as if no matter how hard I pulled, there would always
be something stronger than me tugging him in the
opposite direction.

But now, walking alone by the Hudson after dark, and
staring at the bushes that covered the bank with black
rustling shadows where all kinds of creepy things could
hide, I thought that even if Ben's mind was a million
miles away, it would be nice to have him here. Even
if his hand was so limp I could hardly feel it, I'd like
to have something to hold on to, at least until I climbed
back over the fence and got to where the lights and
people and traffic were.

And when I thought that way, it seemed I could
feel a faint tingling on my palm, just a touch that made
me a little warmer than I'd normally be coming home
in a T-shirt after dark. It was like maybe he was thinking about me too, somewhere thousands and thousands
of miles away, right at that very moment. I held on to
the warmth till I reached the fence. I held it all the
way to the front stoop of our building.

But on the way up the stairs, I lost it because I
had to concentrate on thinking up an excuse for being
late. And somehow, I just couldn't find a good one. I
grabbed my hair with both hands and tugged. The only
idea that came out was how could I pull my hair with
both hands when one of them was supposed to be holding my baseball glove. I stood on the dark landing
outside our door, staring at my palms, slapping them
against my head, and then holding them in front of my
eyes as if I couldn't believe they were empty.

My mother would say it served me right because
I lost everything—jackets, school books, keys, toys. I
had even lost one of my shoes at the May Day picnic.
But the glove was different. It wasn't really my fault

at all because I never would've lost it if I didn't have to worry about May Day and my father and the Underground and Dale.

Dale!

As soon as I thought of him, I remembered how he told me to chuck my glove into the backseat of his car. He must've planned it that way. Now I'd have to meet him one more time. I could almost see his bright bulging eyes winking at me in the dark.

I pushed through the door into our hallway. Dinner smells and clatter came from the kitchen along with my mother's anxious voice, "Josh? Where in the world have you . . .?"

I walked straight into the kitchen. Vera and my mother were sitting over steaming plates at the table by the window. They stared at me. Vera looked spiteful, my mother worried. I walked slow and kind of dreamy over to my chair and sagged against its blue vinyl back.

"Where were you?" Elsa asked sharply.

I knew just what to say. The perfect excuse had popped into my head the second I decided to meet Dale again.

"I . . . I was thinking about Dad," I sighed. "You know, first I was missing him and then it was like we went for a walk together. And by the time we stopped, I was down by the river in the dark."

"Down by the river? After dark? Don't you know they have gang fights there?" Vera exploded. "Don't you know a boy was stabbed under the bridge just last month?"

Elsa gave me a long, hard look. "I don't care what you were thinking about," she snapped. "I want you to promise me not to go down there again. We were both worried sick. Is that what you want?"

"No," I said.

She slapped a plate of meatloaf and mashed potatoes down in front of me. Gravy splattered on the table. She got up, grabbed a rag from the sink, and swiped at the spots. As she passed behind my chair, she gave my neck a quick, sharp squeeze. Her nails dug in just hard enough to hurt. But her hand was warm, and I could tell she wasn't really mad.

13

Elsa said that visiting Grandpa and Grandma was the next best thing to seeing Ben, but I didn't want to go and I didn't want to comb my hair either. In the first place, my hair wouldn't stay put no matter how I brushed it. And in the second, even if my hair did stay combed, I couldn't see it because the mirror over the sink in the bathroom was so high that I had to stand on the toilet seat to catch my own reflection. Visiting Grandma and Grandpa just wasn't worth the trouble.

I liked them and everything, and once we got over there, I always had a pretty good time, and I almost never left without a present. But when the day to visit rolled around, it always seemed like I had something more exciting to do. If Vera and my mother would go by themselves and leave me alone today, I could turn on my radio and listen to the Dodgers' game. I'd open my window and sit out on the fire escape drinking a

Coke in one of our tall aluminum glasses while Red Barber called the plays.

Red had a southern accent, and everybody said Southerners hated Negroes, but Red was different. He treated everybody fairly. He said we had a lock on the pennant even though it was only June. We were playing the Phillies today, Robin Roberts versus Preacher Roe. The game was just about to start. But I couldn't listen because we had to leave.

My only hope was Vera. Maybe we couldn't agree on anything else, but we both thought going to Grandma's was boring. And when Vera didn't want to go someplace, she came right out and let you know. She stamped her foot and screamed in your face. And if you still made her go, she threw a fit. Nobody could throw a fit quite like Vera. Once she worked herself up to one, my mother let her do anything she liked. I kept listening for foot-stomping and door-slamming and other hopeful signs that a fit was in the works, but the only door that banged was the one to the bathroom. Vera was pounding on it.

"Will you stop primping yourself and let me in there so I can get ready?" she called.

To get to Grandma's we had to ride the subway down to 145th Street, then take the D train way up into the Bronx. It was a long, boring ride. But once the subway came out of its tunnel and turned into an elevated train clattering at rooftop level through the Bronx, at least I could look out the window.

Rolling past Yankee Stadium, I caught a glimpse of green turf and flags flying above the walls and people sitting in the bleachers. On our way through the Grand Concourse, where Jody lived, I saw pigeon coops on the black tar roofs and women hanging out laundry and even a man and woman sunbathing together, almost naked. I could see into kitchen windows, or stare down on street corners where the cars looked like Tinkertoys shining in the sun, but finally I got bored again and nodded off until we reached Grandma's station, the last one before the end of the line.

Jerome Avenue ran under the train tracks, and the sunlight came down from above in sharp stripes of bright and shadow. We bought some food for Grandma in Label's Kosher Delicatessen. They had chickens and salamis and pinkish-gray liver sausages and smoked cod hanging from their mouths on hooks and pickles floating in vats of green water almost like fish in an aquarium. We bought a loaf of challah bread and six poppy seed bagels and two sticks of halva candy, one each for Vera and me.

Halva was Jewish candy. It tasted something like vanilla fudge with chocolate ripples and sand in it. I preferred Snickers and Milky Ways and even Hershey bars, but if you were going to eat halva, Grandma's neighborhood was the best place to do it. Most of the stores under the train tracks were Jewish. They had delicatessens and laundries and kosher butchers and little clothing stores selling hats and handkerchiefs and galoshes and drug stores with painful-looking girdles and garters and artificial legs on display.

The stores had funny writing on their windows—Hebrew letters that crinkled and curled and sprouted dots in strange places. You could even see neon signs flashing on and off in Hebrew. Outside the stores, housewives with packages in their arms and fat men in undershirts chattered and called across the street to each other in Yiddish.

Grandma lived a couple of blocks down from Jerome Avenue in a yellow brick apartment house with a shiny bronze plaque outside. The lobby was dark and cool with a polished marble floor and a throne chair with a red velvet seat in one corner. I shoved into the elevator ahead of Elsa and Vera because I wanted to work the buttons. I made the automatic door slide open and closed a couple of times, but Vera gave me one of her looks, so I pushed number six for grandma's floor.

Grandma was waiting in the hall when we got out of the elevator. She gave us all a big hug. She was smaller than my mother but very soft. When she hugged, you kind of sank into her. Vera would only let herself be hugged for half a second, so Grandma gave me an extra squeeze. "Oh, Josh," she said, filling my name with so much feeling that it sounded about four syllables long.

Grandma had wavy gray hair and glasses, and when she wasn't smiling she seemed kind of sad, but I didn't really think of her as old because every summer she went to a big camp for Jewish kids where she worked as the Camp Mother. I didn't know exactly what a Camp Mother did, but I imagined her putting Band-Aids on everybody's knees and elbows and making lots of food for them to eat and if anyone got hurt or homesick and started to cry, she'd give them a big hug like she did to me.

We followed her into the apartment. It was dark near the front door, but then the hall turned a corner and led you past rows of bookcases up to the ceiling. All the books were in Yiddish. They belonged to Grandpa. He was a poet. The bookcases faced the kitchen and the living room, and somehow they seemed the center of everything. The whole apartment smelled of books and cooking and warmth, but more than anything else, it smelled Jewish. I couldn't say what exactly made it smell Jewish, or if I liked the smell or didn't like it, and after I'd been there a while I forgot about it, but especially when I first came in, I always recognized the odor and knew it had to be different from our apartment or else I wouldn't smell it.

Grandpa was waiting for us in the living room. He was a tall man with wispy white hair and a high, domed forehead. I'd never seen anyone with a forehead quite like Grandpa's, and sometimes I imagined millions of thoughts milling around in there, pushing on it from inside and making it bulge out like it did.

Every time we came, we'd find Grandpa sitting at his writing desk under a lamp in a corner of the living room. His desk was piled high with books in Yiddish. He wrote with a fountain pen, making the strange, craggy Hebrew letters in blue ink on thin sheets of paper. On the gray wall above his desk, he had photos of foreign-looking men sitting in cafes or standing in groups with their arms around each other's shoulders and he had a picture of my father when he was young and skinny and holding up a magazine that had just printed his first poem.

"Well, well, well, *kinder*," he said to Vera and me. He stood up and looked down at us and put his hands on our heads to rumple our hair. Vera shied away. She never liked anybody to touch her. Grandpa didn't seem to notice.

"This morning," he said, "I went out and bought something special just for you. But now,"—he bumped his palm against his forehead—"I'm so old and feeble, I forgot where I put it."

He had green eyes, very bright and clear, and he gave them a teasing light as he smiled down at us. "Maybe you can help me find it. I'm sure I had it somewhere. Didn't I put it somewhere in this room, Bubba?" he called to my grandma.

We knew the game. He played it with us every time we came. We had to search the living room looking for our presents while he sat at his writing desk smiling and pretending not to watch. We lifted up the cushions on the armchairs near the windows. We picked up the vases on the windowsill and turned them upside down. I checked under the rabbit ear antenna on the television. Vera looked behind the pictures on the walls.

Both at the same time, we turned to the dark polished dining table against the wall. We lifted up the tablecloth and pulled out the drawers underneath. Vera found a box of dark bittersweet chocolates. I found a little silver top under a pile of letters. The top had a strange four-sided shape with a Hebrew letter on each side. Grandpa called it a dreidel. He taught me the names of the letters. I spun the top on the dark wood of the table. I liked to watch the silver point dance on its own reflection in the polished wood. Vera wouldn't give me any of her chocolates. She put them in her purse and carried them down the hall to the bedroom. She wanted to read. Grandpa went into the kitchen where they were cooking dinner.

I could hear them through the wall talking in Yiddish. I knew lots of Yiddish words from listening to my mother and my grandparents and even some of the people in the Party talk. But I couldn't quite figure out what all those Yiddish words had to do with me.

We didn't go to synagogue and we didn't have to fuss around with all sorts of different plates and forks like Grandma and our house didn't smell like theirs. And even though you weren't supposed to feel that way, I didn't like being Jewish very much, except on Jewish holidays when I got to stay home from school, because lots of people hated Jews and Hitler burned them in big ovens, and I thought we had enough trouble just being communists. It all had to do with God, but I didn't like him that much either because the bad people seemed to win most of the time anyway and a lot of them talked about God while they went around killing you the worst way they could.

I stopped playing with the dreidel Grandpa gave me. I wandered over to the window and looked out at the fire escapes and clotheslines and pigeon spatterings on the bricks of the buildings across the way. We hadn't even eaten dinner yet and already I was bored. I thought about going out to ride up and down in the elevator, or maybe taking grandma's garbage out to the incinerator so I could throw it down the shaft and hear the *whoosh* of the flames. But then I remembered the pile of letters in the drawer of the dining table where Grandpa hid the dreidel. The typing on front had been in English, and inside I'd seen just a glimpse of yellow paper, and something about that yellow paper seemed familiar.

I walked over to the table, lifted the cloth, and opened the drawer. I felt a little guilty about doing it, which was strange because I'd opened the drawer right in front of Grandpa and he didn't mind at all. Even so, I looked around the room to make sure no one was watching, and then I took the first letter off the stack. I sat down under the dining table to read it. There was a low, comfortable shelf between the legs, and just to make everything nice and private, I pulled the tablecloth down in front of me. Now even if someone came into the room, they wouldn't see me reading in my little cave.

As soon as I unfolded the letter, I knew it came from Ben. I could tell by the paper. He always used rough, yellow paper, the kind that you couldn't write on with a pen because it made the ink spread out in ugly blots and blotches, but it was good enough for typing. My dad didn't type very good. He crossed out lots of words and had to stick in others above or below the lines, and sometimes his typewriter ribbon changed from black to red and back again all in the same sentence. But I could read his letter anyway, and it didn't take me long to figure out that it came from Underground. It said:

Dear Mama,

I should have written you a long time ago. And I am sorry. I guess I had the excuse in my mind that I would wait for you to write again. When you didn't, I relied on Elsa's reports on how you are which she includes in just about every letter. I guess the real excuse, even though it isn't good enough, is that it is difficult to write these days and not too much I can say.

Of course I was deeply troubled to hear that Papa was attacked in the Yiddish Writers Union for my beliefs. Please tell him that I am proud of the way he stood up for me publicly despite his own bleak assessment of Soviet policy toward the Jews. As far as that is concerned, the Paper's correspondent in Moscow assures me that while certain individual writers with Jewish backgrounds have been tried and convicted, there is no generalized anti-semitic campaign, nor could there be in a socialist country. Our correspondent by the way is a good Jewish boy who, in fact, sat three rows away from me at Yeshiva.

These are hard days generally and the torrent of anti-soviet propaganda is drowning all voices of moderation. The McCarthy bunch seems to be in control and is quite capable of some big reckless move, some major miscalculation based on Soviet weakness after Stalin's death. It will be touch and go for a while. I'm afraid that for the moment, it doesn't look too good for peace—or too good here at home either. You have probably heard that the people who were on trial here have been convicted. The future is terribly vague and the bright side seems to lie more in the long run than in the immediate months ahead.

It is a shame that Elsa has to live so far from

you. I know she has always been a favorite of yours, and she is very fond of you. Of course, this whole period hasn't been much easier on her than it is on me.

Tell me how you find the kids. From what I can gather, they both seem in very good shape. I certainly agree that summer camp will be just the thing for Vera. Being with other kids from progressive homes should give her more self-confidence and counteract her feelings of being alone and afraid. Josh I'm not really worried about. I'm sure he'll be fine in every way. Elsa worries about the financial obligations for summer camp. But you have already helped her some. So I don't know what else you can do. She was talking about borrowing some from friends.

About myself there is, as always, very little to say. I am well and comfortable and busy. But, of course, I lead a very lonely and dreary life, with not much to do except read and work and work and read. And one does get so bored with one's own company. Yet in a way one gets a little used to it too.

I keep in fairly good spirits and exercise a little, even spend occasional weekends in the mountains during which I can go hiking and talk with friends. I'm watching my diet but I still haven't lost any weight. However, I haven't put on any either, which would be all too easy under the circumstances.

Take care of yourself and I hope this will be a good summer for all of us.

All my
love,

Ben

After I finished the letter, I sat in my cave, brooding behind the white curtain of the tablecloth. I heard my grandma's footsteps come into the dining room. She walked over to the table. I could hear silverware rattling and see her skirt and her thick legs through the cloth. I watched her turn in a circle, as if she was looking all around the room.

"Josh?" she called. "Josh, where are you?"

"Under here," I said, "and I'm not coming out."

She lifted up a corner of the tablecloth and looked in at me, smiling and shaking her head. Then she went back into the kitchen. In a while, my mother came into the room. She put things on the table and arranged chairs around it, and then she said, "Josh, honey, come on out of there now and help us get ready to eat."

I didn't answer.

"Josh," she said, "I'm talking to you."

I still didn't answer.

She lifted up the tablecloth and looked in at me, her black bangs hanging in her eyes, which were half-laughing and half-mad.

"I'm not coming out," I said.

She thought that over. "Well, all right," she said, dropping the tablecloth and turning to go. "Stay there. We'll eat dinner on top of your head. Vera can drop scraps down to you like a little puppy. She'll love that."

"You lied to me," I called, poking my head out from under the table as she walked away.

"What?" She stopped and turned.

"You said there's not enough money for summer camp. So how come Vera gets to go and I don't?"

"What *are* you talking about?" My mother came back and knelt down and smoothed out the wrinkles in her red print skirt and gave me a smile that said I had about two seconds left before she blew her stack.

I threw Ben's letter at her. I meant to throw it at her face, but I couldn't quite make myself crumple it up, so the paper just kind of flapped around in the air and fell at her feet.

"You're writing him and he's writing grandma and everybody knows where he is but me!" I said.

"How in the world? Have you been snooping around in grandma's things?" said Elsa, her voice rising high enough to bring Grandma and Grandpa in from the kitchen.

Grandpa saw the letter at her feet. He saw me sitting under the table with my head sticking out from under the cloth. He gave me a wink and said something to my mother in Yiddish. She answered back. Then my grandmother chimed in, and all three of them started jabbering Yiddish as fast as they could, and the only thing that made sense to me was when my grandma said, "Ach, Ben, Ben, Ben," pressing her hands against the sides of her face and giving a deep sad sigh.

Somehow, that set Grandpa off. He started pacing around the room and talking in an angry voice and waving his arms over his head and stopping every once in a while to look at my mother and shout something about "Stalin." He pronounced it "Sta-leen" and made it sound like the ugliest word in the world.

Then Vera, who had been watching from the door all this time without saying anything, began to stamp her feet and shake her head till her hair flew out every which way and her face turned red and her glasses slipped off one ear and hung down her nose. When everybody turned to look, she screamed, "Will you PLEASE stop talking YIDDISH! If you're going to drag us up here, and subject us to one of these INTERMINABLE scenes, for God's sake, at least speak a language we UNDERSTAND!"

My grandma collapsed into an armchair. *"Oy gevolt,"* she cried. "That I should live to see the day when mine own grandchildren hate to hear Yiddish."

And then my mother must have remembered how

I started the whole thing. She gave me a black, furious look, and I shot one right back at her because she told me she didn't write my father or know his address or anything, and he said right there in his letter that she did.

In the end, we all sat down to dinner. We had borscht with sour cream and poppy seed bagels and gefilte fish and boiled chicken, but no one felt like eating.

14

I only wanted to get my glove back. I mean it was all broken in and I liked it and I knew who had it, so there was no reason to make my mother buy me a new one. Especially since she was so hard up for money that she could only afford to send Vera to camp and not me like my father wrote in his letter.

But I didn't want to give Dale the idea I was eager to meet him. So when school let out on Wednesday afternoon, instead of racing straight up to the park, I hung around for a while down at the corner of 181st and Cabrini watching the buses climb the hill. I stood on a metal grill, looking down through the bars at a grimy row of windows below the sidewalk. Smells of laundry and garbage steamed up through the grill, along with a strange whooshing noise, deep and powerful like the wheezing of a monster that lived under the street.

The same noise wheezed out of basements all over

the neighborhood as if the monster had hollowed out a network of tunnels and secret passages connecting all the cellars in Washington Heights. The metal grills in the sidewalk kept him caged under the street. But every once in a while he broke out and gobbled up a kid who happened to be standing on the bars at the wrong moment. I did a little shuffling dance on the grill to show I wasn't scared. Then I turned up the hill toward the park.

Dale was waiting on the same bench as always. But he looked different today. Instead of a sweatshirt and dungarees, he was wearing a brown suit and a hat with the brim turned down the way the cops do it on TV. His face was shining a little from sweat. He looked so much like an FBI man now I hated myself for not spotting him right away.

"I just came for my glove," I told him, stopping in front of his bench and looking down at the gravel between his glossy brown shoes.

"I got it right here for you," he said, patting a paper bag beside him. "I even rubbed a little neat's-foot oil on it. Not that I needed to. You keep it pretty good." He picked up the paper bag and handed it to me. I looked inside. He laughed. "Whatsamatter, Josh?" You think I'd try and switch gloves on you or something? Hey, if you didn't come today, I was going to drop it off at school. At Mr. Klein's office. I figured you wouldn't want me to deliver it to your house while Elsa might be home. I guess you didn't tell her about our little chat, or you wouldn't be out here meeting me alone. Am I right?"

He said it real friendly. But the idea of him knowing Mr. Klein and the way he said my mother's name gave me this creepy, closed-in feeling like he'd been watching me for months. And somehow, somewhere, I knew I'd seen him before that day when he came up and saved me from Eddie Allen during the fight.

"I gotta get going," I said, tucking the bag with my glove under my arm.

"Just like that?" Dale asked. "You don't even want to toss a couple?"

"Not right now."

"What about the team?"

I looked over at the kids in the sunlight on the baseball diamond. They were kind of floating around in the thick yellow sunlight, dragging their feet through the heat waves rising off the tarmac. They seemed to be doing everything in slow motion, like they were swimming. Sidney out in right field had his back to the batter's cage. He was staring at a pigeon perched on top of the flagpole. He yawned.

"It's too late now anyway," I told Dale, shrugging my shoulders. "I give up. They'll never let me on before school ends."

Dale shook his head. He snorted. "I never figured you for a quitter, Josh," he said.

"No," I sneered at him. "You had me figured for a *stoolie*." I stared him straight in the face when I said it. All of a sudden I was mad. My scalp prickled. I could feel the blood burning in my ears. He smiled back at me. He thought I was funny.

I turned around and stomped out of the park. Dale got up and walked with me. I couldn't make him stop. If he laid a hand on me, though, I was going to kick him right in the shins, FBI or not. But he just fell in step and followed me through the gate.

At the corner he said, "Come on, Josh. Don't go away mad. Look, there's a lot you don't understand about this deal. If it was all up to me, I'd . . . hey, whaddya say we go have a Coke, for old time's sake? Just so we can call it quits with a good taste in our mouths."

I should've kept walking without turning back. But the way he said it made me glance at his face, and then the way he looked made me forget about hating him. Even in his brown suit and hat and everything, he still looked like Dale, with his funny eyes bugging out over his flat cheeks and his mouth tilted in a lopsided smile and sweat popping out on his forehead because he was standing in the hot sun talking to me when he could've been sitting at a desk in an air-conditioned office.

Partly I felt sorry for him. And partly I felt, I don't know . . . kind of excited because even though he was the FBI and I was just this commie kid, I knew I could make him stand in the sun and sweat and smile and play games with me and even plead to buy me a Coke.

We went to the Hilltop Fountain on the corner of 181st and Fort Washington Avenue. The Hilltop wasn't a real great place for talking because the front window looked down on the entrance to the IND subway, and Vera rode the IND home from school. If she looked through the window on her way up the stairs and saw me in a restaurant with a stranger, she'd snitch for sure. But I'd always wanted to eat at the Hilltop because they had a sign outside that showed a huge deluxe cheeseburger with pickles and relish and french fries and a toothpick sticking out of the bun and on top of the toothpick was a blue neon flag that actually waved.

When we went in, the waitress tried to put us in a booth up front. But Dale shook his head.

"Me'n my buddy here, we need a little privacy," he said.

The waitress smiled. She was a plump lady with black glasses and a Spanish accent. She called everybody "honey." The way she said it sounded like "who-nay."

"All right, who-nays," she told me and Dale, leading us down the aisle through the booths to the back of the restaurant. There was a little archway in back, with a pair of steer horns on top of it and a brown curtain hanging down from the horns. Behind the curtain they had a little booth for two.

Dale hung his hat on a chrome pole attached to the side of the booth. He loosened his tie and unbuttoned the top of his shirt and squeezed himself into his side of the booth.

"You hungry?" he asked me. "How about a sundae or something?"

"No, thanks. Just a Coke."

"Come on, Josh. You wanna play with the big kids, you gotta put a little meat on those bones."

I knew it was wrong, but I let him talk me into a cheeseburger. He had one too. We didn't talk much while eating. I was glad about that. I wanted to concentrate on my cheeseburger, on the crisp toasted bun and the wet, spicy splash of mustard and ketchup coating my tongue just before I bit through the pickle into the charred meat. I knew that the cheeseburger was going to spoil my dinner and that I shouldn't be in the Hilltop eating with Dale in the first place, and that made it taste all the better.

From time to time, the waitress came through the curtain with a trayful of dirty dishes that she put on a ledge under a little window opening into the kitchen. I could look through the window at the cooks working over a big stove that glistened with black grease. Above the stove hung knives and pots big enough to chop people up and stew them in.

We were wiping the juice and ketchup off our plates with the last of our french fries when Dale started to talk.

"I love this," he told me. "No kidding. Coming up here to the park and palling around with you in the afternoons. It's the best part of my job. You know what

I'd do if I had my druthers? Coach your whole team. Believe me, there's kids on it who need help even more'n you do. Eddie Allen, for instance. There's a kid who could use a lotta coaching in the fair play department.

"But the thing of it is, Josh buddy, that's just not how it goes in the real world. Maybe you think it's rough being a kid. But wait'll you start earning a living. Hey, what're you gonna do when you grow up, anyway?"

I shrugged. By the time I grew up, they'd have the Revolution and everything would be different. Besides, I was feeling full and maybe even a little sleepy now that we'd eaten. I wanted to get outside and walk around. If Dale had something to tell me, I wished he'd get to the point.

"You better think about it, Josh," he went on, " 'cause once you get out of school, nobody gives you nothing for nothing. Take my boss. You ever seen Jimmy Stewart in the *FBI Story*?"

I nodded.

"Well, my boss's nothing like that. He's one tough old monkey. Always on my back. 'Duerson,' he says—never calls me by my first name, never says 'Agent Duerson' or anything like that. Anyway, 'Duerson,' he says, 'get something out of that little commie brat or stop wasting my time playing baseball up there in the Heights.' He threw in some stuff about baseball bats and what we could do with 'em that you probably wouldn't understand even if I repeated it to you.

"But I can't blame him. He's got the Director on his case just like I got him on mine. A lot of people think it's a blight on the Bureau to have these top commies running around the country where we can't find 'em. It's so hot, we gotta follow every little lead. They'll even let me come up here and fool around with you. But I gotta produce, Josh. That's the thing of it. I gotta have something to show for my time."

Dale stopped and wiped the corner of his lips with his napkin and then licked his tongue over some grease that he missed. "You understand what I'm telling you, Josh?"

"Yeah," I said. "I understand. You're still trying to get me to squeal."

Dale gave me his lopsided smile. He snorted a little through his nose. "Ya got a real way with words, kid. You know that? Maybe you're gonna turn out a writer like your old man. By the way, you haven't—"

"No," I interrupted. "I haven't heard from him or seen him or anything and—"

"And you wouldn't tell me even if you had, right?'

"RIGHT!" I said.

Dale nodded. He unbuttoned his cuffs and rolled up his sleeves. He laid his hairy forearms on the orange formica tabletop and leaned toward me. His shoulders bulged over the sides of the booth. His eyes locked onto mine.

"Even if I gave you something that you really wanted," he asked, with a bright, half-joking twinkle in his eyes, "even if I took you out to a doubleheader at Ebbets Field on the Fourth of July, you still wouldn't help me out?"

"Right," I said again, real loud and quick, without even thinking about it.

"Even if I said we could sit in a special box practically on top of the Dodgers' dugout, where we could see the guys' faces and hear the chatter and probably snag a couple of foul balls for souvenirs? You wouldn't give me just the tiniest hint of a lead in exchange for something like that?"

This time it came a little slower, but I still got it out. "Right," I said.

Dale leaned closer. His eyes got wider, brighter.

I leaned forward, too. I couldn't help it. I felt like we were going to rub noses above the dirty plates on the table. "What if we could go down to the dugout after the game?" he asked me. "What if we could walk right in and meet Pee Wee Reese himself and shake his hand? You still wouldn't play ball with me?"

My mouth was too dry to answer, so I just shook my head no.

"I didn't hear you, Josh," Dale smiled. "Did you say you wouldn't give me a lead to follow even if we could get Pee Wee to autograph your glove? To sign it right in the pocket 'To my buddy, Josh Rankin'? Even if we could get him to autograph a baseball for all the kids on the team so's they'd let you play again? Even if I did all that for you, you wouldn't give me the lousiest scrap of information to get the boss off my back?"

"Right," I said, "right, right, right." But I was chewing on my knuckles so it didn't sound all that convincing.

Dale let out a big sigh. He leaned back in his seat and kind of slumped down a little and grinned at me, showing lots of white teeth.

"Well, you're not making my life any easier, Josh," he said, tilting his head and squinting down at me, "but I'm proud of you. You're a good loyal kid. No one can call you a stoolie. So I tell you what. I'm gonna do all that stuff I said for you. Take you to the game and let you sit in the box and introduce you to Pee Wee and . . . and you don't have to give me a single, blessed thing on your dad. Not one word. You understand me, Josh? You hear what I'm telling you?"

"Yeah . . . ," I said, kind of holding my breath because I knew it couldn't be that simple.

"You don't have to give me a thing about your dad," he repeated. "But you hafta give me something. Anything. Even the smallest little thing. So long as it checks out and I can show it to my boss and prove I'm not wasting my time. That's how the game goes from here on out. I help you. You help me. Everybody gets what they need. And nobody the wiser. Fair's fair, Josh. Whaddya say?"

I didn't say anything. I chewed on my lip. A fly buzzed through the little window into the kitchen, and one of the cooks swung at it with a spatula and missed. Out in the restaurant, I heard the waitress calling "Two deviled eggs to go."

I felt Dale's eyes on my face. I couldn't look up at him. I wished I still had something to nibble on my plate. I used a finger to pick up a sesame seed stuck in a ridge of brown grease. While I was chewing on it, the booth creaked. Dale stood up.

"Think it over, buddy," he said. I saw his glossy brown shoes cross the soiled tiles on the floor. The heels stopped and turned back at the curtain. "July fourth, Dodgers versus Giants," he said. "I'll meet you downstairs in the subway. In front of the turnstiles. Eleven-thirty in the morning. Oh, and Josh?"

"Yeah?" I said, still staring down.

"Look at me when I talk to you."

His voice wasn't loud, but it had a sudden scary edge on it that made me swing my head up in a hurry. He was standing in the archway, one hand holding up the curtain, his shoulders filling the frame, his eyes glaring at me steel blue and cold as gun metal.

"Don't stand me up," he said. "You're in this too deep to back out now."

15

Elsa

Josh was the kind of trusting toddler who would walk off with anyone who gave him a kind word or a pat on the head. I let go of his hand in Chinatown on the first night after we moved to San Francisco, and when I looked around a moment later, he had attached himself to a friendly woman in a long fur coat. He was crooning happily to himself as he followed her up the block, his face buried in the hem of her long fur coat.

Ben had been dispatched from Washington to help the Party publish a daily newspaper on the West Coast. It was April 1947. We were both excited about starting a new life in a new city, far from the pressures of the capitol.

Leo and Kaye helped us find a house to rent—a Victorian on the sunny slope of Twin Peaks. It had high ceilings, ornate light fixtures, bay windows with leaded glass, and many inconveniences to go along with its charms, including rats in the walls.

Ben called them harmless little mice and refused to do a thing about it. He obliged me to attend to all the practical details of our household. No argument in the world could convince him to pick up a screwdriver, a hammer, a paintbrush, or even a pen to pay the bills and balance the checkbook. I had to crawl along all the baseboards in the apartment, dropping poison pellets in the mouseholes, then stuffing them with steel wool. I set mousetraps under the sinks, in the cupboards. Nothing worked. Finally I adopted Ben's approach, which was to loftily ignore the whole business.

We had been married ten years by now, and I knew all about his abstraction, his habit of walking off with his head in the "big picture" when there were menial chores to be done, or emotional demands that had to be met. But he had taken me a long way from the frightened immigrant girl who lived in a gloomy flat above an East-side laundry. When I had time to think about it, I felt satisfied with our lives, with him, with the person I had become by his side.

The whole family seemed to flourish in San Francisco. Vera skipped a grade and a half but still jumped to the top of her class. I enrolled Josh in nursery school. When I tried to leave him the first day, he howled as if his heart was breaking. Then the teacher gave him a red fire engine, and the little traitor became so engrossed that he forgot to wave his mother good-bye.

With both children in school, I began working part-time as a legal secretary for Leo and his partners. We were involved in labor cases and political trials. It was a responsible job that I loved, and it had the added benefit of time off for family matters and party business. Evenings, I wrote leaflets on neighborhood issues and attended classes at the Labor School.

Ben was, if anything, even busier than he had been in Washington. While editing and writing for the *People's World*, he also served as a key liaison in the

Wallace for President campaign. I remember one huge rally down by the ferry building. It seemed that all of working-class San Francisco turned out—the longshoremen, the warehousemen, the maritime workers, the hod-carriers. Listening to their cheers, you could almost believe in victory.

Yet when we took stock of our situation in the aftermath of the 1948 campaign, all we could see were communists under attack, and no one willing to rise to our defense. Russia had replaced Germany as our great enemy. Cold War talk was epidemic. Dozens of committees had been formed to investigate un-American activities. We had, of course, seen such committees before, but now they were armed with new laws, such as the Smith Act, which had been rewritten to virtually outlaw the communist party, and the McCarran Act, which set up concentration camps to hold the newly outlawed reds.

Leo and his family moved back East to aid in the wave of first Smith Act trials. Everywhere our members were pilloried as traitors, expelled from unions, fired from jobs. The FBI visited the mothers in my chapter of the PTA, and they refused to talk to me. Before, we had always reached out to people. We had never felt ashamed of our party. Now we had to spend all our time defending ourselves. "Communist" was a word we no longer dared to use openly.

Inside the Party, a group of hardliners around William Z. Foster and Bob Thompson had come into power. Moderates such as Ben, who had argued for coalition politics and peaceful change within the American system, came in for stinging criticism. Even in meetings among old friends, everyone's voice had become more shrill.

It all came home to me the night Ben and I discussed buying a new phonograph from Sears. Josh had literally played the arm off the old one, listening to sad, slow ballads about cowboys dying young. When the phonograph's arm fell off, he howled as if his own had broken.

Money was perpetually tight, but Sears had an installment plan that stretched payments over six months. When I proposed it to Ben, he vetoed the idea. "Six months from now," he said, looking at me levelly, "there's no telling where we'll be." I knew he was talking about the wave of Smith Act arrests. For months now, the paper had been full of the most dire predictions. Of course, if we were going to be thrown in jail, there was no reason not to leave Sears Roebuck holding the bill for a new phonograph. But that night I was not inclined to see the light side of the matter and neither was Ben. He kept talking about fascism, jail, Germany, repression, the Underground. He insisted that we draw up a legal document specifying who would take custody of the children if we were both summarily carted off to concentration camps.

We were in our bedroom, talking in low voices. Josh must have heard. White-faced with fear, he toddled into our room and pleaded to get in bed with us. We put him in the middle and he fell instantly asleep. An hour later we woke to an acrid smell and an uncomfortable dampness on the sheets. The child was so unnerved that he had wet the bed. Ben fumed and scolded—an indication of how upset he was as he never scolded the children, even for their worst infractions. We had to change sheets, blankets, pyjamas. At last, Josh went back to his own room and we drifted off to sleep, on our own sides of the bed, both wrapped in our own worries. I thought that night about the rats in the walls. I seemed to hear them gnawing through the floorboards, swarms of them, gnawing and threatening to burst out into the children's rooms while I lay there paralyzed, unable to help.

*   *   *

When the order came for Ben to go underground, we had to act very quickly. Twelve people, including the editor of the *People's World*, had been indicted in California. Ben's assignment was to make sure that the paper could go on publishing even in the face of mass arrests. One morning, he simply left for work and didn't come home. For that matter, he had no one to come home to, as we boarded the California Zephyr for New York that very evening.

We did not pack our belongings, sell our furniture, or pay our last month's rent. Friends saw to all that for us. I told the children we were going to spend summer vacation with Ben's parents back East. Josh was ecstatic. Riding trains ranked high on his list of life's pleasures. But Vera knew. Somehow or other she pieced the whole puzzle together and threw a terrible scene in the Southern Pacific Station. She cried and fussed. She made me drag her across the platform. She refused to board the train. I could have cheerfully strangled her.

In Denver, two men in brown suits entered our car and sat across the aisle facing us. I recognized the type instantly—beefy faces, meticulously polished shoes, little brown briefcases, they might just as well have worn FBI badges on their lapels. I mentioned nothing to the children. Josh seemed undisturbed. He ate pancakes with maple syrup for breakfast, lunch, and dinner. He stared endlessly out the window, chattered a mile a minute, made up little songs to the rhythm of the wheels. Vera sulked and whined. She could not sleep at night. She hated all the food and all the waiters in the dining car. She badgered me with questions. What could I tell her with the men across the aisle perpetually listening, watching?

They rode with us all the way to New York. I had hoped to lose them among the crowds at Grand Central. But on the subway up to Ben's parents, I spotted our friends again. They got off at our stop. Their brown hats followed us through the flocks of shoppers on Jerome Avenue. I did not know what to do. We were all exhausted from the three-day trip. We had luggage. Josh kept whining about going to the bathroom. I had to lead them straight to Grandpa's.

What a relief it was to enter the apartment and lock the door behind us. I broke into tears when Grandpa hugged me. He was alone for the summer, finishing a book of poetry, while Grandma helped to run a summer camp for Jewish youth. He wrote a poem about the night we arrived. He called it "My Three Orphans." The first line went:

This night the black wind knocks and three orphans carry candles to my door . . .

16

Mrs. McMahon told us about the play at the end of a hot, boring afternoon. We had been doing free reading practice, and half the kids were dozing over their books. I had been watching a bumblebee bash its head against the window for the last ten minutes.

"Close your books now, children," said Mrs. McMahon, ringing her silver bell to get our attention. "It's time to start our final class project. We're putting on a play for the end-of-the-year assembly. I wrote it myself, and if I may say so, it's a very inspiring story that happened right here in our own neighborhood during the Revolution.

"Now I'm afraid I don't have enough speaking parts for everyone," she said, patting a stack of mimeographed scripts on her desk. "But we're all going to work on this together, even those who don't get a chance to appear on stage. Well then"—she looked brightly around—"who wants to be General Washington?"

All the boys raised their hands. Me too, even though I knew she'd never choose me.

"All right, Vincent," said Mrs. McMahon, handing him a sheet of paper with his lines written on it. "I think you'll do very nicely."

Vincent was the biggest kid in class and played catcher on the baseball team. He was kind of slow-footed and dim-witted and let smaller guys like Eddie Allen shove him around. But no one shoved too hard because when Vincent finally got mad, he'd sit on your chest and sock you in the face and then you were in deep trouble. I had to admit he'd make a pretty good Washington.

"Now, it's the girls' turn," said Mrs. McMahon. "Who wants to play the heroine, Margaret Corbin?"

All the girls waved their hands, but everybody knew Myra Simpson would get the part. She was teacher's pet. When Mrs. McMahon left the room, she always put Myra in charge. Myra had pale skin and a dark blond pony tail that she liked to flick in your face. I guess she would've been pretty if it weren't for her squinty black eyes and the way her nose turned up at the end in a piggy, little snout.

Next Mrs. McMahon asked who wanted to be the hero, Colonel Robert Magaw. Naturally, she chose Eddie Allen. When she picked him, Eddie just gave a little nod and glared at the other kids who had dared to volunteer for his part.

Then Mrs. McMahon assigned the minor roles. There were British soldiers and revolutionary soldiers and John Corbin and someone to say the prologue and a general for the redcoats. I raised my hand for every part, but the more I waved it, the more she ignored me, and the more she ignored me, the worse I wanted to be in the play.

Finally she said, "We have one role left. It's a

small one. Just a few lines. Who wants to be William Demont?"

I flapped my arms so hard I almost flew out of my chair. A couple of other kids waved too, but Mrs. McMahon looked straight at me. She smiled. "All right, Josh," she said, nodding and handing me a sheet of paper. "I think you'll be the perfect William."

My sheet had four lines on it. They were really easy. All I had to say was, "Here are the plans. The front wall is strong. But one lone gun defends the southwest corner. Strike there and they are doomed." I memorized them on the way home from school.

I imagined myself up on the stage in the spotlight in front of the whole auditorium with all the kids and the teachers and the principal and maybe even the parents watching. I didn't care about not being the star. I just wanted to say my lines without stumbling, and after, when everyone came out for a bow at the end, the other kids would put their arms around my shoulders and we'd all bow together and the audience would clap for us and the term would end that way and it wouldn't be so bad after all.

After practicing our lines in class for a couple of days, we held our first rehearsal in the auditorium. It was just Mrs. McMahon and the kids in the cast. Everybody else stayed in our classroom painting scenery or making costumes. The auditorium was dim and almost empty. A couple of bare lightbulbs hung over the stage. Afternoon sunlight peeked through the thick red curtains over the windows facing the schoolyard. Our footsteps echoed when we ran across the bare stage. Mrs. McMahon sat in the first row of seats with the cast around her. She was wearing her black dress and using her yardstick to give directions. She yelled a lot and rapped her yardstick on the back of the chairs, but most of the time she was smiling, and once or twice she even laughed.

When we were ready for the second act, Mrs. McMahon called my name and I went up on stage with Colonel Magaw and Maggie Corbin and the revolutionary soldiers. We stood in a big box chalked onto the boards. The box was the fort we were supposed to defend. Eddie Allen was in charge of defending it. We all had to stand around, shifting from foot to foot, while Mrs. McMahon patiently prompted Eddie through his part.

Finally she said, "All right, cast. Now it's night and the British soldiers are all around. Josh, it's your turn. You sneak out of the fort and walk very quietly to the front corner of the stage. Keep looking around and over your shoulder. Remember, it's dangerous. You don't want anyone to see or hear you."

I tiptoed out of the fort and across the stage. I imagined myself sneaking through the lines of British soldiers ringing the fort. I wasn't afraid of them, but my mission was so important that I had to get through. I remembered the movie of the Alamo where Davy Crockett sent a boy riding through the Mexican lines to get help from General Sam Garrison. The boy was only twelve, and after delivering his message, he rode back to die in the Alamo with Davy.

When I reached the right front corner of the stage, Mrs. McMahon said, "Sidney, now you come out from behind the curtain and talk to Josh."

Sidney came out. As soon as I saw him, I understood everything. He played the British general in charge of attacking our fort.

"Go ahead, Josh," Mrs. McMahon called. "Stand close to Sidney and say your lines. Remember to whisper. Whisper in his ear."

She didn't need to remind me. Suddenly I felt a cold little hand grabbing my throat. "Here are the plans," I croaked to Sidney. "The front wall is strong. But one lone gun defends the southwest corner. Strike there and they are doomed."

"Now pretend to pass Sidney a roll of paper," Mrs. McMahon said. "And Sidney, when you get the paper, pretend to drop money in Josh's hand and say your line."

Sidney played like he was counting coins into my palm. "There you are, Demont," he said. "Thirty pieces. Fair pay for foul work."

"Fine, excellent," said Mrs. McMahon with a little clap. "You two are ready right now today. But let's get back to Colonel Magaw in the fort. Myra, are you all set for Maggie Corbin's big scene?"

I felt strange after rehearsal. Mrs. McMahon had clapped for me and I'd said my lines without stumbling once and Sidney and a couple of the other kids had even spoken to me backstage. I had to admit that acting was fun. But I wasn't quite sure about my part.

I walked home along Fort Washington Avenue. At the corner, I stopped and leaned against the rough gray boulders of the wall to the park. The stones felt warm. They looked chipped and mossy and old. Maybe they'd been here all the time since Washington.

I climbed a flight of steps into the park. The diamond was empty except for a couple of mothers pushing baby carriages across the tarmac. The chess players were leaning across their stone tables in the shade of the trees. The flag flapped and shimmered against the warm blue sky. I walked over to the flagpole. For the first time, I noticed a white marble plaque built into its base. With my finger, I traced the words etched into the marble. They said:

Here on this site, on November 11, 1776, the defenders of Fort Washington fought a desperate artillery duel with the Hessians to defend this, the highest natural point on the island of Manhattan. After three assaults, the fort fell. All defenders died at their guns.

Sweat popped out on my face when I read about all our soldiers dying. Suddenly I knew why Mrs. McMahon picked me for William. This was her way of making me admit I was a traitor in front of the whole school. I thought about how I'd waved my hand and jumped up and down and practically begged her to choose me. I wanted to run right back and tell her I wouldn't do it. But she was probably gone. And saying no to Mrs. McMahon wasn't all that easy.

And the worst thing was that I still wanted to be William. I could imagine just how he'd sneak out of the fort at night and pull his hat down low and wrap his black cape around his face and slink and whisper and glance over his shoulder while he held out his hand for the money.

I shook my head and slouched out of the park. Without even thinking about it, I began to slip from tree to tree. I tried not to let anybody see me. I wished I had a black cape and a hat to pull down over my face. I had to admit it. I wasn't right for General Washington or Colonel Magaw or even for the British soldiers. But I made the perfect William.

The next day, just before we went into the auditorium for rehearsal, I raised my hand and waved it until Mrs. McMahon called on me.

"What is it, Josh?" she asked, gathering up an armful of extra scripts and not really looking at me.

"I ah . . . I umm . . ."

"Speak up. We have a lot of rehearsing and not much time to do it in."

"I don't like my part," I told her.

"What?" said Mrs. McMahon. Her black eyes blinked a couple of times.

"I wanna be excused from the play because I don't like my part." I meant to say it quiet and sorry. But the words rang out loud enough for everyone to hear.

"Why don't we talk about this after rehearsal, Josh?" said Mrs. McMahon. "We can't all be stars you know. Come along now." She smiled, stepping toward the door. "We only have three days left to get ready."

"I don't like my part," I insisted, my voice raising. "And I'm not gonna be in your play."

Mrs. McMahon put down her papers. She walked back to her desk. She brushed at the shoulder of her black dress. She picked up her yardstick. "May I ask why?" she said, giving me a bright smile.

I'd been waiting for that. "Because William Demont's a traitor," I said, my voice going up with every word. "AND I HATE TRAITORS!" I wanted her and everyone in class to hear. My heart was thumping and my scalp prickled and my face felt all sweaty and beet red. I shot a glance over at Eddie Allen. He just yawned and rolled his eyes.

Mrs. McMahon didn't react quite like I expected either. "All right, Josh," she said in a voice that sounded more disappointed than mad. "That's your decision. If that's your idea of citizenship, I'm sure we'll find another William. Stay here and work on the scenery committee," she told me. "Come on, cast," she called to the others, picking up the scripts and heading for the door. "Now that Josh won't help us, we have even more work to do."

That afternoon, Mrs. McMahon made me stay after class until everyone left the room. Then she called me up to her desk. She was ready to go home too. She had a little black hat pinned over her gray hair with a pearl-tipped hatpin. Her desk was all cleaned up with the silver bell standing in its corner next to the black-framed picture of her son in his air force uniform. Her hands were folded in the middle of her ink-stained blotter. They rested on an envelope with Mrs. Elsa Rankin written neatly on the front.

"I want you to deliver this to your mother," she said, picking up the envelope as I reached her desk.

I stuck out my hand, then dropped it. "What's inside?" I asked.

"That's none of your business, young man," said Mrs. McMahon. The corners of her lips curled up for a second in a mean smile, then drooped down into her usual frown. "Just you make sure that your mother receives it. *Unopened.*"

17

When I got home, our apartment had that special waiting quiet of a place where no one's been all day long.
I went straight to the kitchen, took our old blackened
tea kettle, filled it with water, and put it on top of the
stove. I struck a match and held it to the burner under
the kettle. The gas caught with a pop that made me
jump back. I wasn't supposed to turn on the gas when
I was alone in the apartment, but I figured I had about
half an hour before Vera came back. The kettle took
forever to whistle.

I dragged a chair over to the stove and stood on
the seat, holding Mrs. McMahon's letter over the steam
starting to rise from the spout. In the movies, it looks
real easy to steam open a letter, but actually it's pretty
hard. You have to hold your fingers out of the way or
else they'll get burned and if you don't do it just right
the envelope gets soggy and the letters run and the
bottom starts to open before the top.

I guess it was the whistling of the kettle that kept me from hearing the door. But just when I had the seal wet enough to open, I glanced around and there was Vera watching me from the hallway outside the kitchen. She was leaning against the frame of the door, with her books under one arm and the braces on her teeth glittering as she smiled at me.

"Just *what* do you think *you're* doing?" she asked in that happy, excited voice she used whenever she caught me redhanded.

I hopped down off the chair and hid the envelope behind my back. The kettle kept on whistling.

"It's a secret code," I told her. "From Captain Marvel comics. You hold it over steam and the invisible ink comes out."

"Liar!" she said, coming into the kitchen. "I saw you. It's a letter. You're trying to steam open Elsa's mail like a disgusting little spy. Lemme see." She made a grab for the envelope.

I dodged around her and ran to the kitchen door. "It's none of your business," I said. "It's from Captain Marvel. It's a secret code."

"You better let me see," she said, holding out her hand, "or else I'm going to tell."

"Snoop," I yelled at her. "Squealer."

"Spy!" she shouted back. "Just you wait till Elsa gets home." I stormed into my room and slammed the door. The kettle kept on whistling.

I took my glove out from under my bed and sat on the edge of the mattress, pounding my fist in the pocket. I smacked as hard as I could. I wished it was Vera's face I was smacking. I still had one hope. I wanted Vera to run right up and start squealing on me before my mother got a foot in the door. Vera had a knack of doing everything at the wrong time. If she caught my mother when she was still tired and nervous from work and the subway and shopping and all, maybe Vera would get in trouble instead of me.

But this time Vera was smart. She didn't say anything when my mother came home. She helped in the kitchen making dinner. I could hear them in there talking. Running water and cooking noise hid the words, but just from their tone of voice, I knew Vera wasn't squealing yet.

"Josh," called my mother, "dinnertime."

Our kitchen felt hot and narrow even though the window was open and a breeze blew in from the street. Vera watched me all during the meal. I could tell she was waiting for the right moment. Every time she opened her mouth, I choked on my peas and pot roast. But she just blabbed about school and the camp in Vermont she was going to and how happy she was that she and Simone were bunking in the same cabin.

I thought maybe I should bring the letter up myself, but my mother seemed so tired. She always looked pretty to me, with her gold skin and big eyes and her long, thin hands. But her hair wasn't as glossy as usual tonight. It hung down in limp bangs and there were bags under her eyes. For the last couple of weeks she had been going to meetings about the Rosenbergs every night after dinner. She was organizing a vigil. A vigil was when you stay up all night watching someone so they won't get killed. The Rosenbergs were going to get killed on June 19. That was the last day of school.

Every so often, Elsa rubbed her forehead over her left eye. I looked at her. I thought maybe she had a headache. She smiled back and patted my hand. Vera saw it and started to squeal.

"If you're quite rested now," she said to my mother, "I think Josh needs a little parental guidance."

I kicked at her under the table. She kicked back hard enough to rattle the plates but kept talking in a calm, even voice. "He was playing with the gas when I came back from school."

"Josh," said my mother, "if I've told you once, I've told you—"

"It wasn't *just* the gas," said Vera. "In fact, the gas was the very least of it." She paused. "You'll never guess what else your angel boy was doing."

"I don't have time for guessing," my mother said. She stood up to start clearing the table. She didn't like it much when Vera squealed.

"I know you're preoccupied with the vigil," said Vera. "But I suggest that you secure the home front before you rush off to save the Rosenbergs. Why don't you ask my darling brother about the letter he was trying to steam open this afternoon. I saw the envelope quite clearly. It was addressed to you."

My mother turned to stare at me. Her eyes were bright but puzzled. "Well?" she said. "Do you have a letter for me?"

"It's from school," I mumbled, looking down at a pot with a couple of leftover peas floating in a puddle of puke green water. "From Mrs. McMahon."

"May I see it please?"

I brought the envelope from my room. The flap was all puckered up like it had been left out in the rain. Elsa gave me a disgusted look as she opened it.

Vera got up from the table. "I shall retire to my room for a session with Chopin's piano etudes," she smiled.

Mrs. McMahon had perfect penmanship. All her letters slanted the same way, and the capitals had lots of swirls and curlicues around them. Her note said:

> *Dear Mrs. Rankin,*
>
> *As we have not had the pleasure of meeting this term, I would like to extend my personal invitation to our class play. Perhaps you could come to*

the year-end assembly with your son, and stop by
for a chat with me about his progress afterwards.
I'm sure it will be an interesting morning for you.
Sincerely yours,

Mrs. Iris McMahon

"This isn't anything to hide," my mother said after reading the letter twice. "Why didn't you show it to me right away?"

I didn't know where to start. I hung my head and swung my foot against the legs of the table in time to Vera's piano studies.

"Jo-O-osh," said my mother, glancing at her watch. "Please. In fifteen minutes, I've got to leave. What's this about? Are you having some trouble in school?"

"It's about the play," I told her. "Mrs. McMahon hates me because I won't be in her play. She's just trying to get me back."

My mother rapped her hand impatiently on the table. "What play? Your class play? Why don't you want to be in it? You love to act. You're acting half the time and don't think I don't know it."

"She wanted me to play a traitor," I said. "She gave me the worst part on purpose. She's always picking on me."

"And you don't do anything to deserve it, I suppose."

I took a deep breath. Now that I knew about the letter, I had to get Elsa ready to meet Mrs. McMahon. "The only bad thing I ever did was May Day," I said.

"May Day?" Elsa frowned. "What happened on May Day?"

"Mrs. McMahon found out I was going to the parade." Telling after all this time felt like tearing off a scab. It stung and ripped and felt raw to the air.

Elsa shifted the plates and put her elbows on our

dingy plastic tablecloth. She leaned closer to me. I felt myself turning red and starting to fidget under her stare. I remembered how I cried up in front of the class. "I'll clean off the table," I muttered, jumping up and grabbing a dish in each hand.

"Not now. What happened when Mrs. McMahon found out?" Her voice was serious now.

"She called me up in front of the room," I said, feeling the shame shrivel my skin again. "And then she called me a . . . a . . . a *commie!*" I shouted. All of a sudden I was mad. It felt better than being ashamed. My mother couldn't blame me about the letter. It was her fault. Everything. Even about my father. She just wanted him out of the way so she could be with Leo. She didn't even have time for me tonight because she had to rush off to a meeting with him.

"So your teacher called you a commie on May Day," Elsa said, rubbing her forehead. "And right after that they threw tomatoes at you in the parade." She gave me a sad, tired smile. She reached out and put a hand on my face, but I pulled away.

Vera had stopped playing now. I knew she was listening.

"Come over here," my mother said, pushing her chair away from the table and gesturing me into her lap. I wouldn't go until she pulled me in with both hands.

"I don't mind about going to the play, Josh," she told me with her cheek against my ear so I could feel the words coming out in warm wet puffs of breath. "I'm busy, but I should've gone before. And no matter what Mrs. McMahon or anybody else says, I know you're doing your best and it's very hard for you right now. It's hard for all of us. Even Vera."

I wished she'd stop. Under the warmth and the calmness in her voice, I heard the quaver, the tiredness and worry and doubt and even fear. She squeezed her arms around my chest. I could tell she felt lonely.

"Don't hide things from me, Josh. Please," she said. "Any problems you have, you can tell me and I promise I won't get mad no matter what it is. But things like steaming open letters . . . You just can't do that anymore. We have to trust each other. Okay?" She was almost pleading.

"Okay," I nodded. I could feel something wet running along my cheek. I couldn't tell if it came from my eye or hers.

"Especially you and me," she said with another squeeze. "We have to trust each other and help each other. Is there anything else you need to tell me now?"

I shook my head.

We sat there for a while until Vera started banging her piano again. She was doing scales now, going through them very fast and always messing up at the same point and going back to the beginning again. Finally my mother gave a big sigh and stood up.

"Be an angel and do the dishes for me," she said, glancing at her watch. "I've got to run."

18

The assembly was pretty boring. We sat toward the back of the crowded, stuffy auditorium. Lots of other kids had their parents with them. We all had to stand while the color guard marched down the aisle. The flag monitors wore orange soldier's caps and special leather belts with a holster in the middle to hold the end of the flagpole. The teachers stood along the walls and in the center aisle.

After the pledge and the national anthem, Mr. Klein came out and gave a speech about how proud and humble it always made him feel to welcome the parents who had entrusted their children to his hands. He stretched his hands out with the palms cupped together, then folded them back over his big belly.

Then every grade put on a performance. The sixth grade did songs from Broadway musicals with costumes and tap-dancing and a band. The fifth grade held a science fair and magic show. My mother kept sneaking glances at her watch. She had to go to work right after meeting Mrs. McMahon, and after work, she had to go to the vigil for the Rosenbergs. She claimed she didn't mind coming to the assembly, but from the way she kept squirming and sighing in her seat, I could tell she didn't like it.

Finally it was our turn to put on the play. Buddy Ryan came out and stood in front of the curtain to read the prologue. Shifting from foot to foot and rushing through his lines like he had to go to the bathroom something awful, he said:

In Seventeen Hundred and Seventy Six
George Washington's army was facing a fix.
The redcoat DePauls with four thousand men
Had them caught in a trap, a murderous pen.
One hundred bold lads their lives had to give.
But brave Maggie Corbin was destined to live.

When the curtain went up, George Washington and Colonel Magaw were talking in front of a big painted backdrop showing the Hudson River in the snow.

"No, brave friend," said George Washington. "We cannot hold this fort. We must retreat to White Plains. The hour looks dark indeed."

"Retreat?" said Colonel Magaw. "And surrender these heights to the British? Not on my life. Leave me behind with but one hundred men, and I'll hold our fort against all the redcoats in America." Colonel Magaw was wearing a blue cape and a three-cornered hat, but from the way he smirked and strutted around with his thumb hooked in his belt, you could tell it was Eddie Allen. He thumped his chest and snorted to show what he thought of redcoats.

" 'Tis certain death," said George Washington, scratching at his wig. But in the end he galloped off to White Plains and left Colonel Magaw to hold the fort.

The second scene was at night. You could hear someone shouting orders. "Cut those trees. Come on dig. Move those boulders." But you couldn't see anything until the lights came up just enough to show the fort in the middle of the stage with lots of soldiers working around it.

The fort was four big sheets of plywood covered by a painting of rocks that looked like gray faces with chicken pox. William Demont stood in a corner of the fort, dressed all in black. He watched everyone work and made notes on a piece of paper, stopping every once in a while to take a swig from a bottle in his pocket.

"That's him," I whispered to my mother, just as he started to creep out of the fort. "That's who she wanted me to play."

The spotlight followed William Demont as he snuck across the stage. Herbie with ringworm had the part now, and he made it look like William was drunk. When the British general paid him, he got all excited and danced around in a circle like he was doing the whole thing just for money to drink. The audience hissed and booed. My mother reached over and squeezed my hand.

I smiled. I felt glad it wasn't me. But I couldn't help thinking that Herbie didn't understand the first thing about my part.

The British general rode out with a white flag just before the battle started at dawn. "Surrender and live," he yelled to the fort. "Or stand and die!"

Colonel Magaw popped up to answer. He put his hand over his heart and shouted, "Moved by the most glorious cause in the history of mankind, I shall defend this fort to the last ex . . . ex . . . exter . . ." He was supposed to say "extremity." But he had never gotten it out right in rehearsal, and he couldn't say it now.

After a couple of tries, he just waved his hand and snorted to show that he didn't have time to worry about words like "extremity" when there were four thousand redcoats to kill.

The British charged the fort three times from the front, but lots of them got killed. The fourth time, they attacked from the side with William Demont leading the way to the southwest tower. Our soldiers made a lot of noise dying and falling out of the fort.

Colonel Magaw shouted, "They have killed John Corbin, gunner of the southwest wall. Who will serve his cannon?"

"Let me, sir," cried Myra Simpson, stepping up to join him. She had black smudges on her face and a red bandana over her hair and a bunch of tissue paper stuffed down the front of her white blouse. She waved a mop handle in her fist. The mop was supposed to be one of those poles you use to load a cannon.

"A woman," said Colonel Magaw, taking a step backward and throwing up his hands.

"Woman though I be," Myra answered, "I have fought by the side of my husband, John, all through this bloody battle. Now he is slain and I, Margaret Corbin, arise to take his place."

"No," said Colonel Magaw, "I cannot allow . . ."

But just then the British charged again, and Maggie Corbin rushed to her gun and started firing at the enemy. You could see her pumping the mop handle as hard as she could and pulling the string that shot the cannon and putting her fingers in her ears when the boom came and then rushing around to do it all over again. She kept the British from getting into the southwest corner, but they killed everyone else in the fort, even Colonel Magaw.

In the end, the British pushed down the walls of the fort and rushed inside. They danced around and celebrated. Then someone asked, "Are all the rebels dead?"

"Every man."

"But wait," said another soldier. "Here lies a woman. It was she who fought like the devil himself to keep us from the southwest tower."

All the redcoats crowded around Maggie Corbin lying on the ground.

"Is she dead?" the general asked.

"Yes," said the soldier.

"Then we must give her a hero's burial," the general said. "But first bring out the spy."

Two redcoats came out dragging William Demont.

"You told us to attack the southwest wall," the general yelled at him. "And half my army died there. Take him to the gallows."

So the soldiers dragged William Demont away.

And just then Maggie Corbin struggled to her feet.

"She lives. She lives," the British soldiers cried.

Maggie Corbin grabbed for her mop handle and looked around like she wanted to find her cannon and kill a few more redcoats. But she was too weak to stand.

The British soldiers held her up by the arms. And their general said, "Let us honor her and nurse her back to health. For she is the bravest woman that ever I have seen. If all the rebel women fight like her, I fear for the cause of King George." They put Maggie Corbin in a chair and carried her off the stage like a queen.

After the play, we went back to the classroom. We had to wait a long time to talk to Mrs. McMahon. First she was busy with the cast, and even when she came back from the auditorium, she met with all the other parents before getting around to us. I sat with my mother in the back of the room, near the window.

Elsa had forced me to wear a suit jacket and the scratchy wool slacks I hated. With my polka dot tie and my hair all slicked down except for a couple of curls that kept popping up in back, I looked like I belonged in the peanut gallery on the "Howdy Doody Show." I thought of saying that, but my mother was in one of those moods where the less we talked to each other the better.

She was all dressed up for the Rosenberg vigil in black high heels and a straight black dress and a charcoal gray hat that she wore off to the side, like a beret. Everything about her was dark that morning, except the turquoise ring on her finger and a silver pin on her dress and the red lipstick on her mouth.

She kept shifting around in her chair, looking at the drawings and the charts of revolutionary history on the wall, scanning the titles of the *Reader's Digest* primers in our bookcase, reading the lists of class monitors on the wall, and comparing her watch with the clock above Mrs. McMahon's desk. It was after twelve. I was hungry. Out the window I could see the Good Humor truck with long lines of kids and parents around it.

When the room was finally empty, Mrs. McMahon called us up to her desk. She stood to shake my mother's hand. Their fingers touched for just a second. Then they pulled their hands apart and stood looking at each other. Mrs. McMahon was wearing a black dress, as usual, but this one was made of silk, and she had a big flower pinned to the front. The flower had ruffled petals and a sweet smell that didn't go with the chalk dust in the air.

"I'm so-o glad you could come," Mrs. McMahon smiled at my mother. "I'm sure you must be very busy."

"Not at all," my mother smiled back. "What a lovely flower."

"It's an iris," said Mrs. McMahon. "From the mothers of the children in the cast. Wasn't that thoughtful? But please, sit down." She pointed to a chair next to the desk.

"No, thank you," my mother said. "We've been sitting all morning. I'd rather stand."

"Well, then . . ." said Mrs. McMahon. Now she didn't want to sit down either. She pulled herself up straight so she could stare down at my mother. Mrs. McMahon was taller and thicker and she had gray hair and all, but in a way they looked alike to me just then, both of them wearing dark clothes and standing very straight and staring at each other with bright, tight smiles on their faces. I didn't feel like standing just because they were. I slouched down in one of the desks in the front row. Neither of them noticed.

"Well, then," Mrs. McMahon said again, "and what did *you* think of our little play?"

"To tell you quite frankly," Elsa said, "I loved it. Especially the character of Margaret Corbin. A very advanced woman for her time. And the little girl who played her was inspired. I thought all the children were."

"Did you?" said Mrs. McMahon. "Really? I mean . . . you did? I wouldn't have thought . . ." She seemed surprised and even a little worried that my mother liked her play.

"Did you actually write it yourself?" Elsa asked.

"Well, yes. As a matter of fact, I did." Mrs. McMahon blinked and patted the hair over her ear.

"Then you're to be congratulated," my mother said. "You've created a very progressive and inspiring piece."

Mrs. McMahon blushed. I'd never seen her do that before or even imagined that she could.

"Have you ever thought of publishing it?" my mother asked.

"Publishing?" said Mrs. McMahon, taking a step backward and throwing up her hands. "Why, no, of course not. It's just something I tossed off in odd moments for the class . . ."

"You're much too modest," my mother said. "You have talent and your message is important. Especially for young girls. They're so rarely exposed to progressive ideals, to positive, active models for development. Do you have an extra copy of the script? I happen to know a publisher who might be very interested in bringing it out."

"No thank you," said Mrs. McMahon curtly, drawing herself up and shaking her head. "I'm not interested in having my play published by any of *your* friends."

"What a pity." Elsa shrugged and smiled. "Well, I certainly hope you do something with it. And now, if there's nothing else . . ." She glanced at her watch. "Oh, look at that. Almost one. I'm afraid I really must . . ." She reached out to shake hands again and say good-bye.

Mrs. McMahon looked confused. For a second, I really thought she was going to let us get away just like that. But then she pursed her lips and plopped herself solidly down in her chair. "As a matter of fact, Mrs. Rankin," she said, "there are a number of other things . . . Perhaps we'd better start with this." She opened her desk drawer, took out my report card and passed it to my mother.

"Please notice the Unsatisfactory in citizenship," she said.

Elsa looked at the U on my report card. She turned around and saw me slouching in the desk and jerked me up to my feet. "Is this because he refused to be in the play?" she asked.

"Only in part," Mrs. McMahon answered. "He's been having adjustment problems all term long. I thought it was my duty to let you know."

"I appreciate your concern," my mother said. "I'll talk to him about it."

"I certainly hope you will," said Mrs. McMahon. "And while you're at it, you might consider how your own beliefs contribute to his problem. In fact, I'd say they're at the root of it."

"My beliefs? Since we've never had the opportunity to discuss them, Mrs. McMahon, I don't see how you can draw any conclusions whatsoever about the nature of my beliefs."

"Well, you'd be surprised," Mrs. McMahon smiled. "You'd be surprised at what a teacher learns about her students and their home environment. I notice, for instance, that Josh never talks about his father the way the other boys do. What is Mr. Rankin's occupation? *If* you don't mind my asking."

"He's a journalist," my mother said.

"How nice. And what paper does he write for?"

My mother sighed. "Really, Mrs. McMahon, I think we're wandering."

"Then I'll come straight to the point. Are you a communist, Mrs. Rankin?"

My mother sucked in her breath with an angry, little click of her tongue. "This is a classroom, not a senatorial inquisition," she said. Her voice was stiff and cold, and for the first time I heard a little tremor underneath it. "That question is entirely out of line, and I fail to see what relevance it has to my son's education."

"In that case, there's a great deal you fail to see. And I don't believe I've heard your answer." Mrs. McMahon's fingers drifted to her yardstick. Sunlight flashed off its metal edge.

"The answer," said Elsa, putting an arm around me, "is that I believe in standing up for my own principles. Like Margaret Corbin in your play."

"Ah, yes," smiled Mrs. McMahon. "Margaret Corbin. But then her principles were so very different from yours."

"And from yours as well," Elsa shot back. "Unless you plan to write a sequel in which she becomes a teacher who persecutes little children for their parents' beliefs."

"The only thing I plan to write," Mrs. McMahon answered, rearranging the picture of her son in its corner of her desk, "is a summary of this interview for our permanent records."

"Then we'll leave you to your task," Elsa said, pushing me toward the door. "What a pity you can't find a more constructive outlet for your talents."

"How very odd," said Mrs. McMahon, watching us leave with both hands folded on her blotter, "I was thinking precisely the same thing about you."

19

The TV was showing a bunch of Gillette razor blades dancing around in a boxing ring made out of foam. I leaned back on the cushions piled on my mother's daybed and put my glass of Coke on the coffee table and sang along with the commercial. "To *look* sharp . . . dah . . . de . . . *dah* . . . de . . . dah. To *feel* sharp . . . dah . . . de . . .*dah* . . . de . . . dah." I was trying to work myself into a good mood about the end of school and getting out of Mrs. McMahon's class and all, but I just felt lousy. I wanted the boxers to come out and start slugging each other. It was one of those muggy summer afternoons when the whole city smells like rotten eggs.

The bell for the first round rang. The flyweights danced out of their corners and touched gloves in the middle of the ring. And just then, without asking or anything, Vera came along and switched the channel to Edward R. Murrow.

"Hey, I was watching first, snotball," I said. "You can hear the news on the radio."

Vera whirled around to glare at me. Her skirt made a dry rustling noise, like a snake. "You astonish me," she said. "I simply cannot comprehend how anyone who grew up in a household like ours could want to watch two poor exploited workers batter each other senseless for money. Especially tonight! Don't you know what's happening? Don't you even care?

I knew all right. You couldn't help knowing. It was June 19 and the Rosenbergs were going to get the Chair at eight o'clock unless the Supreme Court gave them another stay. A "stay" was when they let you stay alive for a little while longer. Elsa was down at the vigil in Union Square with all the other people who wanted a stay for the Rosenbergs. Vera and I were supposed to be good and cook our own dinner.

I drowned out the news by giving her my two-tone, high-low, Nazi-siren howl. "Bee-BEEP-beep, bee-BEEP-beep, bee-BEEP-beep," I wailed. Vera hated it when I did that. It scared her even during the days when my mother was there. But now that we were home alone and the Rosenbergs were about to get the Chair and all, the noise made her grit her teeth and jam her fingers in her ears. I could see her steel braces glinting in the light from the window. I got up to change back to boxing.

"Just you touch that dial," she said, clacking her teeth. "Go on, you little fascist. Try it."

I knew she'd bite me if I changed channels, so I slipped around to the back of the TV and unhooked the antenna. We had a second-hand Philco that Jody's family had given us when they bought a new one. Reception was crappy even with the rabbit ears plugged in. Without them, Edward R. Murrow's face dissolved into a bunch of buzzing black dots. You couldn't hear a word he said because of the static.

Vera started chasing me to get the antenna back. We ran in circles around the coffee table. I climbed up on top of the bookcase full of the collected works of Lenin in green leather covers and held the antenna over my head so she couldn't reach it. She started to bite my leg. I made a really beautiful jump off the top of the bookcase, across the coffee table, and onto the day-bed. Vera screamed at me for ruining the springs. I bounced up and down as hard as I could. I wanted to touch the ceiling with the tip of the antenna. I was getting really close when the doorbell rang.

Vera stopped chasing me. She put her hands up to her head and stared all around the room with quick little jerks of her head.

"Don't answer!" she said. "It's the police. They've arrested everyone at the vigil and now they're coming for us."

I rushed to the window next to the TV, stuck my head out, and saw a big dark car parked under the street lamp. I jerked my head back. Our doorbell rang again. Vera grabbed me. We stood there in the middle of the room, holding onto each other.

"Hey, come on, open up!" called a deep, man's voice. Fists thudded on the door.

"Who . . . who's there?" asked Vera. Her voice sounded shaky, but at least she could talk, which was more than I could do.

"It's me, Leo."

I let my breath hiss out. I didn't even know I'd been holding it. Ever since the whole business about the address book, I'd been scared around Leo, but I was plenty glad to see him now. I opened the door. He stood in the dark hall, very tall and broad. The shadows collected around his eyes, turning them into big dark holes under his brow. He carried his briefcase from work.

"Your mom sent me," he said. "She doesn't want

you two alone tonight. You're eating over at our place. And sleeping over too."

I gave a little clap. Going to Leo's meant I'd have a chance to see Jody again. It seemed like years since we'd played together.

"Why didn't you telephone in advance?" said Vera, coming out into the hall and talking in a snooty British voice so Leo wouldn't guess she'd been about to pee in her pants a second ago. "I shall need some time to prepare myself. I suggest you have a seat, or wait in the car if that's more comfortable."

"I'll give you about three minutes flat, Madame Pompadour," Leo snorted. "I've got a carload of people back at the house waiting for a ride down to the vigil. This's no time for nonsense."

I ran down the hall to my room. Leo followed. He watched while I got down on my hands and knees and tried to find my pajama bottoms in the pile of sheets and toys and underwear and plastic model parts and empty tubes of glue and paint all jumbled up together on the floor.

"You and I have something to discuss," he said, dropping a big heavy hand on my shoulder.

My stomach flopped. I jumped up and moved away from him because I thought he was talking about his address book. I saw his eyes rove all around my room like he was looking for my secret hiding place. I didn't want to think about what he'd do if he found it. All of a sudden, I couldn't even remember what made me take his book in the first place. I just knew there was no way to give it back now without getting myself in trouble.

"You know what I'm talking about, don't you?" he said, giving me a little shake.

"N-n-no."

"You mean those big ears of yours haven't picked up any rumors about plans for the summer?"

"Summer?" I said.

"That's right, summer. The season between spring and fall? You've heard of it, haven't you?" Leo was smiling now. He took off his hat and scratched at his thick curly hair. I wished he'd just come out and tell me what he meant. But I was beginning to get an idea.

"Are we going somewhere this summer?" I asked.

"Why don't you ask Jody when we get home." Leo winked.

"Can't you tell me now? Please? Is it about the cabin?" Jody's family had a cabin on Bear Mountain in upstate New York. We went there sometimes on weekends. The cabin was on a lake, and it had a fireplace and a rickety wooden dock and a rowboat with an outboard motor.

"I thought that long nose of yours would sniff it out," said Leo, tapping his finger against his nose. "Jody's getting too uppity to spend time alone with the old folks anymore. And you're not going to summer camp. So Elsa and I were thinking . . . but that was before I saw what a slob you are. You're not going to do this to my cabin, are you?"

Leo studied my room again. It seemed especially small and shabby with him standing in it. His head brushed against the sloping, water-stained ceiling. The cuffs of his pressed gray slacks picked up dustballs from the floor.

"I'll clean everything up, I promise." I grabbed my sheet off the floor and threw it over my bed. A couple of bubble gum wrappers and a pair of dirty underpants flew out from its folds.

Leo shook his head and held his nose. "I don't know . . ." He smiled.

But now I was sure. I was going up to the cabin with Jody. Maybe we'd spend the whole summer together, and he'd teach me to dive off the dock and swim. I was so happy, I hugged Leo. I could barely get my arms around his waist. He put his hand on my back and pressed my head against his stomach in a clumsy way. I decided to give him his address book back the first chance I got. If he wasn't watching, I would've gotten it out right then and slipped it into the cushions of the car while we drove over to their place. But that wouldn't work because he could still figure out who took it. Leo was a lawyer. He was smart. I had to be careful. But now I had all summer. Maybe up at the cabin.

Jody lived on the Grand Concourse in the Bronx. It wasn't a snob building because they didn't have a doorman, but it was a lot nicer than ours, with polished marble floors in the lobby and an elevator that went fast enough to make your stomach drop.

Up in Jody's apartment there were so many people I thought they had a Party party going on. Then I noticed that nobody was drinking or passing food around. None of the adults came up to ask me stupid questions about school. Instead of talking as loud and as fast as they could, they all whispered the way you do around sick people. They smoked lots of cigarettes and kept glancing at their watches.

Mainly they worked in the kitchen making sandwiches to take down to the vigil or folding blankets and piling petitions and copies of the paper into boxes that they stacked by the door. They had a bunch of picket signs there too, with thick wooden handles. Leo was organizing rides for people who wanted to go to Union Square. Most of the people were afraid to take their kids along so they left them with Kaye, Jody's mom.

Kaye didn't go to demonstrations much, or to meetings and Party parties, either. She liked to stay in the house and make things. She could make all sorts of stuff like pottery and paintings and rugs for the floor and big pillows with birds and animals embroidered on them. She liked kids too, so she was more or less the official babysitter for everyone, along with fat Peggy Mendolsohn.

There must've been about a dozen kids at Jody's that night. A few of the older girls, like Vera and Simone, helped out in the kitchen making coffee or sandwiches. I went into the living room to find Jody.

I wanted to get him alone and ask if we were really going up to the cabin together and when and for how long. But you could never get Jody alone when there were other kids around. I found him sitting on the couch, surrounded by Lonnie Mae and Davy and a bunch of other kids I hadn't seen since May Day. The couch had purple silk cushions with white cranes embroidered on them. Jody waved and smiled when I came in, but nobody said much because they were watching the news on TV. I flopped down on the rug and leaned back against Jody's legs.

The news showed a reporter standing outside the walls of the prison where they had the Rosenbergs and the Chair. On our TV, the people looked like they were talking to you from another planet where there was a big storm going on. But Jody had a Philco Futurmatic with a sixteen-inch screen. The picture was so clear you could see each brick in the wall. You could see the way the reporter raised his eyebrow and clenched his jaw when he mentioned the Chair.

He said Julius had already packed his belongings and left a note for his lawyer and now they were taking him to the barber to have his head shaved so the electricity could get into his brain faster. But the warden was standing right by the phone in case the Supreme Court or the president decided to call the whole thing off.

After the news, "Your Hit Parade" came on the air. "Hit Parade" was Jody's favorite program. He watched it every Friday night. Usually he got dressed up special for it and rolled up the rug and danced along with all the songs. But he couldn't do that tonight because of the Rosenbergs. He got up and walked kind of slowly over to the TV.

"I guess we ought to turn it off, huh?" he said, putting one hand on the gold knob, then glancing at Lonnie Mae because she was as big a nut for "Hit Parade" as he was.

"Yeah," she said. "I guess we better, huh?"

But by that time, the number ten song of the week was already playing, and I could see Jody's toes starting to tap to the rhythm. Lonnie Mae got up and strolled over to the TV too, like she was going to help him turn it off.

"Well, maybe it wouldn't hurt if we heard just this one," Jody said.

He loved dancing better than anything. Leo kept making him take lessons in boxing and swimming. And I knew he could make the Dodgers for sure if he'd practice baseball a little more, but Jody said he was going to be a dancer when he grew up.

Before he got around to turning the knob, Vera and Simone came in from the kitchen and leaned against the door and stood there staring at us through their thick glasses like we were fish in the aquarium or something.

Simone made a sharp *tsk, tsk, tsk* sound with her tongue, then shook her head at Vera and said, "Well, you really can't expect *children* to comprehend the gravity of the situation, can you?"

"Of course not," answered Vera. "After all, why should *they* care? *They're* not the ones who'll be orphans if their innocent parents are executed."

They kept their voices low like they were just talking to each other. But of course everybody heard. Jody stared down at his toes, which were still beating time to the music. Lonnie Mae got angry. She threw back her head and said, "Well, maybe watching TV isn't gonna help those poor folks. But I don't see you all doing much except standing around looking down your noses and making us feel bad."

"Well, as a matter of fact," said Simone, rubbing her high white forehead, "we have a much more practical idea. Don't we, Vera?"

"We most certainly do," nodded Vera. "*If* you can spare the time from 'Hit Parade'," she sneered, "we would like to enlist your help in writing a petition, a children's petition. A Save the Rosenbergs petition to the powers that be from all the children of the world." Her eyes circled the room and came back to Simone, and the two of them beamed at each other like they had just invented the airplane or something.

"A petition?" laughed Lonnie Mae. "How's your old petition gonna help? Millions and zillions of people have already signed petitions. Even the old Pope signed a petition. And they're still gonna get killed."

"Yeah," I sneered. "What's some lousy petition gonna do anyway?"

And Davy popped up from the couch to add, "How about if we petition the two of you to get your tushies out of here and leave us alone?"

"I second the motion," said Lonnie Mae.

"And I third it," fat Nicky chimed in.

"And I f-f-fourth and f-f-fifth it," lisped Connie, struggling to get the words out through her buck teeth.

Vera turned pink. She tried to keep a superior smile on her face, but it didn't look convincing because her lips pulled back and you could see her teeth grinding together. Simone patted her on the shoulder, but Vera didn't seem to notice. I could see she was just about to burst out crying in front of everybody. I racked my brains to think of some really nasty comment that would make her start.

Before I found it, Jody spoke up. He had just been standing there, very quiet, watching and listening to everyone. But now he said, "Hey, what's wrong with you guys? Can't you hear? Maybe she's right." He looked around at everyone who argued against Vera. "Maybe they will listen to a petition from kids all over the world. And if they don't, so what? Don't you guys even want to try?"

And, of course, as soon as Jody said it, all the kids changed their minds, even Lonnie Mae and me. Jody had been the one who wanted to listen to "Hit Parade" in the first place, and he should've been the one to be angry about all the things Vera said, and in a way we had all been speaking up for him. But if he wanted to stop and do the petition, that was fine with us, too.

"I'll get you paper and things," he said, smiling at Vera. "You tell us how to write it."

So we turned off the TV and sat down to write the petition. Naturally, with Vera and Simone in charge, we couldn't make a nice, simple petition that just said "Please don't kill the Rosenbergs" or something. We had to have a real meeting according to Robert's Rules of Order. Everybody had a chance to propose clauses and amendments and revisions. But in the end, the petition came out pretty much the way Vera wanted because she knew the Constitution and the Declaration and everything. She wrote the final draft with a fountain pen that Jody got from his dad's study. Her handwriting was perfect for a petition—so fancy you could hardly read it. When she was all finished, we signed our names. Then Vera led us into the kitchen to present our petition to the adults.

Jody had a big kitchen with bright yellow walls and a round wooden table and plants growing by the window above the sink. The adults were sitting around the table under a cloud of cigarette smoke. They were listening to the radio, staring at the green glow of the dial like it was a bomb they expected to blow up in their faces.

The second we came in the door, Jody's mom turned off the sound. She was the smallest lady I'd ever seen, hardly bigger than I was. She had blond hair and bright blue eyes that looked straight into yours when she talked. Her voice was sweet and soft most of the time, but when she got angry, even Leo was scared of her. Fat Peggy looked like a hippo sitting by Kaye's side. Herschel was the only man there. He had to walk with two canes because he got wounded in Spain.

"Ahem," said Vera, clearing her throat and staring nervously around like she had an audience of about five thousand adults. "We would . . . that is . . . if it's not an intrusion . . . what I mean is that we have prepared a petition to . . ."

"Vera, dear," said fat Peggy in a tense voice, "it's not really the time for . . ."

But Vera wouldn't let her finish. "Well, we wouldn't dream of intruding on your deliberations," she said. "But we happen to feel this is *important*!" She looked daggers at Peggy.

"Go ahead, honey," smiled Kaye. "Read us what you wrote."

"In that case . . . ," said Vera, adjusting her blue butterfly-shaped glasses and smoothing out her skirt and drawing herself up, "in that case, I should like to read a document entitled, 'A Petition from All the Children of the World to All the Powers That Be,' It has been duly drafted and signed by my fellow petitioners." She turned and glanced at all of us crowding behind her in the doorway. "And it goes as follows:

Whereas, an innocent and inoffensive couple, Ethel and Julius Rosenberg, have been thrown behind bars and menaced with execution for heinous crimes which they did not commit;

Whereas, the two young children of the aforementioned couple are, through no fault of their own, menaced with the prospect of orphanage, which is perhaps the cruelest blow that can befall a child;

Whereas, children all over the world—frightened and saddened by this spectacle of justice gone awry—are moved to reach out to each other and form one great family united in human sympathy despite differences of culture, creed, language, and color of skin;

Whereas, it has ever been the right of children to petition their elders for redress of grievances, and to promise that exemplary behavior will be forthcoming if said grievances are indeed redressed;

We, the undersigned children of the world—residents, citizens, and future leaders of all political and economic systems, do hereby raise our voices, reach out our hands, and earnestly petition the Powers that Be to release Julius and Ethel Rosenberg from vile captivity, to reunite one terrified and unhappy family, and by so doing, to give all families everywhere greater hope and faith in the future. Written at 7:00 pm on the dark night of June 19, 1953.

>*Recording secretary: Vera Rankin*
>*First witness: Simone Hardin*
>*First signatory: Jody Hardin"*

The room was very quiet when Vera finished. Then Peggy blew her nose. She was crying. Kaye had tears in her eyes too. Herschel propped himself up on his canes and wobbled across the room to throw his arm around Vera's shoulders.

"Bravo!" he said. He thumped on the floor with this canes. Vera hated for anybody to touch her, especially Herschel, but she didn't seem to mind now. She was all flushed and smiling.

"We've got to get this out," said Herschel. He turned to face Jody's mom. "They've got to hear this at the vigil. Think what it'll do for morale. We've got to get her down there so she can read it to the whole vigil. Think of the impact. This child's pure high voice, ringing out over the multitude assembled in the dark of night . . ."

Vera puffed herself up. She didn't say anything, but I could tell she liked the idea.

But Peggy shook her head and said, "I don't know, Herschel. It's almost eight. By the time we drive all the way down to . . . besides, it's dangerous. And if they don't get a stay . . ."

"Well, that's precisely my point." Herschel pounded his cane again. "We can't sit here drowning in defeatism. If there's something, anything we can do. And this. The purity of it, the emotion, the militancy . . ."

"Sit down, Herschel," said Kaye calmly. "If they get the stay, it's a new situation, time to launch a new petition. If not . . ." She shook her head.

"Well, at least we can call the paper," said Herschel, glaring at Kaye and Peggy. "Stay or no stay, at least they can run this document in tomorrow's edition. Front page, three columns. You defeatists don't see anything wrong with that, do you?"

So Vera and Herschel went into the study to read the petition to the editor of the paper over the phone, and the rest of us went back into the living room and settled down on the cushions and couches and armchairs or stretched out on the rug to wait. Nobody could think of much to say, so Davy took out his guitar and started playing folk songs.

The guitar was so big and Davy so small that he looked like a bright-eyed little mouse peeking out at us from behind the curved blond wood. And the songs were just the same ones we always sang, the same ones we sang at the May Day picnic, for instance, but tonight, I don't know, I kept hearing how all the words were about people dying or getting stuck in jail or being lonesome or sick or scared and hungry out in the rain. And I got this feeling about things always turning out the sad way no matter how hard anyone tried to make them right. And I could kind of feel this lump rising up in my throat, and the funny thing about the lump was that it made me sing a lot better than usual. I could hear how all the voices, the girls' voices and the boys' voices, blended together with the chords Davy was playing. And I could hear Davy's voice rising above everyone's as he closed his eyes and laid his cheek along the curve of the guitar. And even though it was only a couple of minutes before eight and just turning dark outside, somehow it felt like deep black in the middle of the night, and then we were singing this sad, stupid song I always liked that went:

> *Go tell Aunt Rhody,*
> *Go tell Aunt Rho-o-dy.*
> *Go tell Aunt Rhody*
> *That her old gray goose is dead.*

20

For the first week of summer vacation, I tried to forget about school and the baseball team and Dale and all the stuff he said about going to see the Dodgers' double-header. When any of that popped into my mind, I just concentrated on going up to Bear Lake with Jody. I'd talked to him the morning after the vigil and he said we were going to spend two whole weeks at his cabin, starting July 4. And just to make sure we didn't get bored while we were up there, we were going to go down to Chinatown first and buy enough firecrackers to blow the whole cabin into the lake.

I needed at least a dollar for my share of the fire-crackers, but I didn't dare ask Elsa. If I asked for a dollar, I'd have to tell her what for, and probably she'd give it to me like she usually did. But on the other hand, she might say something stupid like firecrackers are dangerous or we'd set the woods on fire. This was too important to take any chance of letting her ruin it.

Besides, there were lots of ways to get money without telling. I brought all our Coke and seltzer bottles back to Sweeny's for the deposit, and I sold him my whole collection of Batman comic books for two cents apiece. I invented a story about going downtown to the main library and asked for carfare and got an extra quarter from my mother that way. When she gave me my allowance on Friday, I already had a whole dollar.

That still didn't seem like enough so I asked if there was anything I could do around the house. She had me sweep all the rooms and send our newspapers down to the basement on the dumbwaiter and tack down our hall carpet where it was beginning to fray at the edges.

By Saturday, the day before we were going down to Chinatown, I had two dollars and ten cents. That really should've been enough. It was more than Jody told me to bring, and it seemed like plenty when I went to sleep on Saturday night. But when I woke up early Sunday morning and lay in bed thinking about how in just a few hours I'd take the money out of my back pocket and give it to Jody and say, "Here, you buy firecrackers for the both of us," all of a sudden two dollars and ten cents just didn't seem like enough anymore.

I got out of bed and opened my door very quietly. It was just about dawn. I could hear Vera sleeping in the room next to mine. Our hall was dark, except for a patch of gray light about halfway down. The light came from the kitchen windows. The edge of the rays fell on the little telephone table next to the kitchen door. I could see my mother's purse on top of the table. She left it there almost every night. The gold clasp gleamed a little.

I tiptoed down the hall. My mother had a small black purse made out of genuine imitation leather that was supposed to look like alligator skin. When I opened it, a strange secret smell of powder and lipstick and tobacco and pencil shavings and handkerchiefs with perfume and saliva on them came out and kind of curled around my face and made my heart bump a little.

I took out her wallet. She had one ten and two fives and four crumpled green dollar bills inside. I looked up the hall to the room where she was sleeping, down the hall toward Vera's room, then slipped two dollars out of the billfold. I closed the wallet and opened it again and looked at the green edges of the bills inside. They looked just about as thick as before. I put the wallet back in the purse and silently shut the clasp. By the time I got back to my room and closed the door and leaned against it, I felt out of breath, like I'd just run up all six flights of stairs on the way to our apartment.

I stretched out on my bed again but couldn't fall asleep. I felt bad about the money, but I felt glad too. Mostly I just felt too nervous and excited to lie still. As soon as I heard Vera stirring around in her room across the hall, I jumped up, got dressed, and ran downstairs to the street. It was a hot, bright morning. I went up to Sweeny's candy store on the corner and bought a copy of the Sunday *Times* for twenty-five cents.

My mother was in the kitchen when I got back upstairs. She was toasting bagels for breakfast. Her black hair was hanging loose over the collar of her housecoat. The housecoat had a white· lace collar with a missing button and a safety pin in front. I dropped the Sunday paper on the counter by the toaster. She glanced at the headlines, rubbed sleep out of her eyes, shook her head, and smiled at me.

"Such service," she said. "You should only clean your room without my asking, too." She laughed to show she didn't really mind about my room. Then she popped a bagel out of the toaster and said, "Bring me my purse and I'll pay you back."

"It's a present," I told her, patting the paper, "a treat."

"A treat?" She tilted her head to one side and looked at me.

I stared away from her gold-brown eyes. I looked at the sun on her hair. It was funny how her black hair gleamed purple and green and red in the sunshine.

"You did extra chores all week to save money and now you're spending it on my paper?" she asked.

I could tell from her voice she didn't believe it. I started getting all red and prickly and sweaty. I thought any minute now she'd look in her purse and figure the whole thing out and keep me from going over to Jody's for the firecrackers. And that made me mad. I felt myself getting ready to stomp and shout and scream because even though I shouldn't have stolen the money in the first place, I had bought her a present when I didn't need to or anything, and instead of being happy or even thanking me, she was acting like I'd done something wrong.

But just before I blew my stack, she bent down and grabbed me and gave me a big hug and a wet kiss right on the lips and I could smell her warm, sleepy morning odor, as secret as the inside of her purse, and I guess usually I would've liked it a whole lot, but now I squirmed and pushed away and said, "I gotta go to Jody's."

When I got there, Jody was playing in the vacant lot across from his apartment with five other guys. I'd seen them before. They were Jody's gang from school, big kids in the sixth grade. He never told me they were going with us. They were playing with a knife—the game where two guys take turns throwing it in the dirt and each one has to stretch his legs to cover where the knife sticks, and the first guy who can't stretch that far loses.

When I came over, they stopped playing and looked me up and down, and the biggest kid there sneered to Jody, "is *that* what we've been waiting for?"

Jody reached out, grabbed the front of my T-shirt, and pulled me into the group. "Yep," he said, "that's my scuzzy little cousin, all right."

I stared down at the weeds. I wished Jody hadn't called me scuzzy, but I liked the idea of being his cousin.

"Dork on a fork," the big kid sneered to Jody, wiping his switchblade on his jeans. "I bet he doesn't even have any dough. How about it, scuzzy cuz?" He turned to me and shoved his hand in front of my face. "Let's see your money."

His hand was thick and stubby like the rest of his body. He had square shoulders and no neck and a head that looked like it was made for ramming through walls. "Come on," he said, rubbing his thumb across his palm, "fork over or flake off."

I gripped the bills in my pocket. My hand was sweating. I looked up at Jody.

"Go ahead," he nodded. "Donny's holding the money for everyone. He's got mine, too. C-town's a rough place. They've got gangs and everything."

I didn't want to, but I passed my money over— the money I saved, and the money I earned, and the money I stole from my mother to give to Jody. Donny slowly unfolded the bills and counted them.

"Hey, you know what, scuzzy cuz?" he said, stuffing my contribution in his pocket, "you're all right. Whatever happens, stick with me. Get it?"

On the way to the subway, I couldn't talk to Jody or even walk with him because Donny and the other guys crowded me out of the way. They all wanted to be next to him or goof around with him just like the kids in the Party. And Jody treated them the same way he treated us, always smiling and laughing and having a good time himself and trying to make sure they all had a good time too. He even looked around once or twice and spotted me at the back of the pack and winked in that way he got from Leo.

Chinatown in San Francisco always seemed like a happy safe place to me, but New York's was dark and kind of scary. The buildings leaned in close together so the fire escapes almost touched in the middle of the street, and the people stared at us with unfriendly eyes, and the whole place smelled funny.

The shop that sold the firecrackers was on the ground floor of a grimy red brick building with a pointed roof and green dragons on the corners. It was just a little store, tucked in between two restaurants, but I knew it was special right away because its windows were covered with strips of firecracker red paper. Inside, they had a long wooden counter and behind the counter rows of glass bottles like you see in a drugstore, only these bottles were full of black and gray and brown powder or mushrooms or animal horns and some of them had awful things floating in clear liquid like maybe dead babies or snakes.

The man behind the cash register wouldn't even look at us. But down at the far end of the counter, an old Chinese guy was sitting in a chair tilted against the wall. When he saw us come in, he coughed and spit into a bucket by his feet and jerked his head about half an inch at the red curtain screening off the back room of the store.

Jody and Donny led us through the curtain into a roomful of firecrackers. They were spilling out of canvas sacks and cardboard cartons on the floor and stacked in crates up to the ceiling. They had firecrackers as skinny as a toothpick and as thick as dynamite. They had red ones and blue ones and striped ones and silvery bombs with thick green wicks and bottle rockets big enough to fight a war with and roman candles and sparklers. The sharp, tingling smell of gunpowder was so strong it made me sneeze.

A Chinese man stood in the middle of the room. The left side of his face was covered with a thick, black scab. It looked like maybe a box of firecrackers had blown up in his hand. He scared me, but Jody walked right up and smiled.

"Hi," he said.

The man didn't answer. He didn't smile either.

Jody bent over the box of silvery bombs. He picked one up and twirled it around by the wick. "How much?" he asked.

"One piece, one quarter," said the man.

Jody put his head on one side and grinned at the man again. "How about two for a quarter?" he asked. "Or three for a quarter and we'll buy the whole box?"

The man snorted. "Okay, okay. Two for a quarter. Hurry up! Buy and get out!" He peeked through the curtain into the shop to make sure no one was watching.

Altogether we had twenty-five dollars and seventy cents, and we spent every penny of it. We didn't even leave ourselves money for carfare. Jody and Donny did the choosing and each guy got a bagful of firecrackers, all except me because I wanted Jody to carry mine. I carried the punks and wicks and matches that the Chinese guy threw in as a bonus.

We wandered around Chinatown for a while before heading home. The part that felt like the other side of the world with all the smells and stores and signs only lasted a couple of blocks and then it was just shabby brick buildings with sad-looking laundry drying on the fire escapes. I wanted to leave, especially because a couple of Chinese kids were following us. The little one had been waiting right outside the store when we came out with our firecrackers, and then the big one was there next time I looked around.

Nobody else seemed to notice though, and I didn't want to be the only one scared, so I just walked close to Jody and kept looking back every once in a while, and pretty soon there were three kids behind us, and then there were five.

"Hey, Jody," I whispered, jerking my head back. He looked around.

"What you doin' down here?" one of the Chinese guys called to him. "What you got in those sacks?"

We started walking fast. Before there had been lots of people on the streets, but now we were going through alleys between old warehouses with steel shutters closed for Sunday and one of the alleys turned out to be a dead end and when we looked back the Chinese kids were blocking the way out.

They didn't say anything at first, just stood there with the bright light behind them. I could hardly see their faces, but the sun gleamed on their slicked-down black hair, and they looked big and mean and their shadows stretched all the way down to the brick wall behind us.

The kids in our gang clustered together about half-way up the alley. I squeezed in next to Jody. We stood there, staring at the Chinese guys around ten feet away. There was no place to run. The fire escape ladders were too high to jump for. The brick walls leaned in closer and closer.

Then Donny stepped out in front. He walked right up to the biggest kid in the Chinese gang and stared him in the face.

"Get the fuck out of our way, chink," he said.

The Chinese kid didn't look scared. "You wanna get out, gimme that bag." He pointed at Donny's sack of firecrackers.

"Try 'n take it," said Donny.

The Chinese kid grabbed for the bag. Donny tossed it back to us and put up his fists, and then they started circling each other and faking and jabbing but not hitting yet because neither one really wanted to start it. The kids on both sides were beginning to crowd in and yell. I couldn't breathe right or think straight.

It took me a couple of seconds to realize that Jody was tugging on my arm and whispering something about a match. He was whispering to me without moving his lips or taking his eyes away from Donny and the Chinese kid, who were edging closer and punching harder even though they were still just hitting air.

"Gimme a match," he kept saying. "A match. Come on, Josh, gimme a match."

My hand needed a long time to find the way into my pocket.

"Light one," said Jody. "Light it and drop it in."

He was holding his bag of firecrackers open, down by his hip where nobody could see it but me. I spilled half the matches trying to get one out, and if it had been anybody else asking me, I would've spilled them all, but because it was Jody I took a deep breath and struck one hard against the box. The head broke off from the stem. I almost cried, but Jody kept smiling at me and the strange thing was that his eyes had that dark, happy shine they got when he was dancing to Hit Parade and that calmed me down a little.

I struck another match, watched it flare, and dropped it in. Jody waited till he heard a sputtering in the bag, then twisted it closed, stepped forward, and started yelling all at the same time.

"Hey, what're you guys fighting for?" he yelled. Donny and the Chinese kid stopped circling. They looked glad. "You wanna see what we've got?" Jody said, holding out his bag to the Chinese kid. "Here, go ahead, take a look."

Smoke was already sputtering out of the top of the

bag when he threw it. The Chinese guy jumped back into the middle of his gang. The bag landed on the black pavement and sat there hissing like a snake while everyone froze and stared at it and then the whole alley went crazy. Booms and blasts and flashes and smoke and everyone bumping into each other to get out of the way of firecrackers sizzling across the ground and rockets smashing against walls and rattling the steel shutters, and before I really knew what was happening Jody and Donny slammed into the Chinese kids and opened up a big hole in their line and then we were all dashing down the street with their gang chasing us, but they didn't chase all that hard because Donny was bringing up our rear and feeling real brave now and yelling and waving his knife and daring any three of them to fight.

We ran all the way down to the river on the West Side where there were trees and grass and benches overlooking the water. We were all laughing and pounding each other on the back and Donny and Jody were the heroes, but Jody told how I lit the match, and Donny said I could come with them anytime and he didn't call me scuzzy cuz anymore, either.

Jody lit a whole pack of firecrackers at once and threw them into a garbage can, and after the deep hollow booms and the smoke and the spray of red paper like confetti flew out, someone said, "Hey, shouldn't we save them?" But Jody cupped his hand to his ear like he was deaf and said, "Twat say? Cunt hear you. Slight defuckt in my left ear," and everyone fell on the ground laughing, even me although I didn't get it really. And after that we went running uptown along the river setting off firecrackers every which way we could think of.

We put them under cans. We blew bottles to smithereens. We launched rockets at the ferryboats steaming up the river. We found a sandbox and blew half the sand out of it. We threw packets of ladyfingers under passing cars and even dropped cherry bombs into mailboxes. We dug newspapers out of garbage cans and made paper airplanes and attached firecrackers to their wings to make them explode in the air. When we got up to the docks in Harlem, we put cherry bombs in tin cans and threw them off the piers and watched them explode underwater like submarines in the war movies.

And crazy things kept happening, like one of our rocket planes took off, trailing a long puff of white smoke and just disappeared into the sky without blowing up or falling down or anything, and another time I felt this warm, tingling in the butt pocket of my jeans where all the loose wooden matches were jammed in and rubbing their heads together and I swear I saw smoke pouring out and I ran down the street, slapping my ass and trying to get away from the smoke and terrified that flames from one pocket would set off the firecrackers in the other and laughing at the same time because everything was fun that day and sure enough I slapped the fire out before it even burned through my pants.

And the best thing was that when we got back up to Jody's neighborhood in the Bronx, the other kids began to drop out one by one to go home and finally even Donny said good-bye, and then it was just Jody and me walking side by side through the weeds across the vacant lot to his house.

21

Riding the elevator up to Jody's, I realized my head was pounding. It made a deep faraway boom in my ears like cherry bombs going off underwater. I could still smell gunpowder too, all over my clothes and hands. The smell tingled up my nose and into my brain and made my headache worse.

Jody unlocked the front door and headed straight for the kitchen. "Let's eat," he said. The apartment was empty. We could do whatever we wanted, but I just felt like lying down.

"I got a headache," I told him.

Jody was too busy poking around inside the refrigerator to answer. He came out with a carton of milk, an egg, a loaf of Wonder Bread, and a jar of wheat germ. Just looking at food made me feel sick.

Jody filled his glass two-thirds full of milk, poured the raw egg in, added about five spoons of wheat germ, and stirred the whole thing up. He took two slices of

Wonder Bread, nibbled a little bite out of each, and peeled away all the crust. Then he tore the white slices into little pieces and plopped the pieces one by one into his glass. Finally, he took a fork and mashed and squished everything together until his glass was full of white, gooey, disgusting gunk, which he slurped up in one long swallow, smacking his lips and shaking his head to show how good it was.

"I feel kinda sick," I told him, swallowing hard. "I'm gonna lie down."

He finished the last spongy piece in the bottom of his glass, stood up and belched. He was good at belching. The sound came out of the bottom of his stomach and kind of rolled around the room.

"Go ahead," he told me. "I'm gonna listen to music. I got the new one by Stick McGhee. You ever hear it? The one where he goes, 'Drinkin' wine Spo-Dee-O-Dee. Drinkin' wine, wine, wine . . .' He started dancing around the kitchen, still licking the milk mustache off his lip.

I wandered into Jody's room. It was nice and dark. His only window opened on a fire escape at the end of an alley, just like mine. Jody had a double bunk bed, and usually I slept on the top when I stayed over, but this time I lay down on his bed and closed my eyes. After a while he came in and looked at me lying in the dark.

"My head hurts," I told him again.

He didn't say anything, just walked over to the corner behind the bed, fumbled around for a while, and went out carrying a stack of records in one arm, and his portable record player in the other. I thought maybe he was mad. But a couple of minutes later he came back with a cool washcloth and wiped my forehead with it and covered my eyes. He stood by the bed for a minute, humming "Mr. Sandman, bring me a dream, make him the sweetest that I've ever seen . . ." Then he slipped out again, shuffling his feet to the rhythm, and quietly closed the door.

I lay there in the darkness under the washcloth, feeling the headache move off little by little. I started getting that warm sleepy feeling where everything melts into everything else and you can't tell whether your head is lying on top of the pillow or all wrapped up in cotton inside it. I heard Jody playing music softly in another room and thought maybe he was dancing by himself in the dark with his white socks gliding and spinning across the polished floor and his eyes gleaming like they did in the orange flash of the match that he made me light back there in the alley in Chinatown.

When I woke up I could see the twilight turning dark blue in Jody's window. My headache was pretty much gone. I looked around his room—at his clothes lying in heaps on the floor, his ballet shoes and soccer cleats dangling from hooks on the door. He had three posters tacked up on the ceiling. They were dark now, but I knew they all showed dancers. He liked to lie in bed and look up at them and dream.

I wondered what it would feel like to be Jody. I wondered if I slept all night in his bed and woke up in his room if maybe I'd feel like him just for a minute or two. I practiced a couple of times, closing my eyes and trying to clear all the Josh thoughts out of my mind and then looking around and thinking this was my room and the faint fresh smell of Brylcreem and sweat in this bed was my smell, but it didn't work and I felt kind of stupid trying. We didn't have much time left to play together. Pretty soon Leo was coming home. We were all going out to Pasquale's Pizza for dinner.

I got up and walked into the hall. The whole apartment was dark, not black dark like night, but deep blue and shadowy and silent except that I could hear Jody's music playing somewhere—a piano tinkling and a saxophone and a woman singing in a deep growly voice like a man's. I expected Jody to be in the front room where he had lots of space to dance, but the sounds came from the other end of the hall, down where the bathroom was.

I let the music lead me down the hall. I saw light coming from under the bathroom door. It was the only light in the whole apartment. The music was in there too.

I stood outside in the dark, curling and uncurling my toes on the deep soft carpet.

Finally I knocked. "Hey Jody? You in there?"

"Yeah," he called out. "It's okay. Come on in."

I opened the door and there was Jody, stretched out in a tubful of sparkling white soap bubbles. You couldn't see his body at all, just his head sticking out of the foam, his curls plastered to his forehead, his eyes half-closed, his mouth half-open. I mean if anybody ever looked comfortable, Jody was it.

"UUUU-mmmmmm-NNNNN," he sighed.

I stood by the door. Their bathroom had bright orange tiles on the walls. The whole place smelled sweet from the bubble bath. There was nowhere to sit, not even the toilet because Jody had his 45 record player set up on the seat with a thick stack of records on the spindle.

"Well," Jody smiled at me, opening his eyes up wide for a minute, and waving a lazy arm through the bubbles, "don't just stand there. Dive in. These're genuine Swedish soap crystals. Scandinavian Night for two ninety-five a bottle. My mom'd kill me if she found out. But I fill it back up with shampoo after."

All of a sudden I started blushing. It was weird because Jody and I took baths together all the time when we were little, but somehow I didn't feel right about taking off my clothes now with him lying there, watching.

But then again he wasn't really watching either, just relaxing in the white soap crystals, like he was buried in sand up to his neck on the beach. His eyelids were starting to droop down again, and his lips curled into that goofy half-smile that showed the gap between his big front teeth. And I knew he didn't care all that much whether I jumped in the tub with him or not.

That was the thing about Jody. He was always doing something, and whatever it happened to be, he looked like he loved doing it more than anything else in the world and wanted you to have fun doing it with him, but if you didn't feel like it, that was okay too because he'd just go right ahead having fun without you.

I turned my back, stripped off my clothes real fast, and slipped in. The water was just the temperature that makes you groan at first but not hot enough to burn. I leaned back against my side of the tub and found a place for my head between the faucets. My body disappeared into the white foam, but my feet met Jody's and we started playing around with our toes. It was like we were little kids again.

"I'm a crab," I giggled, pinching his foot, "I'm crawling on the bottom of the sea."

We hooked legs and rocked a little to get comfortable. Every time we rocked, water splashed over the brim of the tub. I tried to be careful, but you could never be careful with Jody around. We joined hands and started rocking back and forth singing along to the music. "De-DOO-ron-ron-ron. De-DOO-ron-ron." The saxophone came on and the water sloshed over the tub and the bubbles rose high up to our ears, up to our noses, but even that wasn't high enough, so Jody dumped the whole bottle of Scandinavian Night into the tub and we made waves till we were just about drowning in soapsuds.

They floated in the steamy air and melted like

icebergs on the floor and we blew and threw them at each other and Jody held his nose and dove down under the bubbles and when he came up his head and face were all covered with white like a snowman. I plowed over to his side of the tub and started shaping the foam on his head into a crown and I guess that's what started it.

He held me steady with his hands and knees, and first I was just patting the bubbles into a ring of peaks and valleys around his hair and then I noticed how the bubble crown had colors in it, rainbow colors, jewel colors, and about that time everything started feeling warm and wet and slippery especially when we rubbed against each other and then we were standing up in the middle of the tub and Jody was holding me by the arms saying, "Stand real still. Close your eyes. Don't open till I say so."

I closed my eyes and felt him do something ticklish and shivery and when he told me to look, I had a couple of soap bubble titties swelling out from my chest. The left one stayed up pretty good, but the right one kept sliding down, so Jody put his chest almost against mine and the soap bubbles slipped down between us, and we watched them clinging to both our bodies and sparkling like jewels, green and purple and blue, and just as they slid down to our bellies, I noticed that some of the bubbles were red and Jody's thing was poking up through the red bubbles, standing straight up in a way I didn't even know it could do.

Then Jody hugged me so hard the bubbles popped between us and we started rubbing against each other every which way, and the woman was singing "Daddy, daddy, daddy do," and I could feel his thing trembling against my stomach and he was touching me in a way that felt strange and shivery and closer than I'd been to anybody in a long, long time and I closed my eyes and let myself float in a soft white wave that swirled and whirled us around till I got too dizzy to know where he left off and I began so I just held tight in the deep, reeling dark and right about then the bathroom door burst open.

It slammed against the wall with a crash that made us both jump back to opposite sides of the tub and I splashed down hard on my ass, and when I got to my feet again, there was Leo. He filled the doorway, his shoulders spreading out to both sides of the frame, his face red, his curly hair almost brushing the ceiling, his hands clenching and unclenching.

He glanced at the clothes soaking in the soapy water on the floor, the record player on the toilet seat, the empty bottle of Scandinavian Night lying on its side in a puddle, the two of us standing kneedeep in soapsuds in the tub. Then his eyes stopped jerking around and focused on Jody—only he wasn't looking at Jody's face, he was staring at his thing, which was still standing almost straight up and wearing a little soap bubble crown on top and blushing red like it was embarrassed to be caught. It looked so funny I almost wanted to laugh, but Leo wasn't laughing.

"What . . . ?" he said and stopped and swallowed. His throat bulged against the collar of his red plaid shirt. "What the . . . what the hell're you two . . . ?" But he couldn't get the whole thing out. It was like he kept choking on it, and choking made his voice rise up to a squeaky shout and his face turn a deep raw purple and his hands ball up into fists, and his fists shake at his sides. And then he was flying across the room at us, covering the whole space with one leap, his arms stretching out from wall to wall.

I just stood there paralyzed. But Jody made a run for it. He jumped out of the tub and Leo grabbed his arm and they twisted around in the puddles on the floor so fast I could hardly tell who was what and then Leo had an armful of soap bubbles and Jody was dashing out the door. He raced down the long dark hall, a white streak with soap bubbles streaming off his back. Leo thundered right behind. They ran faster than I ever saw anyone go before. They darted through the bedrooms and around the table in the kitchen and into the living room and then Jody didn't have anywhere else to run because the living room was the last room in the house and there was only one door to it and Leo was blocking the door.

Jody backed up till his legs bumped against the sofa at the far end of the room. Leo moved in on tiptoe, his arms spread out, his breath hissing through his teeth. Jody faked, shifted, threw his hips one way, his head the other. He looked like a white flame dancing against the black windows behind the sofa, but nothing fooled Leo. He kept inching forward, moving so slow it looked like he'd need an hour to cross the rug, then without tensing up or crouching down or anything he threw himself halfway across the room and rammed his head into Jody's stomach and bowled him over and pinned him on the sofa.

Jody never gave up. He kept struggling, kicking, squirming. He wedged his feet up against Leo's chest and pushed till his face went red. But Leo grabbed both ankles in one big hand, jerked them up in the air, jammed them down, and suddenly Jody was flat on his back like a baby getting its diaper changed and all I could see of him was a big white ass gleaming pale and trapped and helpless in the twilight.

Leo went kind of crazy. His arm flew up and down so fast you could only see the blur. I watched, naked and dripping and all covered with gooseflesh, not even knowing how I got to be standing there by the living room door in the dark. I listened to the smacks and grunts and wails. I watched Jody's white ass writhing and helpless and reddening under Leo's hand. My mouth hung open and my breath caught in my chest and I felt the strangest swirling in my gut.

When it was over, Leo stepped back and Jody bounced up off the sofa and onto his feet all in one move, like a steel coil springing back into shape. He ran straight to the door, his face red and ugly, tears dripping from his eyes, snot hanging from his nose. I reached out to touch him, but he shoved past, knocking my hand out of the way. He dashed down the hall to his room and slammed the door, and I heard him pushing furniture around to barricade himself inside.

Leo stood still for a long time, staring out the window at the night, his hands hanging down at his sides, his shirt all wet and wrinkled up and plastered to his back, his head shaking and bobbing out of control like an old, old man's. He took deep breaths and his shoulders heaved up and down and he made a gurgling, choking noise way down in his throat.

Then he turned and saw me at the door. His eyes flashed and he came at me, crossing the room in one long stride. Gooseflesh rippled all over my body. I couldn't breathe. I wanted to run and wanted to stay and knew it didn't matter what I wanted because my legs were rooted to the puddle I had dripped on the living room rug.

Leo grabbed my shoulder, shook me hard, and shoved me into the hall. "Get your clothes on and get back out here," he said in a thick voice. "Make it snappy."

He pushed me again and I stumbled down the hall to the bathroom. It was bright in there after the darkness in the hall. The air smelled of perfume and hot water. My clothes were sopping wet. I squeezed them out as much as I could. My underpants sagged and bagged and chafed between my legs, but I felt safer as soon as I put them on.

Before going back out in the hall, I drained the

soapy water out of the tub and took a few half-hearted swipes at the dark gray ring we had left around the white enamel and picked up the empty bottle of soap crystals. I was wondering if I should fill it up with water when Leo started yelling.

"Come on," he called. "What the hell're you doing in there? Let's get going."

I put the empty bottle back on the shelf above the sink, turned out the light, and hurried down the hall.

Leo was waiting by the front door in the dark. I followed him out to the elevator. I didn't dare talk to him or look up at his face. I especially didn't want to look at his hands. I stared at the walls of the elevator. They were covered with silvery metal. A pattern of thousands of little diamonds was pressed into the shiny metal, and if you squinted your eyes at the diamonds under the lights you could see all different colors, copper and green and gold and red, almost like the soapsuds in the bathtub.

22

Our favorite booth at Pasquale's was way in back, near the jukebox. It had a painting of canals and gondolas and grape vines on the wall. We always took that booth because it was big enough for everybody and because Jody liked to play the jukebox while we ate. After dinner, when the grownups sat around for hours talking politics and smoking, we'd get up and dance. Or at least Jody would dance while Vera and Simone talked with the adults and I practiced baseball slides on the slippery black floor.

Tonight Kaye and my mom and Simone and Vera were in the booth eating salads and drinking Cokes. They looked happy. They'd been at a rummage sale to raise money for the Smith Act victims. My mother had helped organize the rummage sale, and Kaye had painted all the signs and decorated the hall, and the girls had gone down to buy sleeping bags for camp. Kaye was wearing a silky green turban that she bought at the bazaar. It had purple sequins shaped like a half moon in the middle. She always wore strange clothes like that. She used to be an actress before she married Leo.

"Do you like it?" she asked him, patting the green folds and smiling as we walked up to the table. "It's genuine silk. Guess how much it cost."

Leo didn't answer. He didn't seem to like the turban.

"Well it was only two seventy-five" said Kaye. "A real steal but it just sat there on the table all day long. No one else seemed to want it."

"I wonder why?" said my mother. She was wearing a dark gray jersey and gray slacks with a coral-colored belt and scarf. She wasn't that crazy about the way Kaye dressed. Once I heard her tell Vera that Kaye was bourgeois.

"Oh well, at least it's all for a good cause," said Kaye. "We raised almost six hundred dollars."

Leo stood by the booth, not speaking. He was still mad. I could see the muscles of his forearm bulging under his short-sleeved shirt as he leaned one hand on the table top. With the other hand, he brushed the wiry hair back from his forehead. I got an awful elevator-dropping tingle in my stomach because I knew he was getting ready to tell.

My mother patted a place for me next to her on the bench. I slipped in but not too close. It was funny. All the way over in the car with Leo, I'd been shaking and shivering and thinking how much safer I'd feel once I saw Elsa. But now that I realized Leo was going to tell on us, I couldn't even look at her without feeling hot needles of shame stabbing my face.

"Where's Jody?" Kaye asked. She kind of craned her neck to look around behind Leo as if she just realized that someone was missing. "I was counting on him to appreciate my hat. No one else around here has enough imagination."

"Jody's home," said Leo, slamming himself down next to Kaye with a thump that shook the whole booth. "Home in his room. And he's going without dinner tonight."

"What?" asked Kaye. Her eyebrows arched all the way up to the edge of the turban. "Why?"

"Because . . . ," said Leo. He looked over at the girls in their corner of the U-shaped booth, took a deep breath, shook his head, and let the air sigh out. "Never mind. We'll discuss it later," he finished.

"Leo . . . ," Kaye said, an edge coming into her voice. "Have you been at him again?"

"At him? At him? You bet I've been at him. And if I ever catch him doing that again, I'll be all over him so quick . . ."

"Don't shout," said Kaye. She took off her turban and patted her blond hair. "Please. Do we have to entertain the whole restaurant?"

Leo stopped shouting. He clamped his mouth shut and stuck out his jaw and glared at Kaye. He was a big strong man with a big strong jaw, and Kaye hardly came up to his shoulder, but when she got that sharp edge on her voice, he did exactly what she said.

"All right," she sighed after a minute, "the suspense is killing me. What did he do this time?"

"Ask this little angel," Leo said, pointing across the table at me. "He was in it just as deep as Jody. I wouldn't be surprised if he started it."

Everyone stared at me—my mother frowning, Kaye worried, my sister and Simone wide-eyed and starting to giggle together in the corner. I hung my head. I was hoping my mother would reach out for me or at least pat my knee. But she just stared.

I studied the glasses of ice water on the table. Each ice cube had a round hole through the center. The hollows reflected the purple lights of the jukebox. They looked like caves in the North Pole. I wanted to crawl into one of the purple caves in the ice and hide.

"Come on, Josh, don't be shy," Leo sneered.

"We didn't mean anything bad," I muttered. "We were just . . ." I stopped. I didn't know how to explain it. I had a feeling that maybe I shouldn't even try. But they were all looking at me now, waiting, listening. I had to say something. "We were just taking a *bath*," I finished. Somehow the word "bath" came out too loud. It kind of hung in the air and echoed around the booth.

Vera sucked in her breath with a long low sound like a whistle in reverse. My mother moved away from me, only a couple of inches, but enough for me to feel. I hung my head and hated myself for talking. I felt like I'd just stepped in a big, gooey pile of dogshit.

"Leo . . . ," said Elsa. "Leave him alone now. That's enough. You're right. We'll talk it out later."

"Fine," said Leo. "That's precisely what I wanted in the first place. But I'll tell you one thing right now. The trip to the lake is off and I mean *off*." He slammed his hand on the table and made the Coke glasses bounce to show how much he meant off. "Those two aren't seeing each other again for the rest of the summer."

There was a hush. I felt sure people all over the restaurant were listening. My ears burned and froze. Nobody even chewed their salad. They just sat there silent around the table.

"Have you heard the latest about the Nelson case in Pittsburgh?" Elsa asked. "They've put Steve in solitary confinement for the duration of the trial because he refused to reveal names under oath and . . ."

They all started talking at once about cases and trials and acts. They talked about the Smith Act and the McCarran Act and the Subversive Activities Control Board. Vera and Simone whispered and elbowed each other over in their corner.

Finally the waitress brought our food on a big steel tray. She was a fat woman with her hair in a bun, and she scowled at me like she'd heard everything. We had french bread and spaghetti with meatballs and two pizzas—a big one with pepperoni and olives for everyone and a small one with anchovies for Vera.

I loved pizza almost as much as cheeseburgers, but I didn't dare reach out for a slice and no one offered me one either. I sat there slumped way down on the bench, smelling the fresh dough and the tomato sauce and the spices and hearing them all chewing and swallowing and huffing on the hot cheese, and I remembered how I hadn't eaten anything all day long—not even the bagel my mother gave me at breakfast when I was running out the door to buy the firecrackers about a million years ago. I peeked up and saw one soggy slice left on the tray.

"Could you pass the pizza, please?" I gulped.

They all stared at me like I was a cockroach that had just learned how to speak. I caught a glimpse of Vera's eyes glittering behind her glasses. Kaye was the one who finally passed me the pizza, but the sauce was cold by now and the cheese rubbery and the dough too dry to swallow.

Usually they sat around talking for a long time after dinner, but tonight Leo called the waitress right away. While she was clearing the table, he gave Simone the keys to the car. "Go outside and wait," he told her and Vera. "You too," he nodded at me. As we were walking out, I looked back and saw him leaning across the table, talking to my mother, waving his hands.

"You're sick," Vera hissed at me as soon as we stepped out on the street. "You're disgusting. I suspected it all along."

"Shut your trap," I told her, balling up my fist. I wanted to slug her but figured I was in enough trouble already.

*   *   *

When we got home, my mother sent Vera to bed and made me come into her room for a talk. She closed the door and sat down on her sofabed and made me sit next to her. She took both my hands and looked into my eyes. Hers were very big and wet, with gold and brown circles in them and little lines that I never noticed before snaking out of the corners.

"All right," she said in her serious, shaky voice. "I heard it from Leo; now I have to hear it from you. What were you doing in the bathtub with Jody?"

"Nothing," I shrugged. I didn't want to talk about it anymore. I gave a big yawn. "I'm tired. Can't I go to bed now, please?"

"Tired?" she said. "Tired? Don't you dare talk to me about tired. I'm so exhausted I could . . ." Her voice went way up high and stopped. She shook her head. Her long fingers played with the end of her scarf. She untied the knot and took it off. Now she was all dark, with her black hair, and charcoal jersey and the circles under her eyes and the shadows of the lamplight across her face. "I'm waiting for an answer," she said.

"We were just taking a bath," I whined. "I told you already. And then . . ."

"Then what?"

"We made a mess. We splashed water all over the floor."

"Do you expect me to believe this is all about a little water on the floor?" She gave a hard laugh.

"We used Kaye's soapsuds, too. The expensive ones. The whole bottle." I knew how stupid it sounded, but I wanted her to believe it. Just because I said so and she trusted me more than Leo.

"Josh!" She stamped her foot. "It wasn't the bath and it wasn't the water and it wasn't the soapsuds. And you know it. What were you doing when Leo came in?"

"Playing," I said. "Just playing and fooling around. I didn't even know it was bad."

"Well, it is bad," she said. "It's very bad."

I looked up at the painting of sunflowers above her head. It was a bright yellow painting, and it reminded me of how warm and slippery and swirling everything had been in the tub. That was the worst part. I knew from her voice that what we did was bad enough to make her cry, but I also knew I liked it, and that made me feel so rotten inside that I hated myself and everyone else, including her, especially her.

"Were you touching each other?" she asked, tightening her grip on my hands.

"No, honest," I wailed.

"Liar!" She dropped my hand and stood up. She started walking around the room. The soles of her shoes made sharp slapping noises on the floor. She picked up a carved tray on the bookcase, put it down, went over to the window. She peeked through the slats of the shade, almost like she thought someone was watching out in the street. I could see her shoulders shaking.

"Now this time I want the truth," she said, turning back to face me, locking her eyes onto mine, her voice calm again, but serious, awfully serious. "I want you to think very hard and give me an honest answer. Was this the first time you ever played that way?"

"Yes," I said.

"And who started it? Was it you? Or Jody?"

"I don't know," I said. "We were just splashing with the soapsuds and then . . ." I squirmed. She smiled, encouraging. I knew what she wanted. If I said Jody did it first, she'd think he was bad not me and she'd calm down and like me again and let me go to bed and that's what I wanted more than anything else in the world.

But . . . but by then I was mad. Just fed up and furious at her and Leo and Vera and myself and the whole lousy term I'd had at school and the rotten start that summer was getting off to and the way she kept questioning and staring and believing Leo more than me when I was so tired and hadn't eaten anything all day long, not even the pizza, and whatever I did it was all her fault in the first place, and besides she wouldn't hit me no matter what I said, so just to see the look on her face, I shouted, "No, no. It wasn't Jody. It was me. I started it. I did! And I liked it! It's the most fun I've had all summer long."

She took a step backward. Her mouth shut very tight. Her eyes turned yellow and hard. Her hand went up and rubbed the scar under her bangs.

"You're disgusting," she said. "Go to bed. I don't want to talk to you anymore."

I walked to the door but I couldn't stop now. "Well, you're disgusting too," I shot back. "You're just mad because we can't go to the lake with Leo. You like him better than Ben. Why don't you just marry him and stop pretending?"

She put her hands on her hips and glared at me. "That's a stupid childish thing to say." Her voice was cold, scornful. "If anyone's hurting Ben, it's you. You better go to bed now and think about how he'll feel when I tell him."

23

The next few days I spent a lot of time sulking. Except for meals, I stayed in my room with the door closed and the shades drawn. I played with my glow-in-the-dark spacemen. The spacemen had rebelled against Captain Bob. They had captured him and thrown him inside a huge dungeon that I built out of plastic bricks and now they were torturing him to make him reveal his Underground hideout.

Their tortures were terrible. Nothing like beating or shooting or burning or pulling out fingernails would work on a guy as tough as Captain Bob. So they used an atomic-powered vibration beam. They tied him down and put a helmet on his head, and the helmet made a horrible high-pitched whine that got louder and louder till blood leaked out through his ears and all the atoms in his brain split apart and he couldn't remember what was right and what was wrong anymore.

Captain Bob held out against the vibration beam

longer than any being in the known galaxy. They kept turning it up higher and higher, but that was exactly his strategy. He knew that if he could just hold out long enough, they'd turn the vibrations up so high, his prison would crack apart from the strain. Then he'd escape, go Underground, arm himself, and come back to kill them all.

On Saturday, the day after Vera left for camp, my mother came and stood outside the door to my room and heard me making the horrible high wail of the vibration beam. She pounded on the door and said, "Josh, enough already. Will you come out of there and start acting like a human being again?"

I stopped the torture machine but didn't answer.

"Do you hear me?" she called.

"No," I answered. "Go away. Don't come in."

"I wouldn't dream of it," she said. "You can sulk at me as long as you want. But if you don't get out of that dark stuffy room, I'm going to send you to a doctor. To a psychiatrist. For your mind. Do you understand? I want you to go out and get a little sun. Now. This minute."

I went out. I walked up to Sweeny's, down to 181st Street, then up and over the hill to the busy shopping district around Amsterdam Avenue and Broadway. I drifted along with the crowds, looking at the shops, smelling the hot dogs and french fries cooking at Nedicks, watching the traffic grind by in the hot afternoon under the crisscross shadows of the elevated tracks.

Most of the stores had American flags hanging outside their doors or draped in their display windows. All up and down Amsterdam Avenue it was nothing but red, white, and blue. The flags reminded me that tomorrow was the Fourth of July, and that made me miserable. Not because of being a commie or anything. Because of Jody. Because instead of going up to the lake with him like I was supposed to, they had me cooped up in the city for the holiday without even a firecracker to explode.

I started feeling so bad that I turned into Woolworth's to steal something. Woolworth's had about the biggest toy department in New York, maybe the world. It was down in the basement. The model planes alone went on for aisles and aisles, and they also had battleships, submarines, classic and racing cars, rockets and balsa-wood helicopters that actually flew. I strolled along, looking at the pictures on the boxes.

Just past the models came the guns. None of them really tempted me till I saw the pellet pistol. It looked exactly like a German Luger, the kind the Nazis used, with a shiny black barrel and a detachable ammunition clip that held eight plastic pellets. The clip fit into a slot in the handle of the gun. I shot one of the pellets into my palm. It hit hard enough to leave a bright red mark.

The Luger was too expensive to buy and too big to fit in my pocket. But it was just what Captain Bob needed to blow the fort apart after he escaped. I put it back on the shelf and took a turn or two around the birdcage and stationery sections to make sure no one was watching me. The adults hurried by, looking straight ahead at eye level. They would've walked right over me if I didn't move. I felt like I was floating along inside a little bubble that made me invisible.

I swung by the gun section again. Just to test things out, I snatched up a couple of bags of ammo and jammed them into my pocket. Then I went over by the popcorn machine and stood there watching the golden white kernels spew out of the silvery hopper. The smell made me dizzy. The noise of the store surged and faded. I waited for someone to grab my shoulder.

If they got me now, with only a couple of ammo bags in my pocket, I'd probably get away with a warning. But no one bothered me. And the gun was waiting. I could almost feel it drawing me away from the popcorn, past goldfish tanks and coral castles, past bottles of nail polish and rows of bobby pins, past cap guns and ray guns and water pistols and rifles that shot rubber-tipped darts.

Finally I stood in front of the Luger again. I grabbed it and jammed it down the front of my pants. But the sight got caught on my belt band, and by the time I got the gun tucked away, I was so scared and sweaty that I didn't dare look up to check if anyone had spotted me.

The walk through the toy section and up the stairs and past the make-your-own-souvenir penny machine took forever. I had to step very carefully to keep the gun from slipping down or riding up in my pants. I kept feeling a warm tingling on my back like eyes were boring into me and melting the bubble that kept me safe and invisible. Going past the coffee counter, I glanced down and saw the butt of the gun sticking out above the top of my jeans. But by now I was too close to the cash registers to do anything about it.

The gray-haired clerk with a pencil behind her ear swept her eyes over me, then went on ringing up sales. I squeezed behind the fat fannies of the women waiting in line. And then I was in the most dangerous part of all—the area between the cash registers and the revolving glass doors to the street. If they caught you there, they knew you were really stealing. The door was only a few feet away, but I walked and walked without getting closer. I knew my invisibility bubble was gone. Anyone could see me, grab me. I held my breath.

And then I was through the door and out into the sudden heat and brightness and buzzing of the crowds on the street. I broke into a run, twisting past elbows, dodging through the big slow bodies of the adults. I ran up to the Chock Full o' Nuts on Amsterdam and darted across Broadway against the light. I didn't slow down till I reached the RKO theater two blocks from Woolworth's. They were showing *The Day the Earth Stood Still.* I pretended to study the robot in the posters, but actually I was looking at the reflections in the glass to make sure no one had followed me.

Once I knew I was safe, I started skipping up 181st Street. My mother had been right about getting out in the sun. The afternoon was blue and gold and warm, and I was still free to enjoy it, and not only that—now I had the gun. At the top of the hill, I could see the gray steel girders of the bridge gleaming through a gap in the buildings by the river.

I started down, watching the towers sink behind the dirty brick walls. I was concentrating so hard on the view that I didn't even hear the footsteps behind my back until—wham!—a strong hand clamped down on my shoulder.

I jumped about three feet in the air and hit the pavement with my heart banging and my legs ready to run, but the hand still held me tight, and when I whirled around there was Dale. Maybe it was just because of him standing above me on the hill, and the sun shining behind him, but he looked at least eight feet tall.

"Hey, howya doing, Josh old buddy?" he said, still keeping a hold on my shoulder. "Long time no see. Where ya been keeping yourself?"

I squinted up at him. He was wearing his blue Dodgers' cap and a white polo shirt stretched tight across his chest. He smiled his bug-eyed smile at me.

I couldn't answer right away. I had an awful feeling he'd been tailing me ever since Woolworth's. I tugged at the bottom of my T-shirt, pulling it over my jeans to make sure it covered the gun.

Dale's eyes narrowed. His hand shot out and

almost before I knew what'd happened he was holding the Luger in his palm. "You got a permit for this, little buddy?" he asked.

I shook my head. "N-n-no," I gulped.

"Well, if I was on duty," he grinned, spinning the gun around on his finger, "I'd have to run you in. But it just so happens, I'm taking the afternoon off. I came all the way up here to the Heights on my own time. You know why?"

I shook my head.

"Because I missed you, you little twerp," he said, handing the Luger back to me. "I really did. But I bet you forgot all about old Dale? Right?"

"Kind of." I shrugged. I was beginning to get my breath back. Even if he had seen me in Woolworth's, it didn't seem like he was going to arrest me right now. "I thought about you some," I said. "Not a whole lot. You know, just when I wanted to play catch."

"Well, how's about it?" he said. "I haven't touched a ball since the last time I saw you. Come on, I got my stuff in the car." He swung his big arm around in the socket of his shoulder like he could hardly wait to start throwing."

"No. Uh-uh, not now," I said, shaking my head.

"Hey, don't be like that." The smile faded off his face. "I'm not gonna ask you about your dad or anything. This's just for fun. Just between us. Come on." He jerked his head at the stairs leading up to the park. "Why not?"

"Because," I said. "Because . . . I don't have my glove."

"Is that all?" asked Dale. He bounced a little on the toes of his tennis shoes and the lights popped back on in his eyes. "Then run on home and get it. Go ahead. I'll meet you up at the park." He gave me a little pat on the shoulder to get me started.

I ran off down the block without saying anything.

"Don't stand me up, Josh," he called after me.

I really didn't plan to go back and meet him. But once I got home, my room seemed so dark and small and smelly that I couldn't stand being cooped up inside. I slipped the Luger under my mattress and took out my baseball glove. I pounded the pocket, sniffed the oily leather, flexed the soft webbing. Shooting pellets at my fort seemed like an awful dumb way to spend the rest of the afternoon. I was running down the hall to the front door when my mother came out of the kitchen.

"Where're you going now?" she asked.

"Up to the park, to play baseball," I told her.

She smiled. I smiled back. It was the first time we acted nice to each other since the whole mess with Jody.

Up at the park, Dale was waiting with his glove and bat on the bench where I met him the first time. We didn't talk much, just nodded at each other and walked over the gravel, through the trees, and out onto the baseball diamond. The black tar was a little sticky from the heat, but a breeze was starting to blow in from the river and it felt good to run around. We pretty much had the diamond to ourselves except for a couple of mothers pushing baby carriages around the first baseline.

I hadn't played baseball for weeks and weeks, but instead of getting rusty, all of a sudden I was good. It was funny, like I'd been thinking about all the things Dale taught me without even knowing it and now I could throw the ball straight into his mitt with a pop and hold my head down when grounders were bouncing up at my nose, and when he heaved long, high flies, I could turn my back to him and run flat out to chase them down. When we started playing pepper with his fungo bat, I not only hit the ball, I knew how to take nice level swings and slap liners right back into his glove. On the last pitch, he said, "Okay, go ahead, killer. Knock it clean down to Broadway."

I swung, and like I always do when I try to smash it, I closed my eyes, but this time I connected anyway. The bat handle stung my palms and the shock rushed all the way up to my shoulders, and when I opened my eyes a second later, Dale was sitting on his butt with his first-baseman's mitt in front of his face and the ball snagged in the webbing.

"Geez!" he said. "You almost killed me. First you walk around armed and dangerous. Then you try to take my head off with a line shot to the teeth." He stood up and rubbed the back of his mitt against the flat tip of his nose. "What's got into you?"

We walked off the diamond. He squeezed my arm, digging into the muscle with his fingers. "You been eating a box of Wheaties every morning? No, wait a minute, I know. Your dad came back. You've been practicing with him every day."

"Nope. This is the first time since before school let out."

"Well, something's changed. You look like a different guy out there. Forget that kid's team. You're ready for the Dodgers. Say, how about those bums, anyway?" We were walking through the shade of the trees now, both sweating a little from the game. Dale had his arm around my shoulder.

"Six runs in the last inning last night," I said. "And Gilliam's a cinch for Rookie of the Year."

"If he keeps it up for the rest of the season," said Dale. Then he stopped and let go of my shoulder. He cocked his head on one side and looked at me hard. "I don't guess you remember what I said about going out to the ballpark on July fourth, do you, old buddy?" he asked. The breeze blew the shadows of the leaves across his sweaty face.

"I remember," I said, moving away from him. "I

remember lots of things." The sweat turned a little cold on my back.

He reached into his pocket and brought out his wallet. He pulled two tickets out and kind of waved them in front of my face. I could see they were printed in Dodger blue. "Box seats," he said, "right over the home team dugout. For tomorrow's doubleheader. One of 'em's yours if you want it."

I started to reach out, then pulled back my hand and jammed it into my pocket. I looked up at his face. He was still sweating and smiling. But now I could see that cold, hard gray watching me from the bottom of his eyes, and all the good feeling I had about him dried up like a drop of sweat on the pavement.

"What do I have to do to get it?" I asked.

"Just what I told you before," he said. "Give me a little break. A trade. Here, go on. Take it. Take it."

The top part of the ticket was shaped like a base-ball with blue stitching on the seams. My palms itched but I wouldn't touch it.

"Look, let's sit down and talk this over," said Dale. "Come on up to my car."

"I'm not going near your car," I told him. We sat on one of the stone benches under the trees instead. I moved way down to the far end and watched the pigeons pecking at the gravel.

Dale ran both hands at once through his hair and flicked his thumb across his nose and snorted like a boxer. "You think I don't know how you feel?" he asked. "You think I don't wanna forget all this crap about your dad and my job and just go out to the game with you and root like a couple of buddies? But that's not how it works. I been on this case for months and I'm getting nowhere. I'm over a barrel. Can't you help me out? I'm not asking for much. Just bring me some-thing. Anything I can show my boss."

By the time he finished, his voice had a kind of

whiny tone in it and I hated him. I stood up. "I'm going," I said. "Thanks for the game."

"Sit down," said Dale. He said it in his hard voice, and I was sitting down before I even thought about it. He moved in and pushed his flat face close to mine. I shrank back against the stone bench, but he had me trapped.

"You got this wrong, Josh," he said. "You're thinking like a kid. You think you're being loyal to your dad by holding out on me. But your dad's in trouble and I'm giving you a chance to help and you don't have much time left. Now go ahead and take this." He stuffed the ticket into the pocket of my polo shirt.

"If you wanna see the game, you bring me something tomorrow morning. You've got something for old Dale, don't you, little buddy?" he asked, drilling into my skull with the hard bright beam of his eyes.

I looked away. An image of gold letters on a little black book had flashed through my mind and I didn't dare let him see. All of a sudden, I knew what he was after. What he'd been after all along.

"I'll be waiting downstairs in the subway," he said, "right under that restaurant where we ate. At eleven-thirty tomorrow morning. And if you don't come," he said, staring at me with steel gray eyes, "then you hang onto that ticket as a souvenir. A little reminder of how there was this guy who came along and gave you a chance to get on the right side for once in your life. A chance to straighten things out for yourself and your dad, too. And you were too stubborn to do it."

24

All the way back from the park, I was arguing with myself about the game and Dale. I could think of hundreds of reasons not to go. They shouted and whispered and roared in my ears, but somehow, altogether, they made a low faraway grumbling noise, almost like the crowd booing the umpire for a bad call against the Dodgers out at Ebbets Field.

When I got home, I found a note taped to the icebox in the kitchen. It said:

Josh, I had to go downtown for a couple of hours. I should be back by dinnertime. If not, I'll call. I made a tuna sandwich in case you get hungry.

Be good,
Mom

I crumpled up the note and tried to drop kick it into the garbage can and missed. Then I went in my room, closed the door just to make sure, and got down on my hands and knees in my closet. Clearing away the shoes and crumpled-up clothes that I always kept over my hiding place, I slipped the blade of my penknife between the cracks in the floorboards and pried up the loose plank. I stuck my arm under the boards and pulled out my Murillo Cigar box. Four thick rubber bands kept it sealed tight. I sat down on my bed, rolled off the rubber bands one by one, opened the lid, and breathed in a whiff of old cigars and the men who smoked them in faraway places like Cuba where maybe they still had pirates.

Outside I could see sunlight streaking the red bricks across the alley from my window and hear kids on the street. From the clatter and screams, it sounded like they were roller-skating. Or maybe riding down the hill on a coaster made out of skate wheels and orange crates. But in my room, it was already twilight. The gold writing on Leo's address book gleamed up at me from the bottom of the box.

I took the ticket to the Dodgers' game out of my back pocket. Just looking at it made me imagine the crowd, their white shirts and blue Dodgers' caps flashing in the sun as they watched the game. I straightened the corners of the ticket and laid it in the box.

But somehow it looked lonely, lying on the pale green bottom between a prism that I'd stolen from school and a shotgun shell that I found in the woods near Jody's cabin at Bear Lake. So I opened Leo's address book and stuck the ticket between two well-thumbed, thickly-scribbled pages. And just as I closed the book over the ticket, a horrible nasty idea prickled across my scalp. Then the floorboards creaked outside my door and at the same moment, I saw Ben clear as anything in my mind. He was wearing his wool shirt with the holes in the sleeves and staring at me with a serious look in his sad green eyes.

I jumped off the bed, buried the cigar box under the covers, and tiptoed out to look. The hall was empty. I turned on the light to make sure. No one. Nothing but the dark walls and the gray carpet and the telephone table standing outside the kitchen door. I didn't believe in ghosts or anything, but the roots of my hair were still tingling. Even my teeth ached.

I went back in my room and hid the cigar box away under the floorboards. I arranged my galoshes and loafers and sneakers on top of the loose board and gathered a handful of dust from the back of the closet and spread it on the wood and carefully wedged some dirt in the cracks so no one would think the plank had been moved for a couple of years. Then I went into my mother's room to watch TV.

It was around seven o'clock on Saturday night. I sat on the daybed and watched the Roy Rogers show. He had a golden palomino named Trigger and a German shepherd named Bullet and a wife named Dale. It kind of made me laugh that Dale was a man's name and a woman's too. It was like I had a secret joke on him, something I could snicker to myself about if we ever got together again and he started acting scary and telling me lies like helping him was my only chance to keep Ben out of jail. I didn't believe that.

Helping Dale was wrong and I knew it, and if I ever did it, it'd be just because of that. Because it was bad, bad, bad, and so was I.

Elsa came home about eight o'clock. She looked happy. She was wearing slacks and a blouse with red and white stripes. The stripes matched the red earrings dangling under her black hair. She had a bag of food from the A&P. I could smell barbecued chicken. "Turn off the TV," she said. "Come on in the kitchen. I've got something special for you."

I shut off the TV and followed her into the

kitchen. She bustled around, putting food away in the icebox, lighting the oven, taking plates out of the cupboards. I watched from the doorway. She let me stand awhile, then stopped working, dried her hands on her slacks, opened her purse, and took out an envelope. "Here," she said, holding it out to me, "a surprise."

As soon as I touched the envelope, I knew it was from Ben. I could tell from the rough yellowish paper he always used and from the way his old typewriter smudged some of the letters on the address and made others too light to read. The address said: Joshua Rankin, Esquire. That was all. No return address, no stamps, no postmark. It was a letter from Underground. And it was sealed. I felt pretty excited.

"A lot of people went to a lot of trouble to get that letter to you," my mother said, "including me." She stared hard in my eyes. "I hope you understand that."

I saved the letter for the last thing, just before sleep. I read it sitting in my underpants, at the head of my bed, near the window and the breeze from the street.

Dear Josh,

I'm sorry that I haven't been able to write you in all this time but I'm sure you understand why. Even though I can't write, I think about you and it's always the bright spot in my day when I hear reports about you from our friends. I'm very proud of the way you're growing up. Elsa says you're the one she depends on to cheer her up. She needs you to be good very much and so do I.

I know it's hard for you to believe because these are the only times you know, but things won't always be as they are now. We'll all live together again, and then we'll be glad that we were patient through these bad days. Sometimes there are things that we may want to do on the spur of the moment, but if they hurt other people, we have to avoid them. I know you're trying your very best.

Elsa says that you're not having much fun this summer. We'll cook up something good for you, don't worry. Things can change very quickly if you're strong enough to wait. I know it's not much help, but I'm sending you the children's page from the paper. If you're feeling bored, why not try the crosswords or the puzzles? The cartoons by Al Capp are pretty good, too.

Love,
Ben

I felt kind of cheated because the letter was only one page long. The rest was just stuff he cut out from the newspaper. I looked the clippings over in bed, before turning out the lights. The puzzles bored me and I never liked crosswords, but the cartoons were okay.

They were about schmoos and Li'l Abner and Mammy Yocum. Schmoos were friendly little white critters that wanted to make everybody happy, but they tasted good like chicken so rich people wanted to eat them and sell them for money. I tried to keep the schmoos in my mind even after I closed my eyes and let the cartoons drop on the floor, but at the last moment just before I fell asleep they changed into Dodgers racing around Ebbets Field in their fresh white uniforms.

25

The Fourth of July

The sound of firecrackers woke me up in the morning. I must've been hearing them in my dreams because I'd already decided that the noise came from Jody, who was throwing cherry bombs off the pier into Bear Lake and I couldn't get there in time to do it with him but it didn't matter because I was going to see the Dodgers at Ebbets Field.

I felt pretty happy about it as long as I lay in bed with my eyes closed. But as soon as my bare feet touched the floorboards and I saw the hot sunlight in the alley outside my fire escape, I realized that I couldn't go to the ballgame because of Dale and I couldn't go to the lake because of getting caught in the bathtub with Jody and that meant I was still stuck in the city on the Fourth of July with nothing to do at all.

I stood at the window, listening to the hum and rumble of New York, sniffing the car fumes and garbage and the faint rank smell of the Hudson in the hot July air. The firecrackers had stopped booming.

I felt jumpy, itchy. I wanted to get out and do something, anything. Just run around and play so hard that I forced everything else out of my mind. I dug around in my drawer and picked out my favorite T-shirt. It was bright blue, Dodger blue. I laced on my sneakers. They felt so snug and light on my feet I thought I could fly if I got running fast enough.

My mother was already up in the kitchen. She was wearing a dark dress without sleeves. Her hair was combed. She was smoking a cigarette and drinking coffee in the careful way she had when she didn't want to smudge her lipstick.

"I want to do something today," I told her, standing by the table, too antsy to sit down and eat. "I wanna go to the parade on Broadway."

"That sounds fun," she said. "You can follow them all the way downtown. I'll give you carfare to get back."

"I want you to go with me," I said.

"All right. We'll go this afternoon. As soon as I get back from the office."

"The office?" I said. "It's Sunday. It's the Fourth of July. What're you going into the office for?"

"Why do you think I'm going? It's not because I'm dying to ride the IRT on my day off," she snapped, putting her coffee cup down with a rattle. "Leo and I have some Smith Act work to do."

"Leo? I thought he was up at the lake."

"Well, he's not."

"Then Jody must be in the city, too."

"Don't start, Josh," my mother said, "please."

"Can I call him?"

"No."

"Why not?"

She ground her cigarette stub into the ring of spilled coffee on her saucer. The ash sizzled and sputtered. She stood up and brushed ashes off her dark skirt. "Didn't Ben's letter make any difference to you at all?" she asked.

"Difference?" I said. "What kind of difference was it supposed to make?" But just from the way she was looking down at me with her lips pursed up and her arms folded, I knew. She had told Ben all about me and Jody and the bathtub, and that's the only reason he wrote me, and even then he only sent a lousy one-page letter and a bunch of stupid cartoons.

"The Dodgers are playing a doubleheader," I told her. "I want to go. You can take me to the nitecap. After you get back from work."

"Don't be ridiculous. I'm not going way out to Brooklyn," she said. "We'll go to the parade this afternoon. I'll try to be back by two."

"That's too late!" I stamped. My voice squeaked. I felt like knocking over the table with my milk glass and everything on it.

"What *is* with you?" she asked. "When do you want me to get back?"

"Eleven-thirty," I said. "Twelve at the latest."

"I'll try," she said, going into her room and coming back to stand in the kitchen doorway with a folder of papers under her arm. "I can't promise, but I'll try."

After she left, I wandered all around the house not knowing what to do. I went into Vera's room and looked at the sun shining on the black wood of her piano and the locked red box where she kept her diary on top of her dust-free desk. I went into my mother's room and opened the closet to see her dark dresses hanging down from the rack and her shoes standing in pairs on the floor.

I sat in the sunlight at the kitchen table, listening to the hum of the city and reading about today's game in the sports page. We were going up against the

Giants with a chance to move into first if we swept both ends of the doubleheader. But the Giants were pitching Sal Maglie in the nitecap and he threw close enough to shave the whiskers off the batter's jaw so everyone called him Maglie the Barber. Last time we played the Barber, he beaned Pee Wee Reese right in the throat. Our pitcher promised to even the score this time. But there was no point reading about that because I couldn't go.

I crumpled up the sports page and wandered into the bathroom. I looked at my face in the mirror on the medicine cabinet door. My head seemed pointy and the black dots staining the mirror made it look like I had some horrible rash all down my chin and onto my neck.

I closed my eyes, but then I saw little golden letters gleaming in the darkness. I tried not to think about them. I really did. I went all the way down the hall to the front door and opened it and took one step out and told myself how much fun it would be to walk down to Broadway and see them setting up for the parade.

There would be crowds and smells of hot asphalt and cotton candy and floats and bands and drum majorettes in sequin bathing suits tossing their batons up to flash in the sun and maybe even tanks clanking up from the armory on Seventy-ninth Street. But it wouldn't be like the game.

I stepped back inside and locked the door. Slowly, slowly, I let myself be dragged down the long silent hall to my room. It was like I could see the glow of the gold writing on Leo's address book shining up through the floorboards in the closet and spilling out under the door and beckoning me down the hall.

When I passed the telephone table, I reached out to grab it, like an anchor. Once I had the receiver in my hand, I got the idea to call Jody. If I could just talk to him about anything, maybe I'd feel good enough to play outside for a while. I knew Leo wasn't home. He was downtown with my mother. I dialed, but Jody's mom answered the phone, and I didn't dare say anything at first.

"Hello? Hello? Is anybody there?" she asked.

Finally, I disguised my voice, talking real low and putting my hand over the receiver. I threw in a little southern accent just to be safe. "Is Jody the-ah?" I asked.

"No," said Kaye. "Who is this, anyway? Josh?"

I hung up. But the second I put the receiver down, it rang again, very loud in the quiet hallway. I jumped. I let it ring a couple of times. It could be Kaye calling back. Finally, I picked it up.

"Josh, honey?" said my mother.

"Yeah?"

"Look, I'm really sorry, I know it's important to you, but I can't make it back by twelve. You're just going to have to go to the parade alone."

I didn't answer. Now that she called, I realized I'd been expecting it all along.

"Josh, are you there?"

"What do you care?" I asked.

"Listen," she said. "When you hang up, I want you to get out and go to the parade. Don't mope around the house. I'll be back around four."

"So what?" I said.

She sighed. "We'll go out to dinner. At the automat. How about that?"

"Big deal."

"Josh?" she dropped her voice down almost to a whisper, "Leo's in a good mood today. How about if I talk to him about you and Jody? So you could see each other again. Would that help?"

"Yeah, kind of," I said. "A little."

"Okay, I'll do it. I'll tell you about it at dinner. Are you going to go out when you hang up?"

"Maybe."

"No maybe's. Go ahead. Just get out. It's a beautiful day. You'll feel much better."

I slammed down the phone, but I didn't feel mad. I didn't feel much of anything. I just kept hearing a roar in my head. Probably it came from the street and the wheezy old motor on top of our icebox, but to me it sounded like the crowd filing into Ebbets Field. They were shouting for hotdogs and beer and joking with each other and telling me to hurry up. I couldn't hear myself think with all that racket in my head.

I went into my room and got my cigar box out of the closet. The roar surged in my ears when I opened the lid. I put the ticket in the back pocket of my jeans. Then I sat on the floor of the closet, thumbing through the address book.

Leo had hundreds of names in there, some I knew and lots I didn't. They were written in pencil and different shades of ink and scratched out and blotted over so many times you could hardly read them. Some names had no phone numbers and some numbers had no names and on some pages there were just initials that didn't mean anything at all. I looked under R for Rankin and saw my mother's name, but we were listed in the phone book too so I didn't think that mattered. My father wasn't under Rankin. I looked under B for Ben and U for Underground. I even checked T for Thompson to make sure Captain Bob wasn't listed. Nothing.

I stood up and slipped the address book into my sock. But it felt kind of loose, like it might fall out if I had to run fast, so I unlaced my high-top sneaker and pushed the book down around my ankle and then laced up the shoe again good and tight. I took a few practice steps. They carried me out of my room and down the hall, and once I started, it felt like a huge powerful magnet was pulling me toward the door.

I glanced at the clock on the way past the kitchen. It was already eleven-thirty. Dale would be waiting at the subway station. I ran down the stairs. It was a white-hot day outside. The tar on the street was so hot it sucked at the soles of my sneakers. Just as I turned the corner past Sweeney's, I realized that I hadn't locked the front door or even hidden my cigar box away again in the closet. I didn't care. I wasn't ever coming back.

26

The hill up to the subway station never looked so long or steep in my life. Heat waves danced off the pavement making people's legs look rubbery. The buses gasped and groaned as they took the grade. My feet weighed a ton apiece, especially the right foot where I had Leo's address book laced into my sneaker.

Halfway up the hill, I stopped in the shade under the red awning of the Washington Heights French Laundry. I studied the fancy script letters on the window saying EXPERT REMOVAL OF STAINS, JUICE, FOOD AND BLOOD. Somehow, just reading the word "blood" made me decide to run back home and lock myself in the apartment to wait for my mother. But when I started out again, my feet kept going uphill.

And then I was at the top, waiting to cross Fort Washington Avenue. On the other side, I could see the green globes of the street lamps outside the subway station. The sidewalks going down toward Broadway were full of families heading for the parade. They were laughing and smiling, walking fast without hurrying, the way people do when they have somewhere fun to go. Little kids waved flags as they rode on their father's shoulders. Red, white, and blue crepe paper decorated the windows of the stores.

I started down the stairs into the subway station. And as soon as I felt the shadows on my face and smelled the sharp oily stink of the trains, my feet got so light that I almost floated up off the steps because now, finally, I knew I wasn't going home to wait for Elsa, or down to Broadway to watch the parade like all the stupid people up above. I was going out to Ebbets Field with Dale. We were going to sit in the sun all day long and see the Dodgers cream the Giants twice. And whatever happened after the game, this was one Fourth of July I was going to remember for the rest of my life.

Downstairs, in front of the turnstiles, they had a phone booth and cigarette machines along one wall and the entrance to Delia's Beauty Salon on the other. Dale was leaning against one of the cigarette machines, wearing gray slacks and a short-sleeved white shirt that somehow made his neck and arms look thicker than ever. Just as I came down the stairs, he glanced up and our eyes met and his flashed pale blue in the shadows of the station.

"Hey, whereya been, little buddy?" he called, taking off his Dodgers' cap and rubbing sweat off his forehead with the back of his wrist. "I just about gave up on you."

"They don't start till one-thirty," I said, hopping down the last few steps. "We still got time, don't we?"

"Yeah, but we're not gonna see 'em choose the kids for Happy Felton's Knothole Gang."

"Who cares about a bunch of kids," I shrugged.

"I wanna see the Dodgers. Let's go." I started toward the turnstiles.

Dale didn't move. He chewed his gum and made it pop. "Forgetting something, aren't you, little buddy?" he asked.

My stomach flopped. I felt the address book pressing against my ankle. But I just smiled and pulled the ticket out of my pocket and held it up, saying, "No, I'm all set. See?"

The corner of his lip went up. "Yeah, I see," he snorted. "I see you got the ticket I bought you for the game. And I see you got your glove for Pee Wee to sign when we go into the clubhouse afterward. But I don't see anything for old Dale."

He flexed his shoulder and kind of bounced himself away from the cigarette machine and leaned over me. "This ain't the Howdy Doody show, Josh," he said, holding out his palm. "Ante up or the game's over."

"I got that, too," I gulped.

"Glad to hear it," he smiled, patting my shoulder and leaving his hand there. "What'd you bring?"

"Something good. Something you'll like."

"Let's see."

"Right here?" I said.

"Yeah, here. What's wrong with here?" He gave my shoulder a little squeeze.

"You kidding?" I asked, glancing around at the guy in the token booth, and the people coming down the stairs from the street, and the women getting their hair done behind the window of the beauty parlor.

"Kidding?" Dale said, his voice dropping down. "The time for kidding's over." His hand tightened again on my shoulder.

"Leggo," I tried to wriggle out of his grip. He watched, smiling and chewing his gum. "I told you I got something good, didn't I? I just can't give it to you now," I said.

"Oh yeah? Why's that?"

"I can't. I just can't."

His fingers found a nerve in my neck and squeezed. I stopped squirming and stood still under his hand and looked up at him with tears in my eyes.

"I'll give it to you out at the park," I said. "I swear. Don't you see, if I give it to you now, I won't even enjoy the game. And then what's the point of going?" My voice rose up to a squeak. One of the men buying tokens turned to look at us.

Dale's hand got even tighter on my shoulder. He bent down till his pale blue eyes and flat nose were about half an inch from mine. He had a funny smell— of shaving cream and bacon and bubble gum and something bitter as vinegar. I saw a red streak of blood on his jaw where he cut himself shaving. "You're not joshing me now, are you, Josh buddy?" he asked very softly.

"I swear," I said. "I swear on my mother's . . ."

"Never mind swearing," said Dale. "Just tell me what you've got."

"An address book," I said. My voice shook, but in a weird way I felt proud. "An address book from somebody big."

Dale let go of my shoulder. "An address book?" he said. "Not bad. Not bad at all." He took a step back and looked me up and down. "Where do you have it?"

"Right here," I patted my back pocket.

"Okay." He pursed his lips and sucked in air through his nose. "I'll tell you what. I'm gonna trust you. I'm gonna call my boss and set it up so we can meet Pee Wee after the game. But that means I'm sticking my neck out for you." He tilted his chin up on his thick neck so I could see the bristles on his throat. "I'm sticking it all the way out. Understand?"

I nodded.

"And if you make me look bad, I'm gonna get a

whole lot more than even, with you and your whole family. Ben and Elsa, your grandparents, everybody. So if you're just playing some kind of kid's game"—Dale stared at me with eyes that had turned hard and cold as gun metal—"now's the time to fess up, little buddy. Because once I make that call, there's no backing out."

He walked real slow over to the phone booth, bouncing on the balls of his feet and looking back at me over his shoulder. I swallowed and shuffled and shivered even though it was sticky hot in the subway. But I didn't stop him. He went in the booth and dialed a number and talked on the phone staring at me through the glass. I turned away and looked at the women in Delia's Beauty Salon. They were sitting in orange plastic chairs, with sheets around their shoulders and glistening chrome helmets over their heads. The chrome helmets looked like they belonged on the vibration machine I made up to torture Captain Bob. I wished Dale would hurry up.

The subway tracks at 181st Street were so far underground that we had to take an elevator down. The elevator operator was an old black man wearing a green checked flannel shirt even in the middle of summer. He had a conductor's cap on his head and held the door open with huge dark hands.

"Don't push, don't shove," he wheezed in a tired old voice, as the people rushed into the elevator all at once. "What's your hurry? You'll all get where you're going 'fore you wants to anyway."

We had to ride the subway all the way from the top of Manhattan down to Times Square and then over to Brooklyn. When we first got on, Dale took out his sports page and we talked about the starting pitchers and I told him the batting average of each guy in our lineup and he told me some stuff I never heard before about Leo Durocher, manager of the Giants. He said

Durocher made the Giants sharpen their spikes so they could cut you sliding into second base, and besides that, he was a crook. He bet on horses and ran around with gangsters and cheated with other guys' wives, and Dale said he ought to be thrown out of baseball for the good of the game because he set such a rotten example for kids, and I thought so too.

But when we finished agreeing on that, we were only down to 125th Street and I was tired of talking to Dale. I kept thinking about the way his eyes changed all of a sudden from pale blue to steel cold gray when he squeezed my shoulder and said that stuff about getting even. I moved away a little and looked at the signs asking you to vote for Miss Rheingold Beer and warning you not to expectorate on the platform; then I closed my eyes and leaned back against the seat. I didn't really expect to sleep. Mainly, I wanted to get away from Dale and be in my own world for a while, but the rocking and the stuffy heat in the car and the clacking of the rails made me drowsy and almost before I knew it, I was dreaming. When I woke, the train was rattling to a halt at a station.

"Hey, come on, get up," said Dale, shaking my shoulder. "Times Square. We've got to change trains for Brooklyn."

When we finally came up above ground at Prospect Park station, the first thing I noticed was the smell of fresh-baked white bread. It came from a big bakery on the other side of Flatbush Avenue. All the way under the East River, I had been planning to run away from Dale as soon as we got out of the subway. But the smell of bread made me hungry, and I started thinking that since I'd come this far, I might as well let him buy me a big hot dog with mustard and relish as soon as we got to the game. There'd be plenty of time to run away after that.

We crossed the avenue and turned right. The sidewalks were so crowded that Dale reached down and grabbed my hand. Most of the people were heading for the game. They carried picnic baskets and cushions and Dodger pennants and American flags, and some of them had cowbells or penny whistles, and lots of the kids were wearing baseball mitts like me.

After a couple of blocks, we came to the corner of Flatbush and Empire Boulevard, and there it was— Ebbets Field. It looked almost like a huge department store. It had a curved entrance and red brick walls that covered a square block and three stories of high curved windows and banks of lights for night games towering above the walls and rows of flags hanging from the top story down to the green awning over the entrance.

The intersection in front was jammed with honking taxis and drivers screaming at each other in Brooklyn accents. I followed Dale across the street and into the rotunda, which was sweltering hot and packed with thousands of people shoving and pushing and shouting as they fought for places in line at the gold-barred windows of the ticket sellers.

Dale pulled me through the lines to a gate where we handed over our tickets and started walking up a ramp in the middle of a crowd so thick I couldn't see anything but arms and legs and butts and elbows, most of them swinging right in my face. Everyone was shoving and sweating and rushing because the game had already started and it was hard to even breathe in the crush and I held tight to Dale's hand and the ramp seemed to go up forever, and then suddenly, just when I really couldn't stand it anymore, we came through a passage into the huge open space of the stadium and I looked down across the rows of seats and sucked in my breath because there, big and sparkling and close enough to touch, was the diamond. The grass was bright green and the Dodgers were running out across it to take their positions in the field. I couldn't help but squeeze Dale's hand and he squeezed back and just then a hot dog vendor walked past and Dale said, "Well, how's about it, little buddy? Ready for lunch?"

27

Our seats weren't near as good as I expected. Dale promised they'd be right over the Dodgers' dugout where we could see the players' faces and hear everything they said and practically reach out and shake hands with Pee Wee as he trotted in from short. But actually, we sat about twenty rows back behind first base, just under the shadow of the upper deck and pretty close to a big steel pillar blocking our view of the rightfield corner.

I looked at the chipped white paint on the pillar, then kind of curled my lip at Dale and said, "Well, I guess we're not gonna see Furillo snag any liners off the rightfield wall."

He just laughed. "What the heck, little buddy?" he said, slapping me on the back. "You ain't paying, are you?"

"I guess not," I admitted. But I didn't think my ticket was all that free because he wanted the address book after the game, and that seemed a pretty steep price for a seat behind a pillar.

The people next to us were a couple of huge fat guys in sleeveless undershirts. I guessed they were brothers because they both had mustaches and sandy brown hair and they were fat in exactly the same way with their bellies making three jumbo-sized humps under their shirts and the wrinkles on their faces showing that they laughed a lot.

When we first settled in with our hotdogs and Cokes, they kind of looked at us and then sneered to each other and I thought they were unfriendly. But then they started shouting funny things at the home plate umpire in these high, squeaky voices that fat people have sometimes. And when they weren't hollering at the ump, they kept turning around to look at a blond lady a couple of boxes above us and daring each other to ask her for a date. She was wearing pearl earrings and a blue silky Dodgers' jacket and sitting with a man who looked like an Italian gangster because of the way his hat brim curled down over his eyes.

When the "cold beer bottle-a-beer" guy came to our section, one of the fat brothers passed his money to me because I was sitting on the aisle. "Hey, kid," he said, "buy us a couple of Schaeffer's, will ya? And get one for your old man, too."

Dale and I kind of winked at each other. But we didn't set them straight and Dale took the beer, which really surprised me because I knew from the movies that FBI men never drink when they're on duty.

The first game was pretty much a pitchers' duel. The Giants had Hoyt Wilhelm hurling knucklers, and we had Preacher Roe throwing spitballs and curves. Preacher was a skinny, gawky guy with ears that stuck straight out from the sides of his head, and he took about five minutes between each pitch.

He walked around in little circles behind the

mound, tugged at his cap, hitched up his pants, wiped sweat off his face, looked up at the white hot sky and even talked to it like he was begging for help from above. When he finally got himself ready to pitch, the batter would step out because he was falling asleep on his feet from waiting so long.

When they both got ready and the pitch came in, the hitter would foul it off and they'd have to start all over again. But before they could start, Durocher would come charging out of the Giants' dugout yelling to the umpire that Preacher had just thrown a spitter and the whole stadium would boo Durocher and it looked like the game would last till midnight, and I loved it.

I wanted it to go even slower. I wanted it to slow right down till it stopped and we were all stuck there forever in the hot July sun, munching hotdogs and sipping Cokes and booing the Giants and cracking jokes with the fat brothers about the umpires and watching the Dodgers glide over the green diamond between the red, white, and blue bunting on the stands.

I looked over at Dale. He had unbuttoned his white shirt halfway down his chest, and stretched his legs out under the seats ahead. He took a sip from the beer the fat brothers bought him, then licked the foam mustache off his upper lip and shook his head and sighed.

"Put 'er there, buddy," he said, holding his hand out to me. "This's the best Fourth of July I've had in I can't remember when. And you know what? I owe it all to you." We shook hands hard, looking into each other's faces, and then turned back to enjoy the game.

Inning by inning, it inched along slow as the shadows that stole out from third base to cover the pitcher's mound. The Giants scored their only run on a play where their guy was out by half a mile at the plate. The fat brothers started singing "Three Blind Mice" at the umpires and the Dodgers' Sym-phony came down to our section and started playing the trombone and banging the cymbals and kettle drums right along with them, but the umpires wouldn't change their call, and by the bottom of the ninth, with two out, the Giants were still winning one-nothing.

Then good old Jackie Robinson laced a double down the leftfield line. That made their pitcher mad. It was like he forgot all about Pee Wee waiting his turn up at home plate and just kept whirling around trying to pick Robinson off second. And every time he threw, Jackie dove back in, bounced up, brushed the dirt off his uniform, and took an even bigger lead.

The Giants' dugout started razzing Robinson. Someone in there had a high-pitched Southern voice that cut clean through all the noise of the crowd. "Hey, shoeshine boy," he yelled when Jackie bent down to brush off his uniform. "Hey shine. Quarter-a-shine. Come on over and give mine a shine."

Jackie didn't seem to hear. But next time the pitcher threw to second, Jackie tore down the line for third. The second baseman was so surprised that he just stood there, holding the ball like an idiot, and when he finally threw, his peg whacked Jackie right between the shoulder blades. It almost looked like he did it on purpose, but we didn't care because now Jackie was safe on third with the tying run and Pee Wee, our best clutch hitter, was at the plate.

"Suicide squeeze," Dale whispered to me like it was a big secret he didn't want the Giants to hear. And sure enough, on the next pitch, Pee Wee squared around to bunt and Jackie came barreling down the line toward home, only that dirty Durocher had smelled it out and the pitch was too far outside to hit and by the time Jackie reached the plate their catcher, big fat Hermann Franks who must've weighed three hundred pounds, was waiting for him with the ball.

They crashed hard enough to rattle the pillar next

to us, but Franks held the ball and dug it into Jackie's ribs and the Giants won the game and one of the fat brothers said it was getting time for Pee Wee to hang 'em up because he would've hit that pitch for certain sure a couple of seasons ago.

The grounds crew came out to hose down the dust and sweep the basepaths between games, and we went up to use the men's room in the stands. There were huge long lines outside it and I had to pee pretty bad but when I finally got in there and stood next to Dale with about fifty other men in front of this long trough that was clogged up with toilet paper and cigarette butts and overflowing with stinky yellow piss, I couldn't go at all. I had to wait till he finished splashing a thick gushing stream into the trough and walked away before I could get anything out.

But that was just the chance I'd been waiting for, because when I came out of the men's room, I didn't see Dale. I figured he didn't trust me enough to go back to our seats. But I only needed a couple of seconds to disappear in the crowd, and if I was ever going to ditch him, now was the time. Sure I'd miss the second game and my chance to get Pee Wee's autograph. But on the other hand, I'd probably get home in time to have dinner with my mother at the automat. I had money for subway fare and everything. I stood on tiptoe to look through the crowd and spotted an arrow high up on the bare concrete wall that pointed toward the Flatbush Avenue exit.

I took a few steps toward it, then stopped. My heart was banging. I had a creepy feeling of eyes on my back. I looked all around again, and sure enough, Dale was walking toward me, elbowing and threading his way through the crowd. Now that I saw him in a whole mob of men, he didn't look all that big. Lots of other guys were taller or heavier. But Dale looked more solid.

He moved just a fraction faster, walked just a touch lighter, slipped through the open spaces in the crowd before the other guys even saw him. He came up and smiled at me with his bright bug eyes. "Here," he said, handing me a brand new Dodgers' cap. "Thought you'd want a souvenir."

After all, I was glad I didn't miss the second game. The Giants came out swinging. They got two straight singles, and then Al Dark, their shortstop who wasn't even a power hitter, slammed a drive to right centerfield that went over the fifty-foot-high scoreboard, and over the Schaeffer beer sign on top of the scoreboard and over the Bulova clock on top of the beer sign.

"They're tearing up the pea patch," groaned one of the fat brothers. We all laughed because that's exactly what Red Barber said on the radio whenever a rally started.

We had to come back against their pitcher, Sal Maglie, a sidewinder who threw the most vicious curve in baseball. He never shaved before a game, and the sun outlined the black bristles on his jaw as he stood up on the mound, glaring in at the batter like he wanted to brain him.

He made Duke Snider dive for cover on two pitches in a row. The second one whistled up there like it was going to blast poor old Duke right in the ear. He ducked so fast his hat fell off. The ball zipped right under his hat through the space where his head used to be and still hooked in over the plate for a strike. The Giants' dugout jeered and whistled. Duke picked himself up, rubbed dirt and spit into his hands and bashed Maglie's next pitch on a line straight into the upper deck in leftfield.

That's the kind of game it was from the first inning on. I kept promising myself to disappear as soon as the action slowed down, but it never did slow down.

The batters kept ducking beanballs at the plate, and the runners slid into second with their spikes gleaming in the sun, and every tag was like a punch and you could just feel a rhubarb brewing and boiling in the huge bowl of the stadium. The lead must've changed hands half a dozen times. They hit homers and triples and made diving catches in the field and pulled off double steals on the basepaths and made some stupid errors, too, worse than our baseball team at school.

And meanwhile the sun dropped behind the rim of the stadium, and we could see the shadows of the light towers stretching across the outfield like thin black arms and I started thinking that no matter how bad a crook Durocher was, and how much I hated the dirty Giants, still, I had to like them a little too, for giving us a game like this. And just about then, their center-fielder slid ten yards on his belly to scoop a low liner off the grass and rob us of a sure triple, and I couldn't help jumping up on my feet to cheer.

Everybody in our whole section stared at me. I sat back down in a hurry with my face burning red, and it got even redder when one of the fat brothers turned to Dale and said, "Hey, that play killed us. You ain't raising your kid to be a traitor, are you?"

But Dale stared him down and put his arm around my shoulder and kind of pulled me against him and said, "Let me tell you something, buddy. You scratch my kid here, and he'll bleed Dodger blue. That's the kind of loyal fan he is. He just knows a great play when he sees one is all."

So after that, even though we were right in the middle of the best game I'd ever seen, and even though somewhere in my mind I still knew I had to run away, I kind of faded out for an inning or two and just sat there feeling Dale's arm warm and solid across my shoulder and wondering what it would be like if I really was his kid.

I guess because I was looking at the grass in the sunset, I imagined us living way out in the country somewhere, maybe on a ranch in Utah. Dale would probably be real strict, even worse than Leo was with Jody, but that would help make me tough and I'd have my own horse and I'd ride over the range with a .22 rifle in a long leather holster attached to my saddle. I'd learn to shoot real good, but I'd mainly practice on rattlesnakes and tin cans. I'd play outdoors all the time and get tan and hard and learn how to fix cars and all sorts of stuff that Ben could never even dream about teaching me. And after a few years, I'd be a completely different kid. Maybe I'd even change my name and stop being Josh and turn into someone like Randy or Kit, and of course, we'd practice baseball all the time, every day, and . . .

By the time I came out of it, the sky over the leftfield stands was turning dark blue and the lights had come on, making a hot white blur in the hazy air. I looked over at the scoreboard and added up the long rows of numbers and saw we were ahead 10 to 9 heading into the last inning. The Bulova clock above the scoreboard said 8:45. I stood up and stretched. The stands were full, but you could see a few empty seats where people had gone home already.

"I gotta pee," I told Dale. "I'll be right back."

"Now? Can't you hold it for a second?" he asked.

Just then our players came trotting out onto the field. "Now pitching for the Dodgers," drawled Tex Rickett over the PA system, "Number twenty-six, Jo-o-oe Black."

One of the fat brothers covered his face with his hands. "Not Black," he wailed. "Anybody but Black."

"Give 'im a chance, will ya?" I said. "He won thirteen games for us last year."

"That was last year," Dale said.

I sat down. There'd be plenty of time to make my move after the game.

Black walked the first guy and hit the second with a fastball right on the tush, but the Giants didn't even bother making a stink about it because now they had the winning runs on base. I sat there chewing the leather thongs of my baseball mitt while Black made the next two batters pop up.

So now we were one out away from winning and all thirty-five thousand people in the stadium were on their feet yelling at Black to bear down, and Dale and I were standing side by side, screaming right along with them. Their pitcher was next, so Durocher sent in Dusty Rhodes, a pinch hitter who murdered us every chance he got, and on the first pitch, he mashed the ball with an awful crack like bones breaking and we saw a white streak blurring over Pee Wee's head at shortstop. Pee Wee leaped in the air. It looked like he was climbing an invisible ladder because he just kept kicking his legs and rising up higher and higher than anyone could possibly jump, and at the top of his leap, he swiveled his back to the plate and stretched his arm out like it was made of rubber and the ball smashed into his glove and I could see it so clear, the white ball against the dark leather webbing as he hung up there in the air, and it was like magic, like all of us, the whole crowd, me and Dale and the fat brothers and the thirty-five thousand people and the steel pillars and red bricks and holiday bunting of Ebbets Field were hanging up there with him, and then he crashed back down in a heap on the edge of the outfield and the white ball trickled out of his glove across the green grass and while he scuttled after it on his hands and knees, the Giant runners tore around the basepaths, and we each collapsed groaning into our separate seats, and I just knew right then that everything was going to work out wrong.

*   *   *

After the game, when the crowd was grumbling along toward the exits, Dale turned to me and said, "Well, I guess you don't wanna go down into the clubhouse anymore, do you?"

"Huh?" I said. We were sitting side by side, staring out at the grass under the lights. I felt kind of dazed. I had a headache from the sun and the cheering and all. The sauerkraut from my second hotdog had left a coppery taste in my mouth. "Whaddya mean?" I asked him.

"Don't play dumb, buddy," he said, buttoning his white shirt up to the collar and smoothing his hair, which was cut so short it wouldn't get messed if you dropped a bomb on it. "We blew the whole thing," he snorted. "Pee Wee dropped the ball. Snider struck out to end the game. We lost our chance to take over first. You're not gonna tell me you want an autograph from a bunch of clowns like that, are you?"

"You kidding?" I glared at him. "I don't care if we finish last and Pee Wee drops ten balls. We're still the best and you know it!"

"Okay, okay," said Dale. He tugged the visor of the Dodgers' cap he bought me down over my eyes. "I knew you'd say that. Hold on till the crowd thins out and we'll go on down."

So we leaned back and watched the stands empty out. It was getting to be night now, with a couple of stars showing way up in the middle of the sky where the glare from the light towers couldn't reach. The whole stadium seemed sad and dirty, with hotdog wrappers and Coke cups and peanut shells and cigarette butts littered everywhere and the smell of spilled beer drifting up from the hot concrete and even the grass looking green-black and crushed. I knew I had lots of things to think about, but somehow I couldn't concentrate on anything except the way the ball rolled out of Pee Wee's mitt. I just sat there shaking my head about it until Dale tapped my shoulder.

"Okay, buddy," he said, "let's go."

We walked down between the empty rows of seats, crunching peanut shells under foot, and when we got to the first row of boxes, we followed the waist-high barrier around till we came to a gate leading out onto the field. A guard with a billy club was standing at the gate, but Dale flashed his badge and the guard stepped out of the way, touching his cap.

Then we were out on the grass of Ebbets Field, right by the first base line. I could see the chalk marks for the warm-up circle and the cleat marks that the Dodgers left in the turf, and the grass underfoot felt so springy that I would've turned a few somersaults on it if my head hadn't been aching like it was.

Dale led me straight to the dugout. We walked around the railing and down three steps, and then I was staring at the empty rack where the Dodgers kept their bats. I ran my fingers over the bench where they sat and studied the wooden planks on the floor, which were all chewed up by their cleats. I would've dashed over to get a drink from their water cooler, but Dale took my hand and pulled me through a door in the left corner of the dugout and then we were walking down a tunnel that ran back under the stands to the clubhouse.

The tunnel was empty and dark. It burrowed a long ways back under the stadium. Our footsteps echoed as we walked along. I smelled wet concrete and tobacco juice and even old piss, and for just a second I imagined one of the Dodgers rushing back into the tunnel to take a pee between innings, but I didn't like that thought and pushed it right out of my mind.

Dale led me into the gloomiest part of the tunnel, where paint and plaster were rotting off the walls and the clubhouse door was just a dim white patch about twenty yards ahead and the exit back to the field looked like a tiny green keyhole far behind. Then he stopped and gave me a lopsided smile and moved in close till I was backed up against the tunnel wall. He put his hands against the wall on either side of my head and kind of penned me in between his biceps and my heart started banging like the kettle drum in the Dodgers' Sym-phony.

"Okay, Josh," he said. "A promise is a promise." His voice was soft, almost gentle, his face close enough for me to smell the stale beer on his breath. "Let's see what you got. We don't want to keep Pee Wee waiting, now do we?"

I looked down the tunnel to the door of the club-house and it was like I had x-ray vision all of a sudden because clearer than anything I could see the Dodgers walking around in there. They were half naked with white towels wrapped around their waists. Their legs were lost in clouds of mist and white steam that drifted out of the showers and rolled over the floor, and their chests rose up broad and hairy out of the mist. They called to each other in deep booming voices, but no one was really happy because they'd lost twice that day and Pee Wee was sitting all by himself on a bench in front of his locker.

He was hanging his head and staring down at his feet and thinking how he should've caught that ball, and how just a year or two ago he would've caught it for sure, and how maybe it was getting time for him to hang 'em up like the fat brothers said.

And I knew this was the perfect time for me to walk up and ask for his autograph and tell him not to worry 'cause he'd make catches even better than that before the season ended. He'd raise his head and lift me up on the bench and look into my face with his deep brown eyes and tell me that if I believed in myself the way I believed in him then I could do anything in the world I wanted because he was just a scrawny 110-

pound kid hardly bigger than me when he got out of high school and look where he was now.

Then he'd shake my hand and sign my glove and pat my butt and I'd walk out of the clubhouse a completely different kid, not someone who was all messed up and spastic and frightened like me, but a kid who saved Pee Wee's career, a kid who believed in himself, a kid who could do anything in the whole wide world he wanted.

And all I had to do to get that way was to reach down into my sneaker and pull out the address book and hand it to Dale, who was still leaning over me with his biceps brushing my ears and his bug eyes flaring into my face.

Slowly, like in a dream, I slid down under his arms to unlace my shoe. I moved real careful, trying not to jar the image of Pee Wee out of my mind. Dale beamed and nodded at me. He stepped away and slouched back against the opposite wall to give me room.

I got down on one knee and took hold of my shoelaces and started to tug, but I was feeling all dazed and weak and it seemed like too much effort to pull the knot apart right then so I just knelt there on the floor of the tunnel for a second, staring at the torn scuffed toe of my sneaker and at the cigar butt sticking out from under the sole of Dale's shiny black shoe and at the rotting plaster on the wall behind his dark gray pants and, I don't know, everything just looked so gloomy that I shook my head to clear out the tears that were starting to sting in my eyes and while I was shaking my head I caught a glimspe of the grass far down at the mouth of the tunnel, only it didn't look like grass, it looked like an emerald flashing in the dark, and I didn't exactly see it either, I felt it, a bright green shivery shock that flashed through my eyes and along my spine and rippled all the way down to my toes, which were braced against the concrete wall, and before I even had time to think how hopeless it was, my legs flexed and bunched and blasted me out of my crouch and I shot under Dale's arm and raced down the tunnel because all of a sudden I knew, I just knew clear and deep as the green of the diamond, that the only way to believe in myself like Pee Wee said was to get out of that tunnel without giving the address book to Dale.

But he was quick. So quick. His hand flew out as I darted past and before I had taken two steps, he was yanking me back. My mind said quit but my legs kept pumping in a panic, and what happened is that I turned completely around 360 degrees in a circle while he had hold of my shirt and for a split second we were staring into each other's eyes and his flashed cold-killer mad and then I was facing the field again and my shirt ripped and I exploded down that tunnel.

My arms and legs erupted out of control and my head just rode along on top and the patch of green at the mouth of the tunnel was swelling up and getting brighter and closer and they must've been watering it because I could see a soft mist spraying over the blades and the mist sparkled in the light and rainbow-colored drops hung on the points of the blades and I knew that if I could just set foot on that grass Pee Wee would help me get away, and I was so close, I was down to the end of the tunnel, just a step away from the dugout, and then—*wham!*

Dale's hand slammed down on my shoulder. His fingers dug for some jujitsu pressure point in my neck. My legs froze dead in mid-stride. And then he had me, trapped and paralyzed at the mouth of the tunnel.

"You shouldn't've run like that, Josh," he said in a soft, level voice. He wasn't even out of breath. "You shouldn't've broke your word. Now we're not buddies anymore." He squeezed even tighter, forcing me down on my knees.

"Owww, please, okay, okay," I panted. "I give up. I'll give it to you. Just let go."

But he wouldn't. He pinched the nerve till my head started to swim and I didn't know if I was going to black out or throw up and there was only one thing I could think of to make him stop so I gritted my teeth and fumbled with my shoelaces and pulled out Leo's address book. I dropped it on the concrete, and it sat there right on the crack between the dugout and the tunnel, the gold lettering gleaming softly in the light from the field. But Dale still didn't let go.

"Hand it to me," he said. "Pick it up and hand it over like a good little boy."

I picked the book up and held it in my hand above my head. I couldn't even turn to look at him because of the way he was pinching my nerve. He snatched the book and let go of my neck. I bolted out of the tunnel, across the narrow floor of the dugout and up the stairs to the diamond. I got about halfway across the infield before I tripped over my shoelace and sprawled face first in the wet dirt at the base of the pitcher's mound.

28

Elsa

Meetings of the review committee were not optional. Whether it was the morning of the Fourth of July or a rainy night in the depths of winter, once you were summoned, you went. It was like a subpoena. They did not want to hear excuses about a nine-year-old boy who urgently required his mother's presence at a baseball game, which is not to say that I felt good about leaving Josh alone that morning, or about calling back and canceling our plans when the proceedings dragged on into the afternoon.

The accused in this case was Peggy Mendelsohn. Poor Peggy—overweight, overdressed, never married, emphasizing her unattractiveness with dyed blond hair and gaudy rhinestone jewelry on her pendulous arms. For some time now, we had suspected her of being the FBI plant in our club. As if to dispel suspicion, she clung to us with a fawning, cloying persistence. The sole effect was to increase our discomfort at suspecting her without in any way allaying our doubts. It was Leo, of course, who finally brought her up on charges. He was implacable where security issues were concerned.

The meeting was held in the airless, windowless back room of Elizabeth Ulmann's apartment. As chairman of the review committee, Leo presided at a battered wooden desk. The rest of us, three members of the Washington Heights club and myself, sat on folding chairs that flanked the desk and formed a semicircle around Peggy's seat. The room was sweltering and everyone smoked. We were all extremely tense. The Rosenbergs had been executed barely two weeks before.

Peggy treated us to an endless recitation of her contributions to the cause—the tables she had manned at various functions and bazaars, the clothes and jewelry she had contributed to rummage sales, the cakes she had baked for fund-raising dinners, the subs to the paper she had sold to the paper on rainy weekend mornings, the envelopes she had stuffed, the children (including mine) whom she had watched so that other comrades could go out and organize, the abuse she had suffered passing out leaflets in front of hostile factory gates.

At last Leo cut her short. "Can you explain," he asked, in his hectoring courtroom voice, "why you continue to hold your job at the New York City Public Works Department when all our other members have been booted out of the civil service because of the loyalty oath?"

"Explain?" wailed Peggy. "How can I explain why they haven't fired me? Do you want me to resign? I'll do it tomorrow."

"Can you explain," Leo went on, reading from Peggy's dossier (a thick file to which we had all been asked to make contributions), "why you surreptitiously and habitually take notes of personal conversations which you have no business to record?"

"I don't take notes," said Peggy, wiping sweat off

her jowls, the rhinestone bracelets jingling on her arm. "Perhaps I jotted down a phone number. Or an address. Sometimes my memory . . ."

"Would you like to recount," Leo asked, "why you were the last one to leave Jeannette Miller's house the day that her list of contacts inside the United Electrical Workers disappeared?"

"I went back to get my purse," said Peggy. "I forgot it in . . ."

"In her study," Leo prompted. "You very conveniently forgot it right on her desk where the list was kept. Do you know how many of the people on that list have been indicted?" He pounded his fist on the desk. "How many have been fired from their jobs? Evicted from company housing?"

"Leo. Leo, you know me," said Peggy miserably, "I didn't steal Jeanette's list. I would never do a thing like that."

"Do you have anything else to say," Leo asked her. "For example, about the man in the car with a well-known license plate who talked to you outside Jeanette's house that day? Or the one-hundred-and-thirty-nine-dollar Magnavox TV for which you paid cash at Macy's two weeks later? Or about the address book that disappeared from the pocket of my coat at Elsa Rankin's party?"

That last charge was my contribution to Peggy's dossier, and I had made it, against my better judgment, in response to Leo's unmerciful nagging. He was obsessed with the book. Not because of the names it contained—all aboveground members or sympathizers who, he assured me, were known to our enemies from a dozen different sources—but because the very act of losing it undermined his precious authority. It was unthinkable for the head of the review commission to be so careless as to drop an address book on the street. There had to be a scapegoat, a stoolpigeon. And who better than poor Peggy, already under suspicion on so many other counts?

Her eyes, as I somehow knew they would, traveled around the room and locked on mine with an appalling, dreadful sincerity. "The Party is my life," she said. "How can you think I'd . . ." She began to cry, a sight made all the more unbearable by the mascara that melted down her thickly powdered cheeks.

Elizabeth gave her a handkerchief. "It's all right, Peggy," she said. "Go home now. We'll be in touch."

After she left the room, Leo wiped his forehead and turned to Herschel Puriden. "Do you believe her, Hersch?" he asked.

Herschel shook his head.

"Beth?" Leo faced our host.

"If it were any one charge," said Elizabeth, "I'd give her the benefit of the doubt. But in view of the whole pattern . . . No. How can we?"

"Al?"

"It's a hard call," Al sighed, sucking on the stem of his pipe. "You're a lawyer, Leo. You tell me. Could you go into court with what you've got in that dossier and get a conviction?"

We were all surprised. Al was a hard-liner, a protégé of Bob Thompson, the last one we expected to stand up for Peggy.

"What's your point, Al?" Leo asked coldly.

"My point," smiled Al, "is that nowadays we can't afford the luxury of bourgeois debates on guilt or innocence. The question is—are we better off with her or without her? Does she make the movement weaker or stronger? Once you put it that way, the answer is obvious. She causes suspicion. She consumes energy. She has to go."

There was general nodding, a sense of relaxation, a feeling that these unpleasant proceedings were about to come to an end.

"Elsa?" Leo turned to me, expecting the vote that would make our decision unanimous. He looked quite handsome in his white short-sleeved shirt with his tanned muscular arms cradling Peggy's dossier. His eyes held not a hint of doubt, no recogntion that we, too, could be brought up on charges and expelled for what had passed between us.

I felt a wave of revulsion for him, for myself, for these proceedings, and of course for Peggy. Whatever she may or may not have done with the FBI, I simply could not forgive her for taking up so much of my time on this particular Sunday afternoon when the desperate sound of my son's voice kept ringing in my ears.

I wondered briefly what Ben would do, yearned for the comfort of his mind, his voice, his way of calmly analyzing dilemmas, finding in their deepest shadows some pinprick gleam of hope. Yet at the same time, I thought how terribly like him it was to be absent at this moment, at so many moments, when I needed his support.

In the end, rather than sit in Elizabeth's back room and argue till midnight, I bowed my head and went along with Peggy's expulsion.

29

I ran. Away from the stadium, away from the lights, away from what I'd done with Dale. I ran into the darkness of Prospect Park, through branches and bushes that whipped at my face, around the big stone monuments that leaned along the shores of the lake, and then out onto the streets again.

I ran till I found a subway station. The man in the toll booth stared at me real hard. He had a shiny, soggy-looking face the color of bubblegum after you've been chewing it for an hour or two. "Out kinda late, ain'tcha, sonny boy?" he asked me. I slapped down my dime, grabbed a token off his tray, and dashed through the turnstile. Arrows pointed uptown and downtown. I didn't care. I just wanted to get on a train.

I came out on a platform. A white eye-stinging mist rose up off the tracks, smelling of hot metal and grease. The only other person on the platform was a man bundled up like a big black bear in a winter overcoat and hat. He was talking to himself like a crazy man. "I swear it to you. Emile . . . ," he said, holding up one finger and waving it in the air, "I swear it on my grave . . ." Then he stopped and sniffled and wiped at his eyes like he wanted to cry. "If you think . . . if you think for just one moment, Emile . . . I swear I'll . . ."

When the train came, the crazy man got on one of the cars in the middle, so I rode all the way up front. I didn't see anyone else on the train. We rattled through dark tunnels and pulled into lonely stations. I wondered how late it was. Midnight? After midnight? I slumped down on a bench and hugged my arms around myself and started feeling a little sleepy but fought against it in case the crazy man came to get me.

My eyes drooped down anyway, and for a second or two I dreamed I was back in my narrow little bed under the sloping stained ceiling of my room. I could hear my mother clattering plates in the kitchen for dinner. But then I jerked myself awake and saw my reflection shaking in the windows of the train. And I realized I couldn't go back home, not tonight and not ever, because the one thing my mother and Ben and all the people in the Party hated was a traitor-squealer-stoolie-rat. And that's exactly what I was for giving the address book to Dale.

The train was going fast, too fast. I kept expecting it to slow down and pull into a station any minute, but it just picked up speed and more speed and swayed and clanked and blasted down the tracks like it had broken loose and wasn't ever going to stop.

The wheels screeched so loud I had to put my fingers in my ears. And then I heard another screech, even higher and lonelier and angrier than the train. There was no one else in the car, and the shrieking echoed in my skull no matter how I plugged my ears, so I knew it had to be coming from my own mouth. I stumbled over to the little window in the front door of the train and squashed my lips hard against the glass and that stopped it okay for a second.

But then I saw my face hanging out there in the blackness, getting slapped and slammed by the railroad ties, shivering and splitting apart and coming together as the tunnels branched and twisted, and my mouth was all flattened down and bent out of shape from howling and red lights flashed in my eyes and my hair stuck up every which way like I'd just stepped on the third rail and I looked a thousand times uglier than Vera ever did in the worst of her tantrums and I knew that was my real face, my true face that no one could see but me, and I sucked in my breath and howled my heart out.

The train shrieked right along with me. The conductor had jumped off at the last station and left the throttle locked on full and the crazy man and I were the only people still on board and the train was just going to run faster and fiercer out of control till it exploded itself to smithereens against a wall and there was nothing I could do to stop it. I saw the lights of a station up ahead and people waiting on the platform and I screamed to warn them, to tell them to run. I had to warn them if it was the last thing I ever did. But it was too late, they couldn't hear, they didn't move, and then the brakes gave a great groaning hiss, and the train jerked and swayed and rolled to a stop at the very end of the platform, and as the doors sighed open, I realized it wasn't the people in the station I had to warn. It was the people in the address book.

I stood in the alley, panting and holding my side, and stared up at the fire escape. It zigged and zagged all the way up to my window on the sixth floor. Through the slats I could see the moon hanging up in a narrow patch of sky between buildings. It looked dead white and squashed out of shape like a softball that had gotten slugged too many times.

I took a running jump at the ladder and missed by a mile. I tried to drag a garbage can over so I could stand on the lid and jump from there. But the can weighed a ton and squawked something awful when I pulled it.

I started climbing the wall, pressing my cheek against the still-warm bricks and inching up toehold by toehold. Finally my fingers closed over a ledge. From there, it was easy to reach the fire escape. My sneakers hardly made a sound running up the ladders. On the fourth floor, I looked through an open window and saw a man and his wife snoring under the sheets. She had fallen asleep with one fat arm hanging down to a seltzer bottle on the floor. The nozzle glistened through her fingers.

By the time I reached my window, my heart was banging. I had to stop and catch my breath. The lights were on in my room, glowing warm and yellow on my collection of jet fighters and the spacemen guarding the fleet and the Indian blanket thrown across my bed and the piles of shoes and underwear and comic books sprawled across the floor. Everything was right where it belonged. Everything except the cigar box. It sat by the closet door, with the lid open and something silvery gleaming at me from the bottom.

I tried the window. The wood creaked and the glass rattled a little, but I forced it open. I had to hurry. I had to get in, leave a note to warn Elsa about the address book, and get back out again before she caught me.

I swung my legs across the windowsill and tiptoed over to the little bookcase where I kept my crayons and pencils and notebooks for school. I grabbed a red pencil and ripped a page out of my binder, but before I could write the first word, I heard footsteps hurrying down the hall. Then my door swung open. And there was Elsa.

She stopped in the doorway when she saw me. She was crushing a pack of Camel cigarettes against the torn lace around the collar of her housecoat. Her feet were bare.

"Josh?" she said. "Josh! Where've you been? What happened to your . . . ? Oh, I was so worried!" Her eyes gleamed at me from deep circles. She held out her arms and rushed to hug me, but I jumped back toward the window, dropping the note, throwing up my hands.

"Never mind all that!" I said. "You've got to warn them. Warn everybody. Right now. Tonight!"

She reached for my cheek.

"Don't touch me!" I yelled again. "Can't you hear! Can't you listen! You've got to warn everybody in Leo's address book. The FBI has their names. It's coming after them. Right now. While we're talking!"

She dropped her hand and looked me over from my tangled hair to the rip in the toe of my sneaker. Then she took a deep breath and sat down on my bed. "I don't know what you're talking about," she said, trying very hard to keep the shake out of her voice. "I want to know where you've been. And how you got those scratches all over your face. And why you pop up here after midnight, muddy, filthy, frantic, and full of nonsense about the FBI. Now just calm yourself down and come over here." She patted a place next to her on the blanket.

I threw one leg over the windowsill. I had warned her. If she didn't believe me, it was her fault, not mine. She couldn't blame me anymore. But she would, they all would. They'd blame me for everything for the rest of my life, and it wasn't fair. None of it. All I wanted to do was go to a doubleheader on the Fourth of July, and if I couldn't go with anyone but Dale, then she and Leo and Ben and all of them were just as much to blame as me—only they wouldn't admit it and that made me mad. It made me so mad I wanted to tell. Not just to warn her about the address book, but to tell everything, the truth. And if she hated me for it, I'd just hate her right back and run down the fire escape and never see any of them again, ever.

"I found Leo's address book," I said. The blood was beginning to roar in my ears like the crowd out at Ebbets Field, not cheering, but taunting, daring me to go on. "I found it the night of the party. I found it and hid it. Here! In my room, in my cigar box under the closet." I pointed to the box.

Elsa put the knuckles of one hand against her lips and held the other out to me almost as if she was begging me to stop before I said one more word because right now she couldn't quite see or understand or put it all together but she could feel it, sense it coming, the way I did way back on May Day when Mrs. McMahon was just about to call me commie. Only now it wasn't me cringing and whimpering and feeling afraid. Now it was her turn. And no matter what happened, I wanted to see the look in her eyes when I told. I wanted that more than I ever wanted to go to the game with Dale.

"I found it and hid it and gave it to the FBI," I said. "To a man named Dale. Remember him? He's the one who played baseball with me in the park. He's the one who had time to take me out to the Dodgers' doubleheader today while you were too busy with Leo."

Elsa stood up. Now she was right where I saw her with him that night. A hard yellow gleam collected in her eyes and focused slowly in on me, growing brighter and hotter and colder and sharper every second, and I just glared right back, letting her eyes peel off my skin layer by layer till they got down to the face I saw in the subway.

"Now they know all about everything," I said.

"And none of this would have happened in the first place if you hadn't been kissing Leo that night in the dark."

She sucked in her breath and swung her arm halfway across the room and slapped stars in my eyes. The room was still swimming when I heard her say in a very clear, cold, calm voice, "You're a disgusting little stoolpigeon and I can't stand the sight of you." Then she slammed the door and left me alone.

I looked out the window at the fire escape. I told myself to start running. If I could start right now and keep running all night and the next day and the next, then maybe what I'd done and knew and told to Elsa would never catch up. But somehow I was already out of breath. My side ached and my knees felt wobbly and the soles of my feet burned like I'd been running for years. And my bed was close, so close, with the saggy mattress and the two pillows and the soft flannel blanket. And even though I had no right to sleep there, my bed was the only place I still had strength to go.

I slept for three days. It wasn't nice sleep that made you forget and feel healthy. It was more like being buried in the muck on the bottom of the Hudson with the tide tossing you around and slugs and eels and bloodsucking worms slithering all over your body. But at least it was dark and safer than what was waiting for me up above.

Elsa came in once and dragged me into the kitchen for a bowl of soup, then shoved me into the bathroom where a hot tub was waiting. I fell asleep in the water. When it turned cold, I managed to stand up, run back to my bedroom without drying off, and shiver myself to sleep again.

Finally, one morning or afternoon or whatever it was, I heard a soothing familiar southern voice droning on and on with crowd noise rising and falling in the background. I opened my eyes and saw the dial of my Hopalong Cassidy radio glowing in the shadows of my room. The voice was Red Barber calling the Dodgers' game. I knew it was a trap, but I stretched out, put my hands under my head and settled in to listen.

Elsa came in after about an inning with a glass of milk. "Who's winning?" she asked, passing me the tall, dented aluminum cup I always drank from.

"We are," I said between greedy swallows. "Six-nothing."

"Is it almost over?"

"Why?"

"Because after the game, we're going out for a walk. You need some sun and so do I." She reached behind the bed and lifted my window shade. Bright noontime light leaped across the floor.

"I don't want to go," I said, shielding my eyes. "I'm still sleepy."

"Well, I'm not asking if you want to go or not," Elsa smiled on her way out the door. "Just get yourself ready after the game. And I mean *right* after."

We walked along my morning route to school. I stared at the red brick towers blocking the view of the river as if I hadn't seen them for months. Elsa kept tossing her head and shaking out her black hair and lifting her face up to the sun. She was wearing a turquoise jersey tucked into a wide white belt pulled tight around her waist.

We came to P.S. 187. The big brick building seemed asleep, with blinds drawn across all three stories of windows. A few blocks past school, we entered the stone gates of Fort Tryon Park. Up above, on top of a grassy hill, the Cloisters sat glowing like a storybook castle with a purple banner hanging down from its battlements in the afternoon sun.

We sat on a stone bench on a wall and looked out

over the park and the river. We could see the cliffs of New Jersey and the roller coaster on top of the cliffs and both towers of the George Washington Bridge down toward our house, and up in the other direction, the Hudson widening out and gleaming under the high white clouds. We could even see where the dirty brown East River hooked around and linked up with the Hudson to cut Manhattan off from the Bronx.

"I sat right here once with Ben," my mother said, taking a couple of tinfoil-wrapped sandwiches out of her bag and passing one to me. "It was a long time ago. Before you were born. Before we were married. Before everything." She stared out at the clouds for a minute, with her chin cupped in her hands and her long fingers lacing up into the blackness of her hair.

"He read me a poem he wrote when he was just thirteen, only a few years older than you," she sighed. "It was something about the holes in a poor boy's coat." She rubbed her forehead like she was trying to remember. Then she glanced down at my ragged sneakers. "No, it wasn't his coat," she smiled. "It was his shoes. It was about learning to see beauty through the holes in a poor boy's shoes."

I didn't answer. I unwrapped my sandwich. It was cream cheese on black rye. I took a big bite. It tasted salty. I guess I was crying. We sat side by side on the bench and ate.

They caught Captain Bob Thompson. He was hiding out with three other guys in a little town called Twain Harte way up in the mountains in California. The FBI raided the cabin with about a hundred men carrying pistols and tommy guns and tear gas, but they were still so scared of Captain Bob that they chained him to a tree and made him stand out in the sun all day long. Then they took him to Alcatraz. And he had hardly been locked up on Alcatraz for a week before they got some crazy stowaway sailor guy who used to be a Nazi from Yugoslavia to bash his brains out with a steel pipe while they were lining up in the cafeteria for breakfast.

Captain Bob didn't die. But he was hurt. He was hurt real bad. The papers said they didn't know if he'd ever be able to walk again, or talk, or even think. They said his arrest broke the back of the whole communist underground.

I started to hate myself something awful, but Elsa said it wasn't my fault and couldn't ever possibly be. She said the people in Leo's address book were all aboveground, rank-and-file members and there's no way that any of them could've led the FBI to Twain Harte and that if any of them did, they were responsible, not me, and besides, I had plenty of real things to feel sorry about without inventing stories to distract myself.

I wanted to believe her. I really did. But I just kept thinking of Captain Bob lying in the prison hospital with his head all mashed out of shape and wrapped up in bandages till it looked like a big white poison mushroom, and the only times I could get him out of my mind were when I was listening to the ballgame or reading science fiction books from the library. I started reading a lot that summer, thanks to Vera.

She came back from camp toward the end of July all tanned with sun streaks in her hair and bumps of titties starting to stick out from under her shirt, and somehow her head seemed to balance a little lighter on her neck, maybe because she'd lost her awful blue butterfly glasses during a hayride they took one night in Vermont. I was actually kind of glad to have her home because it had been pretty gloomy living all cooped up with just Elsa and me and my secret.

Vera seemed too busy yakking about camp and planning her wardrobe for school next year to pay much attention to me and that was just what I wanted, too. But one morning, when I was sitting on my bed stirring the dustballs on the floor with my toe, she came in and said, "Well, for heaven's sake, if you're going to mope around inside all day and become a recluse, you might as well read a book for a change. Would you care to accompany me to the library? I don't suppose you could find the way on your own."

She was right. I didn't know the way or have a card or anything. But actually the library was close, just up past the Hilltop restaurant and down 181st Street to Broadway. I started going there every day. I liked sitting on the cool linoleum between rows of towering bookshelves that dimmed the light and blocked all the bad thoughts out of my head. I always left with an armful of books and started reading them on my way home, hardly bothering to watch where I walked.

One afternoon, a car honked at me as I stepped off the curb outside the Hilltop restaurant. I didn't think anything special about it. I just pulled back my foot and went on reading about the gigantic man-eating spiders of Venus without looking up.

But then a voice called, "Hey, little buddy," and my head jerked around, and there was a shiny gray Ford sliding over to the curb with Dale's flat face and bright bug eyes smiling at me out the open window. "Let's see if you can still catch," he called, tossing a ball my way.

I dropped my books and grabbed for the ball and bobbled it a couple of times before holding on. It was a brand-new official major league hardball. With an autograph on it. Pee Wee's autograph.

I glanced from the ball to Dale. He was watching me with a kind of strange sad half-smile on his face that I'd never seen before. Then he winked, revved up his car, said, "Thanks for nothing, kid," and drove away.

I tossed the baseball up and down. I needed both hands to carry my books and I knew I should throw it away but that ball had Pee Wee's signature and I couldn't just leave it there on the street for some other kid to come along and find when I had gone through so much trouble to get it. I looked around at the people rushing past. No one seemed to notice. Finally I sighed and shrugged and jammed the ball into my back pocket and felt it rubbing against my hip as I gathered my books and headed down the hill toward home.